SEND THE DOG

When you are sure you are being followed, you can do something about it, step into a store, jump on a bus, get lost in a sea of humanity or traffic.

Except it was nearly midnight in a deserted part of the city. There were no open stores, no buses, no sea of humanity.

Okay, still.

You can draw a gun. (Mine was home.)

You can turn around and shout, "I see you, you cowardly scumbag, hiding in the shadow of that building!"

You can pretend you're going home and lead him to the Sixth Precinct.

And, if there's absolutely no other choice, you can send your dog to talk some sense into the bastard. . . .

THIS DOG
FOR HIRE

A Rachel Alexander and Dash Mystery

CAROL LEA BENJAMIN

A DELL BOOK

Published by
Dell Publishing
a division of
Bantam Doubleday Dell Publishing Group, Inc.
1540 Broadway
New York, New York 10036

All the characters and events portrayed in this work are
fictitious.

ISBN: 0-440-22520-5

Reprinted by arrangement with Walker
Publishing Company, Inc.

Printed in the United States of America

Published simultaneously in Canada

January 1998

10   9   8   7   6   5   4   3
WCD

For Judy Nelson,
wherever you are, honey.

Acknowledgments

Many thanks to:

John Douglas of Partners & Crime Booksellers, whose enthusiasm and encouragement helped me to sally forth into a new genre

Marty Berkowitz, Ph.D.; Richard Siegel, M.S.W.; Polly DeMille, R.N., B.S.N., M.A.; Bonnie Wilcox, D.V.M.; John Laub; Jan Bella Berkowitz; Larry Berg; and Captain Arthur Haggerty, who so generously shared their expertise; with a hug for Joe Celentano, M.S.W., whose genius was the inspiration for an important part of this book

The Bomb Dogs and their handlers at the Sixth Precinct, Greenwich Village

Alice Quinn, a friend in need

Evelyn Abrams, who taught me, by her sterling example, how to listen

Ann Loring, for her boundless enthusiasm and unfailing support

Los Angeles Food and Fiction Club and NYC's Loose Women's Book Club

Gail Hochman, my wonderful agent

Michael Seidman, Zen master with a blue pencil

with a hug for Job Michael Evans (you're still the favorite)

and love to my family; Stephen Lennard, my sweetheart; Victoria and Stephen Joubert; Jennifer Gutbezahl; Mimi Kahn and Dick Goodman; Flash, the Border collie; and Dexter, a stand-up dog if ever there was one

1

Ordinary Secrets

GREENWICH VILLAGE IS a place full of secrets, back cottages hidden from view behind wrought-iron gates and down long brick passageways and little Edens way up high, secret gardens growing not on the ground but on the roof, retreats concealed from the prying eyes of strangers.

There are other secrets here as well, sexual secrets, passages across the gender lines that I thought, once upon a time, were immutable facts of life. But in this neighborhood of writers and artists, the facts of life were long ago rewritten, familiar images redesigned.

And more and more of late, the secrets indigenous to this place, once visible only to willing participants, are coming out, out of the closet, out of the clubs, out in the open for all to see. Even those who'd rather not.

Still, it's usually a case of live and let live.

But not always.

We have our ordinary secrets, too, the kind every neighborhood has, envy, jealousy, greed, lust, anger, all seething unseen under the surface. And like the other secrets lying doggo among the twisty, tree-lined streets between Washington Square Park and the Hudson River, these too are invisible, until one day they fester up to the surface.

Secrets are what interest me, particularly the ones that eventually compel seemingly normal people to start obsessing about murder.

My name is Rachel Alexander. I'm the Alexander in Alexander and Dash, private investigation. I get first billing, but Dash, my partner, is the real teeth in the operation. He's a pit bull.

Before I got Dashiell, I worked as a sneaky, lying, low-life, underhanded undercover agent, betraying the confidences of people who befriended me in order to get the information I needed to solve cases. The work suited me, and I liked the odd hours, but after a couple of years I decided I was no longer willing to split the client's check with an agency. That's when I started my own business, doing all of the above and worse, but exploiting myself instead of having it done for me by strangers.

I don't know how to explain my occupation any more than I can explain anything else about my life. I just have always been more interested in what's in the hamper than what's neatly folded in the dresser drawer. It's not that I don't ask myself, particularly when Dash and I are out on an especially seedy stakeout, what's a nice Jewish girl like you doing in a place like this? But I tend to think it wouldn't be all that different had I gone to medical school. Only then I'd be asking it while delicately sticking a gloved finger up some poor guy's ass.

That's one of the few places I haven't had to look for evidence. So far.

It had finally stopped snowing, and I was getting ready to take my dog out for his afternoon constitutional. I had one of my Timberlands half on when the phone rang.

"Get that, will you?" I told him, hopping in the direction of the phone.

Dash took the phone off the receiver and walked toward me with it in his mouth.

"For *me*?" I asked.

He dropped it on my unlaced boot. Thank God for reinforced toe boxes.

I cradled the phone in my neck, barked "Hello," and kept struggling with my boot until I figured out the good news. It was work.

The caller identified himself as Dennis Keaton. He was a pretty unhappy-sounding guy, which isn't unusual: Happy people don't usually hire detectives. He asked if he could see me right away about an urgent matter.

I told him he could.

I had an urgent matter myself. I was dead broke.

I could never see the sense in wasting money on an office when most of the work I have to do is done elsewhere. In winter I meet new clients at James J. Walker Park, on Hudson Street. There's a ball field there where the neighborhood dogs gather to play when it's off-season. It seems to me the proper ambience for my work, even when people do scoop.

Dashiell was dancing impatiently at the door, so I told this Keaton fellow where to meet me, grabbed my coat, my camera, and a notepad, and headed downtown.

2

It Began to Snow

DENNIS KEATON ENTERED the park, carefully adjusted the gate so that a garbage can would keep it from blowing open, and looked around for a second, then, with a walk that announced his sexual orientation, headed in my direction.

He was tall and reedy, but not your typical what-a-waste, gorgeous gay guy. First of all, his nose was much too big. His skin was okay, but pale, even for midwinter in New York. His eyes, which according to the rest of his coloring should have been a to-die-for blue, were an unrevealing steely gray. His uncombed mop of curls reminded me of an apricot-colored standard poodle I had trained for a lady rabbi, the Reverend Janet, back when I was the Kaminsky of Kaminsky and Son Dog Academy. Bernie, the Golden I had then, was the son. That was before I got married, before I got divorced, and before

I decided to go from getting growled at to getting shot at, escalating what my shrink called my rabid counterphobia.

"Rachel Alexander?"

As soon as he opened his mouth, I saw that his teeth were crooked, too.

I was leaning against the back fence and patted the spot next to me in response.

He wore a brown leather bomber jacket, a small loop of red ribbon, carelessly attached with a safety pin, a long white aviator scarf around his skinny neck, and, despite a temperature in the low thirties, no hat. The rest of his ensemble deviated from code—shapeless corduroy overalls and ancient brown oxfords, both dappled with spots of black paint.

He took a deep breath and let it go. "A friend of mine, Clifford Cole, has been murdered," he said. "I was told you might be able to help me find out who did it."

He looked to be in his mid-thirties, but who knows. In this neighborhood, there's more illusion than reality. For all I knew, I was looking at the aftermath of a face-lift, a dye job, a perm, and liposuction.

"That's police business," I said. "Why would you want to pay for something you can get done free?"

I glanced at Dash, who was doing the doggy two-step with a flirtatious husky bitch.

"It's been two weeks since Cliff was killed—perhaps you saw it in the paper, if you had a magnifying glass. There's been virtually no interest and no progress."

I nodded. Most people talk more freely if they have evidence that someone's actually listening. The more information I can get before I start asking a lot of questions, the more revealing it tends to be, though it could take a while to figure out precisely what has been revealed.

"Since . . . the body was found on the Christopher Street pier, the police are treating it as a gay bashing."

"And you say?"

"Cliffie never cruised the waterfront. He has, God, I'm still having a lot of trouble with tense, he *had* a lover, but even before Louie, he didn't. It just wasn't his style. Besides, there are other things that signal it wasn't a random killing. The hour, for one thing. The estimated time of death was between four and six in the morning. Cliff was a painter. He has the loft above mine. He was a day person, up with the sun and right to work. It always floored me, because I'm up early trying my best to avoid working for as long as possible. And I quit as soon as I can manage to without excessive guilt. But Cliff was one of those people who could go on and on. His stamina was phenomenal. The energy in his work was just enormous, but well controlled. After he worked, he'd get cleaned up and then he'd go out with Magritte, they'd go out for hours. That's the other thing," he said, his voice suddenly sounding as if he were in a movie on television from which off-color words had been bleeped. "Magritte is missing. He wasn't at the loft, and he wasn't with Cliff when he was found."

He took out a handkerchief and blew his big nose.

"Magritte? The train coming out of the fireplace? And the pipe? *Ceci n'est pas un pipe*, right?"

"Yes, but this Magritte is a basenji. The barkless dog?"

I nodded. Anyone who'd worked as a dog trainer would know basenjis, one of the two quintessential brat dog breeds. Until rottweilers got so popular, basenjis and fox terriers were two of the mainstays of the industry.

"I've been at the loft, of course. We had each other's keys since Magritte was a puppy. I had him a lot of the time. You couldn't leave him alone for more than an hour or two. He'd get really destructive, and he'd make an awful racket."

Tell me about it, I thought. But I let him keep on talking.

"Louie couldn't stand him. So Cliff never took him to Louie's. And Louie never stayed at the loft. He was so pissed when Cliff began talking about getting a dog, and it only got worse. I think he was jealous. So Magritte stayed with me whenever Cliff stayed over at Louie's. He's always been sort of my dog, too. Anyway, it was only natural, when the police came—they spoke to everyone in the building— to go upstairs and get Magritte. That's when I saw he was gone, and his collar and leash weren't hanging on the hook where Cliff and I always put them. I thought maybe Cliff had taken him with him. Maybe he ran away after Cliff was hit. Maybe he was stolen. He's an immensely valuable dog, a champion and a son of the top-winning basenji in the country."

I nodded, careful not to interrupt.

"It was never an issue for Cliff, the money, I

mean. He kept turning down requests to use the dog at stud. He always talked about it ruining his temperament, you know, making him aggressive with other males. But honestly, I think he just didn't want the dog to love anyone but him. He got a gigantic kick about Magritte winning in the ring, so he'd let Gil handle him at the shows. Morgan Gilmore, he's the handler who's always shown Magritte, he's fabulous with the breed. But that was it. I mean, I don't think he thought about the dog loving *me*, because he had to have *someone* to take care of him when he couldn't. So I think he just accepted that. But no one else could get in there, could get between them. God, he just loved that little dog to death."

He began to talk faster, as if he needed to relieve himself of the burden of carrying this information all by himself.

"He didn't care about making money hiring him out at stud. He used to fight with his handler about it all the time, because he, Gil, said he'd take care of it, and Cliff wouldn't have to mess with it or worry about it. He said it wouldn't change him, Magritte, that he'd be the same. But Cliff was adamant. What I'm trying to say is that if someone stole the dog on purpose, like if *that* were the point, that would mean whoever killed Cliff knew about Magritte. Gay bashing, you live in this neighborhood, you know a lot about gay bashing, it's random. The event may be planned—after all, you have to remember to put the baseball bats in the car before you leave Jersey—but the victim isn't preselected. Anyway, if the dog were with Cliff, wouldn't he have been hit, too?"

"You mean beaten to death?"

"I'm sorry. I'm doing this ass backwards. I didn't tell you one of the most important things. Clifford wasn't beaten. This was vehicular homicide."

"He was run over?"

"Hit at high speed from behind about two-thirds of the way out onto the pier. At least, that's where he was found."

"Do the police think he was actually hit there or that the body was dumped there?"

"Oh, no, they found enough evidence, they said, at the scene to be sure it happened there."

"Well, I guess we can rule out your garden-variety hit-and-run. Cars aren't allowed on the pier or, for that matter, except for official vehicles, in that whole waterfront area. Did he have any enemies, that you know of? More apropos, do you know of anyone who might stand to gain from his death?"

"I don't know of any specific enemies, not someone who'd want to kill him. Are we talking sane or crazy here? As for money, he plain didn't have much, not that I know of. His art was barely selling. He would trade pieces sometimes, you know, with artist friends. But he didn't actually sell much, and when he did, the prices were really low, a thousand or fifteen hundred at most. Ironically, his first break was about to happen. I guess you'd have to say, *maybe* about to happen. He had just signed his first contract with a gallery weeks before, not a great contract, but still a contract. He was getting his work ready to be in his first group show when he was killed. As far as I know, the loft is mortgaged to the hilt. It's not as if he owned anything worth *killing* for. Except Magritte, I guess. But now he's gone, too."

I took the notepad out of my pocket and began to write down the things he was telling me. When I finished writing, I looked up at the dogs. Dashiell was humping a little Jack Russell who kept turning around and snarling at him. It wasn't a pretty picture.

"Look," Dennis finally said, "the case is open, but I'm as sure as I can be that nothing much is being done, because of the location of the crime, the hour, and the sexual orientation of the victim. But this just doesn't fit the pattern of a bias crime. Well, perhaps there was bias involved—when isn't there?—but I can't accept the conclusion that it was a random crime. Even the money in his pocket was peculiar. A thousand dollars, separate from the rest of his money. And left on the body. Not taken. The bottom line is, I need to know who did this. And I need to find Magritte," he said.

He looked away. Maybe to watch the Jack Russell trying to get even.

I waited.

"The longer he's missing, the less chance there is we'll find *him* alive."

"Hadn't we better get moving?"

He turned around, looking like a deer caught in the headlights.

"You'll take the case?"

I nodded.

"Oh, shit. I didn't ask what you charge."

"It's five hundred a day plus expenses for me and a straight fifty for the dog."

"Fifty a day extra for finding Magritte?"

"No. Fifty a day extra for Dashiell. And I absorb his expenses."

A line appeared between Dennis's gray eyes.

"You mean if I hire you without the dog it's only five, plus expenses, of course?"

"Right. But I don't work without him. It's a jungle out there, and I need to know at least one of the animals is on my side. Do you know what I mean?"

"I do," he said, making a sound with his nose that would have gotten a tsk-tsk from my mother, the late but, if possible, still perfect Beatrice Markowitz Kaminsky. "Precisely. Okay—let's do this. When do we begin?"

"How about now?" I slipped off a glove, put two fingers in my mouth, and blew hard, making the sound of air coming out of a balloon.

"Needs work," he said. He whistled loud enough to wake the dead.

It must be a sex-linked trait. And, Lord knows, I haven't had any of that in a while.

"Thanks. Anyway, I'll need access to Cliff's studio, if possible. I'd like to spend some time there with Dashiell. I have lots more to ask you, but we can do that on the way."

"Does Dashiell actually . . . *do* things, I mean, besides protecting you?"

I looked down at my dog. The top of his head had been slimed by one of the other dogs. His big meaty mouth was agape and panting, a loop of drool draped delicately over his worm-colored lower lip. And he was covered with dirt.

"You thought he was just a pretty face?"

Dennis Keaton's smile was nervous and lopsided, the left side of his mouth moving up at the corner, the right side staying where it was. I got a good close-up view of those crooked teeth.

"Let's go," he said, pushing off the chain-link fence. "We can stop at my place for the keys, and I guess you'll be wanting an advance, or do I see too many movies?"

"I have no idea how many movies you see, but I see too many bills. I require a thousand-dollar advance."

Now *he* nodded.

He seemed like an admirable fellow, my new client, taking on responsibility in a world where most people prefer to shirk it. It appeared he wanted to do right by his friend, a friend whose murderer he wanted found at any cost. And in the midst of his grief, he was even worried about a little basenji.

I wondered what the real story was.

"Suppose we find Magritte, what then?" I asked while opening the loop of Dashiell's nylon slip collar. "Who would he belong to now that Clifford is gone?"

"Why, me, of course. I thought I made it clear that he's always been sort of my dog, too."

"I see," I said.

So it wasn't quite as noble as it appeared, I thought. Then again, it hardly ever is.

I slipped the collar onto Dash, and when I looked up, Dennis was holding the gate for me. What next, I thought, is he going to place his hand in the center of my back and steer me across the street? How does anyone know how to behave nowadays!

It began to snow. Huge white flakes were falling on and around us as slowly as if we were in a dream, and suddenly all the sounds were muted. Even the Hudson Street traffic sounded far away.

I wondered if it had been snowing the night Clifford Cole had died.

"Can we make a detour?" I asked.

"Where to?"

"I need you to show me where Clifford's body was found."

I had a stack of bills waiting on my desk at home. A case was exactly what I needed, and now, thanks to Dennis Keaton, a case was what I had. If I had a normal occupation, I'd be happy. But I don't. And I wasn't. I'd have been a fool not to think that the homely man with the goofy smile walking quietly at my side might himself be the killer I was hired to find.

Hiring the PI to throw everyone off the track is not unheard of, particularly when someone hires a woman in what's clearly a man's profession. Sometimes it's because they think a woman will fail, and failure is precisely what they're after, at any cost.

Whatever the truth would turn out to be, it would emerge as it always did, in frustratingly small pieces, progressing so slowly I'd want to scream, or give up, or get a job selling jelly beans in the five-and-dime. Instead, I'd keep picking away at things until the scab came loose and all the ugliness underneath finally showed itself.

My mother always told me not to pick at scabs because, if you did, you'd get a scar. I never listened then, and I never listen to the voice of reason now. I just have to find out what's under things, the secrets, the motives, the little twists and turns the human mind can take that make something repugnant seem plausible. And when I'm finished poking around where I don't belong, when the answer is finally visible, the crime solved, I think about Beatrice and what she told me, that the wound will never heal properly, that the scar will be permanent, and that chances are I'll be even unhappier when I get where I'm going than I was before I began.

3

I'll Draw You a Picture

THE CHRISTOPHER STREET pier sticks out stiff and straight into the Hudson River like an accusing finger pointing at New Jersey, the state with the worst drivers and the highest cancer rate in the country. I unhooked Dash's leash and let him run while Dennis walked me to the place on the pier where Clifford Cole met his killer and his maker on a cold winter night two weeks earlier.

"It must have been here. The officer I spoke to mentioned that," he said. I followed his gloved finger to the spray-painted sign on the concrete barricade, a comical face with a sad expression, the mouth a wide *M*, the sparse, spiky hair like an off-center crown of thorns, and next to it, "Punk's Not Dead."

I looked around the pier. Where was the dog? I wondered. Was he alive, or as dead as his master?

If I looked over the barricade and into the river, would I see him floating there, bloated beyond recognition? I decided not to, not with Dennis there.

Dashiell was marking the pier. He was never one to ignore masculine responsibility. When I turned around to look at Dennis, I saw that he was looking up to avoid crying. I wondered how many times he had been told that big boys don't cry, that part of *his* masculine responsibility was to avoid showing any vulnerability, as if he weren't part of the human race, such as it is. I took the Minox out of my pocket and snapped a couple of quick shots of the pier.

"Let's get out of here," I said. "I've seen enough for now."

Just before we turned off the pier, I noticed another spray-painted sign.

Beware of Muggers. Don't Be Caught Alone.

"What a place to die," Dennis said.

I didn't respond. I had seen too many worse places, places far from the fresh, fishy smell of the river and the sweeping, open views north and south, places that stunk of urine, feces, vomit, blood, places so dehumanizing and frightening they could have wiped out every decent vision the victim had ever seen, and perhaps the worst place of all to die a violent death, one's own bed, the place for the sort of sleep you wake up from.

I hooked on Dashiell's leash and we headed for SoHo.

One-sixty-three Greene Street was an AIR—Artist in Residence—loft, which meant that only qualified artists could live and work there and that the tax abatement would make the cost a little cheaper, but nothing in SoHo was what you could call cheap. A lovely five-story cast-iron building with Corinthian columns, it was painted white, unlike its drab neighbors. There was an art gallery, Haber's, on the street level and four floor-through artists' residences above. A fabric designer named KiKi Marr who Dennis said had been away since before Christmas was on two, Dennis had three, Clifford Cole's loft was on four, and a choreographer named Amy Aronson was on five.

We walked up to Dennis's loft, a deep, wide space, open in the front, facing east, where there would be wonderful morning light, and divided in the back for living.

Dennis's living room was separated from his studio area by a long, low bookshelf painted teal green and some hanging plants so that it would still get the light streaming in from the enormous windows facing the street. By now it was close to four, and the afternoon light was all but faded in the bedroom and kitchen areas.

Dennis turned on some lamps and went to put up the kettle for tea. We had come in frozen from that long walk in the snow. While he waited for the water to boil, he sat down to write me a check. I thanked him, slipped it into my wallet, and took out my notepad.

He hadn't said what sort of artist he was, and oddly, I thought, there was no clear sign in the studio area except that there were drawing boards and stools, three of them, rather than easels. The art hanging on the pale peach-colored walls was obviously done by many artists, and of those where I could see a signature, none were his.

"Was Clifford close to his family?"

"Well, his dad is dead. His mom lives in Maryland, in Frederick. That's where Cliffie grew up. You should've heard his drawl when he did Barbara Fritchie." He smiled to himself at the memory. "I never used to think of Maryland as the South, you know," he said, "but Cliffie always said it was. He said it surely was."

I had no problem with that. To me, the South started below Canal Street.

"His mother's only been here once," Dennis said. "It was a couple of years ago. Cliff de-gayed the loft and brought everything down here. So I wouldn't say they were too close, no."

"Has she been here since his death?"

"No, only his brother has. He called the next night to ask when I could let him in. He was very quiet, you know, polite, and apologetic about bothering me. It ended up that I left the keys at Haber's for him because I wasn't going to be home when he could come by."

"You never met him?"

"No—never."

"And he didn't have a key?"

"I offered to make him a set, but he said not to bother, he'd just be there a short while and leave the keys back at Haber's. He kept saying that I shouldn't trouble myself. I said anything he wanted was fine with me, wouldn't be any trouble. Shit, the man had just lost his only brother. I didn't mind helping him out, but he said he didn't want to take up any more of my time and that I'd been too kind already. I guess he just wanted to be alone."

"What about the service? Did he say anything about that?"

"He said the service would probably be in Frederick because it was difficult for his mother to travel."

I made some notes, then noticed the silence.

"The truth is, I don't think they want to have any of *us* there. Peter didn't say exactly when it would be, and he certainly didn't ask if I'd come. As far as I know, he never even called Louis at all, not even to say he was sorry. Perhaps he was afraid if his mother met her son's friends, she'd finally have to wake up and hear the Judy Garland records playing. Some people would rather live in denial than know what's going on in their own family. Well, my dear, what would the neighbors say!"

"But Peter knew about his brother, didn't he?"

"How could he not know? He'd have to be blind. Mothers and fathers, especially fathers, that's different. I mean, you could show up for Thanksgiving dinner in *drag* and your parents could miss it. But not a brother. Even if they didn't talk about it, he must have known."

"But you don't know for sure? Clifford didn't talk about Peter, like after he'd seen him? He never mentioned anything they talked about?"

"No. But I didn't find that unusual. I never talk about my family to my friends. Just having to *see* them is more than enough."

Tell me about it, I thought.

"Families, oh, you know. I mean, *they*'re the ones who ought to be in the closet. They're so em*barr*assing."

The kettle had been boiling for a while. He got up and went to the kitchen.

"Dennis, had Peter come up from Frederick?" I asked when he returned with two mugs of tea.

"No, he lives in Jersey," he said, "the *Garden* State." He rolled his eyes. "Fort Lee, I think. He's a teacher, married, two kids, boys. You know, a *nor*mal life. That's all I know. I mean, do *your* friends know your family?"

I took a sip of tea.

"Cliff used to meet Peter uptown, for dinner, once in a while, just the two of them. But not seeing your family too often isn't so unusual. You don't have to be gay to find family relationships stressful."

"This is true," I said. "Dennis, can you give me addresses and phone numbers for Cliff's family and friends?"

"Cliff's address book is upstairs, on his desk."

"And Louis, his lover? Where does he live, in the area?"

"Mmmm, Louie. Louis Lane, believe it or not. He lives on West Fourth Street, near Washington Square Park."

"Is Lane his real name?"

"Is Alexander yours?"

"It is now."

He raised one eyebrow.

"I got it the old-fashioned way—I married it. How did Louis Lane get his?"

"Made it up, for all I know." He suddenly looked uncomfortable.

"Perhaps he wanted something more memorable than his family name."

"Or less ethnic."

"You don't approve?"

He looked away for a moment.

"It was Polski, not that it's any of my business. At least that's what Clifford once told me, but that was after a major row, so maybe Cliffie was just being a bitch."

"I take it you're not terribly fond of Louis Lane."

"Miss Thing? Talk to me after you meet her," he said, rolling his eyes. "I wouldn't want to color your opinion."

Yeah, yeah, I thought.

"What about the handler, that was Morgan Gilmore, right?"

He put his hand up to his forehead and leaned his head into it. "God, I have to call him. He doesn't know about Magritte. And it's what"—he looked at his watch—"the second, less than a week until Westminster. Magritte is entered. I hope he's okay, wherever he is, I just hope he's okay."

I made a mental note to walk around the waterfront area and look over the barricades the next day, but the idea of finding the basenji that way didn't thrill me.

"Who found the body, Dennis? Did the police say?"

"Yes, as a matter of fact, the officers who interviewed me said it was a homeless man who hangs out on West Street."

He proceeded to tell me about the derelict, Billy Pittsburgh, who occasionally earns five or ten dollars and a cup of coffee by wandering into the Sixth Precinct, just across Tenth Street and up the block from where I live, and giving them the location of a wrecked car, a broken store window, or, in this case, a body.

There was a lot more I wanted to know from Dennis, but it was time to see Clifford's loft. I closed my notepad, stood up, and picked up my coat.

"I better get going on this. We don't have any time to waste."

Dennis picked up a set of keys from the top of the bookshelf and handed them to me.

"The round one is for the downstairs door, and the square one is for the loft."

"Can I hang on to these?" I asked. "I'll need to come back here, and I don't want to have to bother you. I sometimes get obsessed with things in the middle of the night and have to check them out, and where I have to check might be Clifford's loft."

"This might help, too," he said, and he took out his wallet and pulled out a worn-looking photograph of Magritte.

I looked at it, nodded, and put it carefully into my wallet.

"By the way, Dennis, when was the last time *you* checked the loft?"

"Three or four days ago. You can't imagine . . . Well, anyway, I had those keys made for you. I figured you'd want to spend time there alone. Too many movies?"

"Probably not enough. Life's too depressing to deal with reality every minute of the day. Sometimes I hate reality."

"Me, too. That's probably why I do what I do. Wait up."

He went to the back of the loft and returned with a book in his hand.

"Here," he said, "for the next time you need an escape from reality."

It was called *Too Big*, and it was written and illustrated by Dennis Mark Keaton. The huge dog on the cover, an Am Staff, looked a lot like Dash.

"Thank you."

"So—how will I know what's happening?" he asked as I headed for the door.

"I'll send you a report, once a week. What's your fax number?"

"Believe it or not, I don't have a fax. I use a messenger service."

"Don't sweat it. I don't have a fax either," I said. "And I hate to write reports. It makes me feel I'm back in school."

I turned the book over and looked at the back cover. A little girl with straight brown hair and round glasses was hugging the big dog, and they both looked deliriously happy.

"Not to worry. I'll call you. Or I'll just draw you a picture from time to time."

I stepped out into the hallway.

"And Dennis, don't hesitate to call me—anytime— if you learn anything new, anything at all, or if you just need to talk. That's okay, too."

I reached into my coat pocket and pulled out a business card and some lint.

"Okay. Good," he said, looking at the card.

It was pretty stark as cards go. It said, "Alexander and Dash, Research Assistance," and the phone number.

"Research assistance?"

"Right. You need some information. We're going to do the necessary research for you."

"I thought you were a PI."

"Maybe you *do* see too many movies," I told him.

I turned to go upstairs, and Dashiell bounded on ahead.

"Rachel," he called after me. "Ditto about calling me. Anytime is okay, day or night. I can't sleep anyway."

4

We Rode Downtown
in Silence

AT FIRST, THE blinking red light of the answering machine was the only thing I could see. After a moment, when I got used to the dark, I found a light switch and was startled to discover myself dwarfed by the immensity, power, and beauty of Clifford Cole's paintings, which were hanging and standing everywhere.

I rolled back the tape so that I could hear Cole's messages. There were only a few since Dennis had been here. The one from the National Dog Registry took an easy preference to the others. My heart began racing, even though the dog who had been recovered wasn't my own. In fact, I hadn't even seen him yet.

Or had I? He was the subject of some of the canvases that were wherever my eye went as I called the 800 number that had been left on the machine a day or two earlier.

I explained my relationship to Magritte and apparently said enough of the right things to be given the name and number of the man who claimed to have him. A few minutes later I had spoken with him, and Dashiell and I were on our way.

Henri Plaisir lived in a walk-up on West Nineteenth Street, in Chelsea. After buzzing us in, he and Magritte waited in the open doorway while Dash and I climbed the three flights trying hard not to breathe in too much of the musty smell of the old tenement stairwell. Henri extended his hand to shake mine. For a moment, Magritte stood still as a statue at his side. I had the photo of him Dennis had given me in my wallet and had seen several much-larger-than-life portraits of him at Clifford's loft, but none of this had prepared me for seeing him in the flesh.

He was immaculately clean, almost sparkling, a little foxy-faced boy with small rounded-at-the-top triangular ears and dark, alert eyes. He was a ruddy chestnut brown with white points on his face, chest, paws, and tail, handsome, elegant, and with an uncanny presence, especially considering he weighed not much more than twenty pounds. He was clearly the kind of dog judges say "asks to win," the kind of creature you somehow find yourself drawn to look at, no matter how many other dogs are around. It was no surprise at all that he was so successful in the show ring.

Henri, as he had asked me to call him on the phone, swept us in with a broad gesture of his arm. Magritte came to life. He play-bowed to Dashiell, and all four of us stepped into Henri's one small, neat room, kitchenette on one wall, pull-down bed on another, two bookshelves, a small TV set on top of one of them, a round oak table with two matching chairs, and two doors, one presumably the closet and the other the john.

Late on January 20, Henri's story began, the evening of the day Clifford Cole was murdered and less than a dozen hours after his body was discovered by Billy Pittsburgh, Henri had stopped at Metrometer, the taxi garage on Charles Street, just east of Washington, to have his meter checked. It was there that he first saw the little brown-and-white dog who, cold, dirty, thirsty, hungry, and frightened, had ducked into the open garage.

Henri was from Haiti but had lived here since he was in his late thirties. He and his brother had saved for years to buy a taxi medallion, and now they shared the cab, each working a ten- or eleven-hour shift. That way they got the most use out of it and usually didn't even have the expense of a garage, he said. He had just parked the cab half an hour before I got there, and his brother would take it out at midnight.

He appeared to be in his mid-sixties, a little taller than me which meant he was five-seven or five-eight, about 165 pounds, with close-cropped salt-and-pepper hair, rough-textured, clean-shaven, dark coffee-colored skin, and soft brown eyes. He was wearing a weimaraner-colored cardigan with pockets, the kind I remember from when I was a kid, like the one Mr. Werner who ran the candy store wore, and beige twill pants with a crease. He had just gotten home from parking the cab when I called from Clifford's loft.

"I wasn't looking for a roommate at the time. I just thought my meter was running awful slow, awful slow. But there he was, and the man, he say to me, what am I going to do with this little boy when I close? I don't want to put him out in the weather with his short fur and all this traffic. And I say to him, I only have another hour or two to drive. What harm can it do if he sit in the front with me? I bend down just so." He knelt to show me. "And he just come right up to me. He make this funny sound. Not a bark. He never bark once in all the time I got him. Like a trill in his throat, he make. And I just lose my heart to him right there on the spot. Can I offer you a cup of tea, Rachel?" he asked.

I nodded.

"I didn't see the tattoo right off," Henri said as I sat at the little table. "And there was no collar, so no tag. But I figured that if I was so taken with this little boy, someone else must be heartbroken. I never thought anyone had throw him away, but that he got lost somehow. So I begin to take him with me every day. I never got such good tips," he said, shaking his head. "No, sir.

"I put some signs up, near the garage in the West Village. But no one call me. On the third day I have him, I was not going to drive the cab, so I decided to give Jimmy here a bath. I been calling him Jimmy, and he likes the name very much, don't you, Jimmy?"

Magritte looked up when Henri addressed him. Then he went back to bringing all his toys to

Dashiell. There were quite a number of them, considering how short a time the dog had lived here.

"So, that's when I found the tattoo, and I wonder why someone would tattoo numbers on the inside right thigh of a dog, so from then on, whoever I pick up in the taxi, I ask them. I figure someone will know, and then I will know.

"The day I called it in, Rachel, my fare says to me I should pull over, and he looks at the tattoo and he says, 'Nine digits, it's a social security number. You have to call the National Dog Registry in Woodstock. They'll have the name and address of the owner.' So I am so happy to get my question answered and to learn something new. And I am so sad that I will lose my friend Jimmy here. He's been good company for me.

"He even know the number, this man, 1-800-NDR-DOGS. His German shepherd, he say, is tattooed also. So I call it. And so here you are."

He sipped his tea, I ate most of the cookies he had placed on the table, and then we sat in silence for a while, watching Magritte wrestle with Dash.

"You wouldn't think that big one would be so gentle," Henri said. "Not even a growl when little Jimmy jumps all over him."

I nodded, my mouth too full of Pepperidge Farm Chessmen for me to speak. One of the reasons people are so afraid of pit bulls is that they usually don't growl, even when they have ample reason to do so. If there's anything scarier than a dog making a racket, it's a silent one, especially if he's not making a fuss because it's clear he knows he doesn't have to in order to get the respect he's after.

"Listen, Henri," I said when there was nothing

left to eat, "I'd like to offer you a reward. My client is going to be so thrilled. I just can't tell you what this will mean to him."

I reached into my coat pocket for my wallet. There was a fifty tucked away behind the picture of Dash, for emergencies.

"I don't want your money, Rachel." He shook his head back and forth and reached his hand out to pat my other hand. "It's been a privilege to have little Jimmy here with me."

"It's not my money, Henri. As I told you, I'm not Magritte's owner. That young man was killed, and I work for the new owner. And he, my client, would be happy for me to give you something." Of course, I hadn't told Dennis what I had discovered yet. I wanted to have the dog before I got his hopes up, to see for myself that he was okay. And even though the call had come through NDR, I wasn't about to send him out to retrieve the dog when its disappearance might have been connected to a murder. Somehow, when I heard Henri's voice on the phone—I pay a lot of attention to the sound of people's voices—I lost most, but not all, of my caution.

"No, no, I couldn't take it," Henri said. "It would give Jimmy here the wrong message." At the sound of his name, Magritte, aka Jimmy Plaisir, jumped as sprightly as any cat and landed on Henri's lap. Henri began to scratch the dog's chest very gently, stroking him again and again, and I noticed how still Magritte stood on his friend's lap and how he closed his eyes to concentrate on the pleasure.

"How about expenses?" I asked. "That's certainly fair."

"Well, he did chew up some shoes for me," Henri

said. He began to laugh. "I didn't tell you that part, did I? Oh, he can be a devil, this one."

"I know exactly what you mean," I said. "I used to train dogs for a living. We call these 'brat dogs.' "

"I like that," he said.

I lifted the saltshaker and placed the fifty and my business card under it.

"If you should hear anything that might relate to the murder, Henri, you can call me anytime. I should be getting him home now. I can't thank you enough. Who knows what would have happened to this dog without you?"

It was nearly eleven when I was ready to leave Henri's apartment with Magritte. Henri kept one toy, a bug-eyed green frog, "for memories," he said, "and in case he come back sometime to visit his friend Henri." He insisted I take the rest of the toys, as well as half a bag of Science Diet and two cans of Kal Kan chopped beef. Then he decided he had better drive me to SoHo, because how else was I going to get there with a bag of food and toys and two dogs? and anyway, he said, it would give him a chance to give Jimmy one more ride in the cab.

We rode downtown in silence. Henri and Magritte were in the front. Dashiell and I rode in the back. Of course, the meter was off, so every few blocks someone stepped out into the street and tried to flag us down. Henri had asked where I live, and when I told him I lived in the Village, he insisted on waiting for me and driving me and Dash home. It took a bit of work, but I finally convinced him that Dashiell needed one more walk anyway, that I'd be perfectly safe walking anywhere with a pit bull, and that, if worse came to worst, I no longer had enough in my wallet to worry about. At that he laughed and finally agreed to let me off at the loft.

I hadn't done any of the work I had planned to do at Clifford's loft, and I was too tired and much too hungry to start now. But as I hiked up the stairs with Dashiell and Magritte, I felt I had done well for my first day on the job. I hoped Dennis wouldn't be spoiled and think the rest of the work would go this well or this quickly. And I hoped he wouldn't catch on immediately that I hadn't done anything at all to recover Magritte except listen to the messages on Clifford Cole's answering machine, just as he would have done had he gone to the loft before me or even with me.

What is detective work if not, at least in part, doing all the obvious things, looking at mail and listening to messages, talking to people who knew the victim, talking to people in the neighborhood and in the area of the crime scene in the hope that someone saw something, even if, at the time, they didn't know if what they saw was significant, and just stabbing around in the dark, hoping to find something somewhere that will point you toward the light? Finding Magritte was wonderful and satisfying, but what, if anything, did he have to do with the murder? As for finding the answer to that and every other question, I hadn't even begun.

5

You Don't Know Me

IT WAS A cold walk home. I unlocked the wrought-iron gate and followed Dash down the narrow covered brick passageway between two town houses into the large, square garden, in the far left corner of which is the brick cottage Dash and I gratefully call home. Though it sounds grand, it isn't. What is grand is the deal I got.

Sheldon and Norma Siegal, who own the town house on the left and the cottage, are rarely around, so more than a tenant, they wanted a caretaker, someone to watch over the house whenever they're away. In exchange for services rendered, the rent I pay is nominal. Which is exactly what I can afford.

The cottage has two floors of living space and a basement for storage. There are two small bedrooms and a bathroom on the top floor, a living room with a fireplace and a small, open kitchen on the main floor, and one big room, with another bath-room, downstairs.

Downstairs is where I keep all the things I still haven't unpacked since I moved here four years ago. I simply haven't found the need for good crys-tal in my current lifestyle.

The house works well for us, storing all the books, files, and rawhide bones we need to keep us reason-ably happy. But best of all is the garden, wonderful when it snows, because Dash gets to make the first paw prints, terrific in spring when the perennial herbs and flowers return as if by magic, amazingly cool in summer, especially in the evening and at night, and mysterious and sad in the fall when the cycle draws to an end in a blaze of beauty, all hid-den from Tenth Street and the rest of the world.

I unlocked the door, flicked on the light, fed Dashiell, and went straight up to bed. I had the tape from Clifford Cole's answering machine in my coat pocket, where I had put it before leaving the loft, replacing it with a new tape I found in the drawer of the table the machine sat on. I had wanted to hear it again, but suddenly the day caught up to me and I could no longer think of anything but sleep.

There were only three messages on the tape, any-way. The National Dog Registry, someone sell-ing home delivery of the *New York Times*, and a squeaky-voiced lady who wanted to mate her bitch to Magritte, that adorable little stud.

Dashiell was already asleep. I closed my eyes and thought about Dennis's reunion with Magritte. I had knocked on the door and when he asked who was there I had said, It's me, Rachel, I'm ready to draw you that first picture. When he opened the door, the basenji dog had squealed. Dennis had bent down, and the little dog had kissed him all over his face. I thought about the look in Dennis's eyes, when he finally could take them off his dog.

I also believed my dog to be the best thing since indoor plumbing. I had rescued Dashiell from some wrong headed, mean-spirited young entrepreneurs I had run into on a case, people who planned to make money fighting him when he grew up. I liberated him in such a fashion, let's say, that I didn't take the time to get his pedigree.

Sometimes when the right dog finds you, he has papers. Sometimes he doesn't. Hey, I have papers. My divorce document. It's not much to curl up against on a cold night. A dog is much better suited for that job.

Hugging Dashiell, I fell asleep happy, but I woke up in the middle of the night with a start. Was it a dream that woke me? I couldn't remember. All I could remember was that sign at the pier.

Don't be caught alone.

I almost always was, more and more of late. I was thirty-eight, suspicious, competitive, too independent on the surface for the taste of most of the men I met, and under the surface, much too frightened to suit my own.

Even if I could have fallen asleep again, it wouldn't have been worth lying there and rehashing my whole life before I finally got fed up enough to sleep. I got up and went into the spare bedroom, a little two-by-four job where I did my paperwork.

Dennis's book was on the desk where I had tossed it earlier. I took it onto the guest bed, slid under the blankets, and began to read about Antonia, who was five and who had always wanted a dog, ever since she was four and a half. When she finds Eliot, she is sure that he was meant to be hers.

"I guess it wasn't meant to be," I told my sister, Lillian, after the divorce.

"Well," she said, meaning "bullshit," meaning she thought I had fucked up again, "what are you going to do *now*?" meaning now that I had ruined my life, just as she always knew I would.

"Move back to the city," I said. "I never should have left. And get a dog!"

"You're not going back to dog training, are you? Why don't you get a normal job, Rachel?"

"I don't know," I said, thinking of how much I hated going backward.

I had closed the school and moved to Westchester so Jack and I could have a "normal life," whatever that was. What had I been thinking! But it was done, and now I'd have to go forward. But to what?

"Look, maybe until you think of something else, Ted could—"

Oh, God. I was filled with panic at the thought of working in the garment industry.

"Well," I said, wanting to make her as miserable as she had just made me, "I've always wanted to be a detective."

It was simply the most annoying thing I could think of on such short notice.

"Rachel, have you completely lost your mind!"

I had a strong suspicion it was a rhetorical question, so I didn't bother to answer her.

"You know, I can really see myself doing investigation work. Jack always said I was the nosiest bitch he ever met, or maybe that was just during the financial disclosure part of the divorce. Anyway, the hours would suit me, and I wouldn't have to wear panty hose."

"A *detective*," she bellowed, "so now that you're finished being Clyde Beatty you're going to become Dickless Tracy?"

Just like that, for the first time in eight months I started to feel like myself again.

"Oh my God, Rachel, tell me you're not serious."

"I can't. I am."

Of course I wasn't. Not yet, anyway. I was just having some fun for a change.

"Rachel!" She was fairly hysterical by now. "Rachel—you wouldn't. You wouldn't dare!"

That's when I knew it was *bashert*, meant to be. I never could resist a dare from Lillian.

I looked at Dennis's ink and watercolor wash drawing of Eliot, realizing as I did that the black stains on his pants and shoes had probably been made by india ink. I mean, was I a born detective, or what?

And what was Lillian carrying on about? This was only my second stab at what she calls the dirt-bag professions. She needn't worry about the other three. Selling insurance has never appealed to me. I'm more interested in who than how much. And on my worst day I'd never consider real estate or the used-car business. Sure, I follow people, eavesdrop, go through people's garbage and read their mail, snoop, distort, deceive, and misrepresent. I even do a little B & E if it's absolutely necessary. But, hey, I have my pride.

I looked at Eliot again, a mountain of a dog, big, square head, thick and stolid, uncropped flying-buttress ears, large, meaty mouth, closed and serious for now. I studied every part of him, the massive chest, the strong, straight legs, the neat, large, rounded feet, so like Dashiell in every way except for coloring. Eliot was a brindle. Dashiell, except for the black patch on his right eye, is white.

"Please may I keep him, Mommy, may I, Mommy, please?"

"He's too big for you to walk," Antonia's mother said, as sensible as my big sister, Lillian.

"He's too big for us to feed."

"And where will he sleep? He's much too big to sleep in your bed."

But there they are, on the last page, in Antonia's bed, and, see, they fit just fine.

Bashert, my grandmother Sonya used to say.

I closed Dennis's book and dropped it onto the floor.

"You don't know me," he had said when he called me.

Was that just this afternoon?

"I got your name from someone in the neighborhood, but you don't know her. You did some work for her cousin about a year ago. Ellen Engel? And now I need your help. I need it badly."

Jack had said it, too, the first time he'd called.

"You don't know me."

There was a silence then, as we both waited.

"I got your number from your brother-in-law. Ted."

"Oh," I had said, my voice catching in my throat.

I closed my eyes and thought about the last message on the tape from Clifford's answering machine.

"You don't know me," a woman's voice had said, "but I have a beautiful basenji bitch, pointed, she just needs one more major, and I was interested in Magritte, you know, if you hire him out at stud."

Sex, it can fucking ruin you.

6

It Looked Like an
Enormous Bowling Ball

IT WAS SO cold when I got up, I could see my breath indoors. One disadvantage of living in the cottage is that I get to pay my own heat bill, and by necessity and nature I'm cheap. If Dashiell were a malamute, I could say I keep the place as cold as the inside of a refrigerator to prevent him from blowing his coat. But the truth is, if he were a malamute, he'd blow it anyway. You really *can't* fool Mother Nature.

I went downstairs and opened the front door for Dash. A moment later, he was back with the *New York Times*, which gets pitched over the locked gate in an electric blue plastic bag.

It was going to be cold and windy with a chance of snow toward evening, the homeless were causing safety and sanitation problems at Penn Station, Tiffany's was advertising a diamond bracelet for about the price of a one-bedroom apartment, and a man in Oregon had poisoned his wife, who, the *Times* reported, had survived to testify at his trial, in his defense.

I fed Dashiell, got dressed, and headed downtown to Clifford Cole's loft.

Where Dennis had warmed the cavernous space with color, Cliff's studio area was white—tin ceiling, walls, and wooden floor all done in a shiny enamel so that when I arrived, the sun was bouncing off whatever surface it hit, except of course the paintings, where the light seemed to become absorbed into the canvas. The paintings apparently had not been touched since the murder, and I made a note to find out who owned them now. Then I took some photographs of the studio.

All the paintings in the large room were Cliff's, all huge, some telling their story in three or even four canvases. There was one set of three canvases, hung so that there were only inches between where one stopped and the next began, that took up the entire north wall of the huge space. The first canvas showed a pale blue wall with a window. Out the window was a single branch with buds, a March branch, and on the pale wooden floor a yellow and black ball, the kind that squeaks when squeezed. The second canvas showed more of the same place, blue wall, no window this time, a single wooden chair with a black baseball cap with a red B on it hanging over the left-hand corner of the ladderback, a green frog under the chair, the same kind Henri had gotten for his Jimmy dog and then kept "for memories." The third canvas showed the blue wall, the pickled whitish wooden floor, and the back end of Magritte, as if he had been caught walking out of the picture. In the lower right-hand corner of the last panel of the triptych, Clifford had printed the title of the painting in small, neat letters, all lowercase: *out, damned spot.*

There was another painting of Magritte on the south wall, this one called *rising son.* It showed another underfurnished room. Even the paint was used starkly in these portraits. The color was rich, but the brush strokes were very even, and you could see the texture of the canvas as part of the painting. At the top of the portrait, you could see the white-socked feet of the basenji, as if this time Magritte were floating up out of his own portrait.

There were two paintings standing against that wall, both done at the beach. In one, an oversize close-up of part of a wooden beach house, painted in shades of gray: you could see through the large window that it was raining *indoors.* The small printed title read *home, sweet home.* The other painting showed Magritte leaning out the window, elbows on the sill, a cigarette dangling from his tight lips, like the lonely men you see looking out of tenement windows in the city. Even Magritte was done in gray, so that the painting resembled a black-and-white photograph. It was called *he never read the surgeon general's report.*

I began to wander around the loft, just to get a feel for the space and to see where things were. I wanted Dashiell to take a look at things, too, the way dogs do, with their noses. So as I walked and he sniffed, every once in a while, I told him, "Smell it, good boy!" to let him know he wasn't just being nosy, he was working. I never know what Dash will come up with, but I always know that it will be very different from what I can "see." I put the kettle up, took out a big white mug, and found a box of Earl Grey tea bags. It was a cook's kitchen—good equipment, lots of expensive, shiny copper-bottomed pots hanging above. There was no microwave, but there was a Cuisinart and a professional-size mixer.

Dash and I continued wandering while the kettle heated. Cliff's bedroom, facing west, was high enough to get good light even though it faced the back of a building on Wooster Street. There was enough space for the light to filter down, enough to give the room a lovely cast, but not enough to blind you when you were trying to sleep. The bed, unmade, was a double, and the sheets and quilt were white, as were the walls, the floor, the rug, and the long, low painted dresser.

There was a four-panel painting hanging over the bed, tilted *up*. In the first three panels there was a man asleep in a bed, in the very bed beneath the portrait, down to the last detail. Those three pictures were identical but for one detail, a slight change in the position of the head on the pillow, a dark head of hair poking out from the white quilt, the face not visible. In the last panel, the bed was rumpled and empty. Somehow I was sure the mysterious man was Louis Lane, that in this way, he did indeed sleep over.

Above the dresser there was a smaller painting with a dark, brooding, and sexually suggestive look, a Diane Arbus–y portrait of two young boys, one on each side of the canvas. The empty space between the boys gave the portrait a palpable tension. Both boys looked ahead, at the viewer, as if unaware of each other. They were nude. The boy on the left was a cherubic-looking six- or seven-year-old, with large, apprehensive hazel eyes. The boy on the right, the older of the two, a ten- or eleven-year-old, had a lewd expression on his face. In the usual spot, it said *les and mor*.

Cliff's work was more intellectual than emotional, more Magritte than Matisse. Even the disturbing pieces had a coldness to them; they were either fascinating or clever but kept the viewer at a distance rather than embracing him, rather than bringing him into the painting or into the heart of the artist. Whatever emotion was visible was well controlled, as if the hurt could be displayed visually but without the accompanying feeling. I wondered how the work reflected the man, but it's not possible to put together a person from the pieces of his life. You can't even come close.

At the side of the bed there was another Magritte, the Clifford kind, the chestnut-and-white dog flying over the rooftops of what appeared to be Paris, a basenji angel with creamy, feathered wings. I wondered if Louis had seen *good boy*, and if he had indeed been jealous of his demanding, adored rival.

I opened the drawers of the nightstands and pawed through the dead man's personal stuff—condoms, K-Y jelly, handcuffs, nothing unusual.

I opened the closet and looked at the clothes, good-quality pants and jackets and lots of them, not the kind of clothes I'd expect to find in a poor artist's closet. Jack, who dressed like a peacock when he wasn't filling cavities (no pun intended, the man is a dentist), had introduced me to designer clothes, and now I could tell without even checking the labels. Cliff was apparently slight; his butterscotch-colored suede jacket fit me perfectly.

When I heard the kettle, I put Cliff's jacket away and went back to the kitchen, adding up in my head the cost of what I had seen in the closet, then opening the cabinets and toting up how much Clifford had spent to outfit his kitchen. Poor artist indeed. Perhaps the man had a patron.

Louis Lane?

I took my tea over to a desk that sat in a little in-between area, open, of course, because it had no window. It was a cozy nook with a desk, a rich, red oriental rug, red walls, and a red velvet chair, someplace to read, listen to music, watch videos, pay the bills.

There were two drawings and a painting in the den that were not Cliff's—a lovely pencil sketch of Magritte, signed "Jan Bella," a pen-and-ink nude, male, signed "D. K." (the D. K. who was helping me pay my bills?), and a smallish watercolor head study of a sweetly handsome young man with a halo of curly hair, signed "john."

I sat at the desk and began to open drawers, and what I found told me that there were some pretty important things that Dennis Keaton did not know about his friend.

The first file I found was the one for Clifford's Fidelity Corporate Bond Fund. His current investment was in the neighborhood of $200,000, give or take a few thou.

The next file was an IRA, with Dreyfus. That was only valued at $22,611.16, but hell, the man had only been thirty-two.

His checkbook—Chemical Bank Select Checking, which, according to the brochure of bank costs in the file, required a minimum balance of $25,000, entitling Cliff to free checking, free telephone transfers, the privilege of larger ATM withdrawals, and a shorter line when he had to show up at the bank in person—had a balance of $44,682.13 in savings and only $132.11 in checking after a cash withdrawal of $1,000 made January 18, the day before he died. Clifford had neatly recorded the withdrawal both in his checkbook and on the bottom of the previous bank statement. But I hadn't needed to see that to know he was an obsessive-compulsive personality type. I had seen his pots.

I had also found money in many of his pockets, along with small sandwich bags for picking up after Magritte. As with every other New York City dog owner, every pocket, including the ones in his tux jacket, had plastic bags in it, because even if you've been out to a black-tie event, you still have to walk your dog and scoop when you get home.

Magritte's papers were in the desk, too, neatly filed like everything else. He was four and a half. His health was protected by the Murray Hill Animal Hospital on East Thirtieth Street. He had, I noticed, been vaccinated against Lyme disease, which probably meant he was taken out of the city regularly, perhaps to outdoor dog shows, and his rabies shot was up to date. He was indeed a champion of record, American, Canadian Ch. Ceci N'Est Pas un Chien. Clever, Clifford, mighty clever, I thought, and then, when the next certificate was in my hand, I was filled with admiration. It seems Magritte had a C.D., a Companion Dog degree, which meant he had satisfactorily performed all the

basic commands off lead at three different AKC
obedience trials and under three different judges,
no small feat for a basenji.

There were photos in the file, too. In all three,
Magritte was stacked, meaning he was standing in
show pose, and a handler, a tall man with a ponytail, presumably Morgan Gilmore, was holding the
show lead taut and beaming. The judge was in the
photos, too, holding the blue ribbon and whatever
bowl or platter Magritte had won at each of the
three shows.

I found Cliff's gallery contract, signed by Veronica Cahill. Most interesting, there was even a
copy of his will in the file drawer, with a note saying
the original copy was filed with George Rich, his
lawyer.

The most recent check register showed regular
monthly payments to a Dr. Bertram Kleinman. I
checked the medicine cabinet. There was no AZT,
DDI, Bactrim, or even Flagyl. It didn't appear Cliff
had active AIDS. There was no Prednisone or allergy medication.

Was Dr. Kleinman a chiropractor or a shrink?

From the amount of the checks, and the little
drawings on them, two men emoting in kind, my
guess was that Clifford Cole was in some sort of in-
teractive therapy.

A gay man in therapy—what a surprise.

After another thirty or forty minutes of poking
around, I took Cliff's will, the gallery contract, his
address book, and Dashiell and headed for the closest copy shop, returning everything to where we
found it before heading back for another look at
the Christopher Street pier. But when we left the

loft, I decided to walk over to the gallery first, just to take a look around and see what I might find out.

The Veronica Cahill Gallery was on the fifth floor of a wide ten-story brick building on West Broadway between Prince and Spring. To get to the gallery, you take one of those elevators that open on either side, depending upon which side you push the button, which depends upon which of the two galleries on each floor you are going to. The elevator opened right into the gallery spaces, which, like most of the West Broadway spaces, were large and bright.

The current installation at Cahill was called Dots, and the most enigmatic dot for me was the single sculpture placed in the middle of the gallery's white floor. It looked like an enormous bowling ball, but without the holes. It was titled *Black Dot*. The price on the title card was $25,000, and amazingly, there was a red dot on the card, signifying that this lucky dot had found a home. The paintings were also fairly large, although there were a few small ones toward the back of the gallery. They consisted of various canvases painted either white with one or more black circles or, for variety, black with one or several white circles. Prices were all in the ten-to twelve-thousand range. Several of those were sold as well. To each his own.

Dashiell and I had been welcomed by a short young blond with the proportions of a twelve-year-old, no hips, no tits, dressed all in black but, happily, without a dot on her outfit. He was offered a dog biscuit, and I was told about how fabulously well this young artist was doing, asked if I knew

"Tess," if I had been at the opening, which was fabulous, if I was a collector, and then followed around as I looked at paintings, as if I might, if not watched carefully, slip one into my pocket.

The more I looked, the more I began to wonder if the red dots signifying sales were all real or if perhaps the gallery put out a few to make people think their current installation was hot and start a buying frenzy.

"This is nice," I said, trying to look sincere, "but what I really love are paintings of dogs. I sort of, you know, collect them."

I gave her the perfect opportunity to hard sell me a Clifford Cole painting. She fumbled the dot, but made a slight recovery.

"I don't know what's going to be in the next show. But would you like to be on our mailing list?"

I signed a false name in the book, thanked the young woman profusely, turned down a second Snausage for Dashiell, and headed back to the Christopher Street pier.

7

I Began to Dig Carefully

I WANTED DASHIELL in a work mode, so I kept him on leash until we were on the pier. Then I pointed down the pier, told him, "Find it," and let him go.

I pulled up my scarf so that it covered my nose and mouth and walked back to the Punk's Not Dead sign, the one closest to where Clifford had been struck. The sad face with spiked hair was still watching over the place where he had lain until the police came to zip him into a body bag and take him away.

The wind was cold and stinging. Loose snow swirled in circles, rose up momentarily, and fell back to the surface of the pier. On a summer weekend, dozens and dozens of gay men would come here to lie in the sun. In winter, it was a lonely place.

Dashiell was working the southern side of the

pier. He would work the perimeter first, then quarter the pier and work each quadrant separately, in each case looking for something that didn't belong. That meant he would not alert if he found a condom. The pier was littered with them, both over and under the snow. Nor would he stand and bark for me, his front feet popping up off the ground with each woof, his ears flapping up and down in the wind he himself would create in his excitement, for beer cans, broken glass, cigarette butts, even underwear. These were all local weeds to him, things indigenous to the area.

Two types of things would get him to "call me." He'd signal for anything out of place, like a button, a wallet, or, say, a gun. In this case, it was unlikely he'd find anything of value. It had been too long since the murder, and the pier was too open and too populated. But Dash would also be looking for anything that had a smell reminiscent of anything at the loft. He had nosed around Cliff's clothing and his shoes. I had even dumped the hamper for him, letting him smell crotches and arm holes, places where the scent would be the most powerful. He had picked up other scents as well, those he would find personally interesting.

I didn't really expect there'd be anything on the pier after all this time, but Dashiell had made some wonderful finds on previous cases, things too well hidden, intentionally or by accident, or too small for me to have discovered. After glancing back at him, now rounding the corner to work the far end of the barricade, I stood at the south fence and looked out over the Hudson.

I could see the Statue of Liberty, far to the south,

and Jersey farther west. The water surrounding the pier where you first walk onto it was frozen, but out here the Hudson was flowing, the light giving it a lovely silver cast.

I began wondering about the money, all that money, and where it came from, and why Clifford's friend Dennis didn't know about it.

Well, as my sister would say, hands on her hips, if your friend was busting his butt to make it, unable to have the freedom to paint, as you did, would you rub it in his face that you didn't have to be concerned about expenses?

When I heard Dash signal, I began to run. He had made a find. It was probably nothing of significance to the case, a cigarette lighter or an old shoe someone had left on the pier. But I needed to get to him quickly and to praise him to the sky. He couldn't discern what would be important and what wouldn't. Sometimes *I* couldn't at first. The only way to motivate him was to praise for every find, and hope like hell, if there was something there of significance, eventually he'd see that, too.

He was at the most westerly point of the pier he could reach, the last few feet blocked off by the chain-link fence. The sign there, this one official, warned of danger—Area Unsafe, Keep Off—but I could see where the fence was cut. This was New York, where warnings went unheeded.

Dashiell was sitting now, facing a snowdrift that had accumulated against the fence, just to the right of the warning sign on the other side. He always waited for me, never trying to bring me what he found. If he retrieved the item, were there prints, he'd blur them. In a different setting, a field or woods, if he brought me what he found, I'd never see the site to be able to look for other signs and clues. Most important, because I loved my dog, if I allowed him to pick up what he found on a search, he might get hurt. He could pick up—and drop—a gun, which might go off. He could find something toxic, something sharp, something that, when disturbed, would leave nothing in its wake but a huge hole and the smell of smoke.

When he saw me running toward him, he stopped barking. As soon as I reached him, he was on his feet, dancing excitedly as he looked from me into the snow piled against the fence and back, again and again.

I began to dig carefully, cracking through the crust, then brushing away the snow, a little at a time, with my gloved hands.

I felt it before I saw it, and the moment I touched it, I knew. As I lifted a piece of it carefully free of the snow, I could hear it, too, a faint, metallic tinkle. I cleared the rest of the snow more quickly, and there, tied to the very bottom of the fence, was a red leather leash, now wet, stretched, and twisted. Still attached to the leash clip was a red leather collar, complete with a small bell, fairly intact, and in my estimation, just about the perfect size to fit around the neck of a twenty-pound dog.

I knelt on the pier and opened my arms for Dashiell, folding him to my chest as he came for his hug. I slipped the Minox out of my pocket and photographed the leash and collar where it was before untying it and stuffing it into my pocket with the camera. Dashiell danced around for more praise, which he got as I checked the area as carefully as I could and then headed for home.

If the collar and leash Dashiell had found were Magritte's, then Clifford had definitely taken him along to the pier. But why? As a pickup aid? Lord knows, more people talk to me when I'm with Dashiell than when I'm alone. So was Magritte tied to the fence while Clifford had sex? If you took a rough count of the condoms that littered the pier, it was certain that, despite the weather, Clifford wouldn't have been the only one having sex out here.

I needed to talk to Louis Lane and see how they were getting along. Was it spite that brought him here, or hunger? And what about all that money? Why did he come out here with so much cash in his pocket? Did he simply have so much he was careless? The money in so many pockets back at the loft would lead me to think that might be the case.

Suddenly, I was famished. Craving a ham and melted brie on sourdough bread, I headed for Anglers and Writers, across from the ball field.

New York's laws prohibit animals on public transportation and in places where food is served, but since Dash, who schmoozes the old people at the Village Nursing Home when I am between cases, is a registered service dog, and perpetually in training, the restriction doesn't apply to him.

Being a detective is a lonely life, but at least I never have to eat out without a date.

8

You Don't Really Belong
in This Family

GETTING INTO BED with the copy of Clifford
Cole's will, gallery contract, address book, and a
yellow highlighter looked to be the most promising
evening I'd had in a long time.

The original will, which dated back to when Clifford was in his mid-twenties, was mostly the legal
jargon that makes what should be three or four sen-
tences go on for pages. Most people that young don't
write a will, especially if they don't have kids. Unless their money is family money, and part of the
deal when they get it is that it stays in the family.

In the original document, Clifford left everything
to his beloved mother, Adrienne Wynton Cole, and,
should she predecease him, to his beloved brother,
Peter David Cole. This could mean that his father
had already died when the will was written or that
the money came from his mother or her family in

the first place. Of course, once he had the money, in whatever form he got it, lump sum, generous allowance, untouchable trust where he could draw a set amount of the interest, or whatever, no one could require him to leave it to a person of their choosing. So he was either young or very honorable, or both. Or perhaps no one he preferred to leave the money to had yet come along. Follow the money. It was the first law of investigation work.

I turned to the next document, one of two codicils, both much more recent than the original will. It left the little African basenji, Ceci N'Est Pas un Chien, who apparently was not yet a champion, to Dennis Mark Rosenberg, aka Dennis Mark Keaton.

People are usually most defensive, my shrink used to say, about things that hit too close to home. Now, Rachel, she'd say after an outburst of denial, what's *really* going on here?

Of course, Dennis could dislike Louis for any number of other reasons. It's not uncommon for people to be jealous of their best friend's lover. I wondered if Dennis and Cliff had been lovers before Louis came onto the scene. Or even afterward. I checked the date of the codicil, but it turned out the one I had just read was the second. Perhaps when I checked to make sure I had everything ready to be copied I had gotten them out of order. The first of the two codicils was two years old, and left Clifford's entire artistic estate to Leonard Polski, aka Louis Lane. The Magritte codicil was dated a year and a half ago, five and a half months later.

If Cliff wasn't accepted by his family, he still kept faith with them financially. He probably knew he had to anyway. His will would be contested if he didn't, that is, unless he had been leading one of those normal lives your well-meaning relatives always tell you about, a life with a spouse of the opposite sex and children.

Dennis thought Cliff's "problem" was a problem for his family. Had they told Cliff, the way families do, that he could change if he wanted to? Had they offered to pay for therapy?

Would they have wanted either Magritte or Clifford's paintings? I wondered if his mother or his brother would have come to his show, had he lived long enough for the gallery to actually install it.

I thought about the coolness in his paintings, perhaps because he felt apart from his natural family, felt Magritte, of *rising son*, and his other heirs, Louis and Dennis, were his real family. If he left the paintings to Louis, he must have felt good about the relationship, at least at the time the codicil was written.

I picked up the gallery contract. How much of the post-eighties art world bust of the pay-the-piper nineties was reflected in Clifford Cole's contract with the Cahill Gallery I didn't know. I had never read a gallery contract before. I knew that a lot of the SoHo galleries had closed, and the remaining ones were often empty, run by people as desperate as the woman who had followed me around the Dots installation at Cahill earlier in the day. I have always found it amusing when someone tries to talk you into buying a so-called piece of art that costs more than your yearly gross.

There were still some wonderful things to see in the downtown galleries, works like Clifford Cole's that would linger in memory, where the range and ability of the artist actually merited the space his work occupied. Unfortunately, much of what was on display for eighties prices made me want to call the bunko squad. But there's no such thing, other than for forgery, in the art world. It's not a crime to produce derivative, dull, or simply poor "works," as the contract calls what the artist produces. It's simply a matter of taste.

Clifford's first contract was surprisingly short and simple, free of the jargon of wills, mortgages, and divorce documents. The gallery would determine the price, and the artist could not sell comparable works for less. The gallery would receive 50 percent not only of the price of works sold at the exhibition it would install but of any sales made by the artist from his studio that were a direct result of the representation and the exhibition at the Cahill Gallery, and even any nonrelated sales made out of the artist's studio for the duration of the agreement, which was one year. It was sort of the same deal real estate brokers love home owners to sign, stating that if the owner sells his home during the time of the broker's contract, even in cases where the broker has done nothing but sit on her ass and never advertised or shown the house, she will still receive 6 percent of the sale price. Nice work if you can get it.

The Cahill Gallery got first pick of all of Cliff's art, which meant that Cliff—now Louis—couldn't sell anything without giving the Cahill Gallery half the money, even if they never gave Clifford a show. I wondered what Leonard Polski would do with his inheritance. I hadn't seen most of the paintings. They were draped and standing in a huge storage

closet opposite the den, and the light in the closet
didn't work. Next time I'd bring a flashlight and
look at the rest of Leonard's loot.

I flipped through Clifford's address book. There
were lots of names of galleries, other places he had
probably sent a padded manila envelope with his
résumé, slides, SASE, and lots of hope. I liked his
work a lot better than much of what I see in SoHo,
but there was no way I could judge if it ever would
have become hot enough to sell. Often that has as
much to do with an artist's life or who he knows as
it has to do with his ability or originality.

I wondered if Clifford had gotten depressed
about his inability to sell his "works." He had
probably been elated the day he signed the contract. That had been November 16, which would
mean he had been working on things for his show
since then. There had been no date set, no promise
of how soon it would be or how many of his works
would be included. Most shows were up for a three-
week period, during which there would be an opening, often stacked with the artist's friends and
sometimes, like the invitations, paid for by the artist.
But then you had the chance to hope, and who could
put a price tag on what that was worth? There might
be a sale, a visit by a critic, a positive line in the
press. You might, after all, have a chance.

Peter Cole did not live in Fort Lee, but Woodcliff
Lake. I found Morgan Gilmore's number, too. He
lived in Greensboro, North Carolina. I marked
it with the highlighter, then put it on the nightstand
with the rest of the papers.

In the morning, I'd try to reach Louis Lane. After that, I'd start looking for Billy Pittsburgh, who,

I suspected, was using a name other than the one he had been given as a child.

What did it all mean, all this name changing? I had even done it myself.

When I took Jack's name, I had thrown away my own. I had detached myself from my past and my family. When we split, I chose to keep his name, not my own, even though I had used it for less than a year. I had set myself adrift. I had even rejected my profession, taking a job with the Petrie Detective Agency on lower Broadway, run by two brothers, Bruce and Frank.

I didn't actually meet the older Petrie, Bruce, until I had been working at the agency for two and a half months. He was obsessed with electronic equipment for both surveillance and criminal activities. Every few months or so he'd surface from his windowless back office and show us the specs on the latest eavesdropping equipment, voice-changing telephone, letter bomb scanner, or microcamera in a key chain.

It was Frank who had hired me to work as a junior undercover agent trainee, meaning I would do the same work as the regular agents but for much less money, because, as he so wisely explained, what if you're following a guy and he goes into the men's room and there's another way out? And when I presented the same scenario with a woman being followed, he had shoved some papers around on his desk and said he couldn't sit around all day and waste his valuable time arguing with me, there was work to be done, and did I want the job or not? I said I did. When I got home, I called Lili.

Why do you want to put yourself on the outside

looking in? she asked, one of her usual rhetorical questions. No, she said, changing her mind, for you, that would be an improvement. You won't have time to press your nose against the glass. You'll be too busy looking inside other people's garbage cans to even wonder about how normal people live. You don't really belong in the family, she said.

Family, Dennis had said, *oh, you know*.

Frank Petrie had put a tail on me right after he'd hired me, a real geek.

Hey, you never know, the Pinkertons could have sent me to find out all his secrets.

The tail was so ugly, you couldn't miss him from a mile away. It did not require a genius to figure out what was going on. I called Frank.

"Next time," I told him, "send someone less memorable."

"Good work, kid," he said. "You might not be a total loss after all."

Now, why couldn't anyone in my own family ever say anything that supportive!

9

You Can Never Be Too Paranoid

I WOKE UP to the sound of my own voice coming from the office. I hadn't remembered to turn down the volume on the answering machine, which I leave on high during the day so that I can monitor calls from anywhere in the house. Living in this city, you can never be too paranoid. At least that's what my shrink always used to say.

The next thing I heard was Dennis.

"Rachel, it's Dennis Keaton. Please call me. I have something important to tell you."

I picked up the phone. "Hey."

"Have you seen the *Times*?"

"Not yet, Dennis. I was asleep."

"Oh. Sorry. I forgot other people do that," he said.

Great. My mother had been reincarnated as a gay guy.

"Can you hang on?" I asked.

"The C section," he said. "Page nineteen, I'll hold."

I went downstairs, opened the front door, and sent Dashiell for the *Times*.

To most people, a C section is a cesarean. If you live in New York City, it's the arts section of the *Times*, the part your husband the dentist hands you while he reads the international, national, and local news and checks the value of his holdings in the business section. I found the article on page nineteen and picked up the cordless extension in the living room.

"So—'*Not* the Death of Art. Murdered artist Clifford Cole's works will be on display in his first one-man show this weekend at the Cahill Gallery in SoHo, a posthumous installation of the artist's paintings, drawings and sculpture,' " I said, reading from the article that Dennis could probably recite by heart. "I guess Veronica Cahill finally figured out what installation is going to follow Dots."

"What are you *talking* about, Rachel?"

"I stopped by the gallery yesterday, just to take a look, and they had this installation called Dots, the most god-awful stuff you ever saw. Well, no, I guess we've both seen worse. Anyway, I told the salesperson I sort of collected dog art, I had Dashiell there, and she failed to sell me a Clifford Cole. She said she didn't know what the next show would be. But apparently Veronica Cahill figured out a good way to get some mileage out of the contract she signed with Cliff. The way it's put here," I said, referring to the article, "well, the notoriety will at least bring people in, maybe even critics. Death makes good copy, or so they say."

"Do you believe this?" Dennis said. " 'An up and coming star of the downtown art world, cut down by human hatred just as his career was taking off.' Where do they get this garbage? She never even guaranteed him she'd put *one* of his pieces in a group show. Now she's his fucking *patron*. Excuse me while I go get a bag to throw up in."

There was nothing but silence on the line for a long moment.

"Listen, Dennis, this is good, isn't it? I mean, wouldn't it be worse if no one ever saw Cliff's paintings? They're quite wonderful."

He didn't respond.

"Dennis?"

"You're right, I know it, it's just that . . ."

"I know. He didn't get the support when he was alive, and he won't get to hear the applause, right?"

"Right," he said, "and someone else will get the money."

"Louis."

"Louis?"

"Louis."

"I thought his family . . ."

"Louis."

"Now I'm really going to be sick. Rachel, I bet Louis is behind all this publicity, this exploitation. I bet he engineered it!"

"It's possible. It should certainly increase the value of his inheritance. Let's keep our mouths shut and our ears open." That's the second law of investigative work. But I sometimes have trouble with the mouth shut part. I thought Dennis would, too.

"Dennis, don't tell anyone you hired me or what I do."

"Oh, God."

"What? Or should I say *who*?"

"I told Louis."

"Shit. Anyone else?"

"No. I *swear*."

"Okay. Let's keep it that way. I have to lie sometimes. Do you understand?"

"I never thought about it. I'm not exactly experienced in this sort of thing. Sorry. I'll watch my mouth. I promise."

"It's my fault, Dennis. I fucked up. I should have told you. It just means Louis will be, well, more guarded with me."

"You're not thinking that *Louis*—"

"It's possible. He did gain from Clifford's death."

"Not nearly what he lost."

Now it was my turn to be silent.

"You'll be there, at the opening?" he asked.

"Definitely. I wouldn't miss it for the world. Would you?"

"Clifford would kill me if I did, no matter what it took. Sorry I woke you, Rachel, but you said I could call anytime, and, shit, it's ten-thirty."

"No problem. I was up late reading Clifford's address book. His brother Peter lives in Woodcliff Lake, by the way, not Fort Lee."

"Same difference. It's all Jersey," he said.

"Dennis, while I've got you on the phone, I need to ask you something. You said Magritte's collar and leash were missing, right?"

"Yes. They weren't on the hook, and I didn't see them anywhere else."

"What did they look like?"

"Red leather, thin, buckle collar, not a slip, four-foot leash. Oh, and Cliff had hung a little bell on the collar. He liked the way it sounded when Magritte walked. Why?"

"Dashiell found them, on the pier. The leash was tied to the back fence, way low, buried in the snow. So he *was* there. Dennis, I'm sorry, but it looks as if Clifford took Magritte and went out to meet someone. Why else would he be on the pier at that hour?"

"You mean, he took Magritte out to help him hit on someone and then tied him up while he was having sex? That's so cheap."

"It's done all the time, Dennis. Let's get real here. Well, it may not be done all that often with a dog in tow, but guys are out there fucking in all kinds of weather and at just about any hour after dark. Am I right?"

"Okay, okay, I hear you. You're right. The police are right. So he had Magritte with him, and Magritte carried on while Clifford had sex. Magritte wouldn't have taken this lying down, you know. He had this thing about not being stopped from what he was doing. So if you took him out to walk, you better keep walking, not tie him up and fuck. That wouldn't have been part of his agenda."

"Dennis, I didn't say Magritte was *happy* to be tied up on the pier. And I know you're not happy to hear this."

"Never mind that. We're after the truth, aren't we? So, the way I figure it, why take the dog? He only would have made a racket. He'd have sounded like *he* was being murdered. That's just the way he was when he was thwarted. People think these dogs are quiet because they don't bark. Trust me, they're not quiet."

"Dennis, I can't say for sure why Cliff took Magritte with him, but you have to admit, a dog is a great icebreaker. No pun intended."

"Okay, okay, I understand, but what about the money, the thousand dollars?"

"Clifford wasn't quite as poor as you thought he was, Dennis. There's apparently money in the family."

"And the thousand?"

"Maybe he was just careless about money, since he never had to worry about it. Or maybe, like a lot of guys, he liked to carry a lot of cash. I read once that women will walk around with twenty bucks on them and feel fine, but that a majority of men don't feel right unless they've got at least a hundred bucks in their pockets. Maybe he needed the money for something the next day and forgot it was in his pocket. He left cash in lots of his jacket pockets, Dennis, not a thousand dollars, but cash. There was a fifty in his jean jacket. He seems to have been careless with money. Not irresponsible, but careless. Again, maybe because it wasn't in short supply when he was growing up."

"None of this makes any sense."

"It will. Give it time."

"But we know Magritte was there. That's definite. And that he was left there. We know that, too," he said, trying to take comfort in the fact that we had learned something about the night Cliff was killed.

"Apparently. The money was left. The dog was

left. Maybe something went wrong. Who knows? We don't know the point of this, do we? But it's my guess that Magritte was there at the time of the murder. From the looks of the leash, he jumped around and couldn't break it, but finally backed out of the collar. What if, let's say, Cliff had had a row with Louis, a big one, and maybe he went out to find someone for spite. It happens."

"Rachel, I—"

"Dennis, you know how people driving by always stare at the pier when they're waiting for the light to change. They hate what they're going to see, but they're compelled to look, like when you pass a car accident. Okay, suppose some nut job was driving by on West Street, no one's around, and he sees a couple of guys in flagrante on the pier and loses it. He turns his car around, shoots back uptown, drives onto the waterfront area and back to the pier. Maybe by then, the other guy has left. Cliff is on the way to untie Magritte, and this poor excuse for a human being drives onto the pier and runs him down. He wouldn't take the chance of getting out of the vehicle and checking his pockets. He wouldn't expect to find so much money. Money isn't the point, is it? He probably got the hell away as fast as he could. He probably never even saw Magritte tied up at the far end or heard him over the car's engine."

For the second time he made that sound with his nose that would have caused Beatrice, the perfect one, to hand him a clean, ironed handkerchief.

"I'm not ready to give up yet," he said. "Are you?"

"Of course not. I mean, even if it turns out to be that it is what it looks like now, maybe we can catch the bastard. Maybe I can find a witness. The opening is tomorrow night. Let's see what we learn there, okay? By the way, has the gallery been in touch with you about getting the paintings?"

"No. They're probably working with Louis. He's known Veronica for years. That's how Cliffie got past the manila envelope and slides stage. Louis introduced them. Anyway, the art is his now, isn't it?"

"Yes. And he can get it? He has keys?"

"He may be there right now, for all I know," Dennis said. "Yeah, he has the keys. God knows why. He almost never came here. He claims he's allergic to paint fumes. And dogs. Okay, so I'll see you at the opening?"

"You bet! Get to work, Dennis. You'll feel better."

When I hung up, I needed to do something to clear my head, so I climbed on my exercise bike and began to pedal rapidly. I had gotten the habit of working out when I was a dog trainer, hauling around dogs that sometimes weighed as much as I did. It's not really brute force that gets the job done. A great deal of getting through to a dog has to do with winning its respect, which is often done mentally, but it doesn't hurt if you can impress the dog physically when necessary, stopping him or moving him, if not with your irresistible personality, then with a little muscle and some swell timing.

I had told Dennis if he did something he'd feel better. But I had, and I didn't. I couldn't stop thinking about the Christopher Street pier, how lonely it must have been that night, how dark. I wondered if there had been a moon.

I thought about the sound of the place, too, the wind, the car, the little bell on the dog's collar, the sound it would have made as he pulled and twisted, trying to break free, and the mournful yodeling of that little dog, Magritte.

10

It Should Only Happen

DESPITE THE FACT that my mail assured me I had won seven million dollars and therefore no longer had to work for a living, Dash and I headed for the waterfront to try to find the homeless man known as Billy Pittsburgh. After all, back before I became filthy rich, I had given Dennis the hope there might be a witness, hadn't I?

When the last thing you want to see is a homeless person, like finally you met a guy who's appealing, interesting, single, straight, and uninfected—it should only happen—and you're wearing your black knit coatdress with the deep V neck and matching cigarette pants, your mother's sparkling marcasite pin, sheer black stockings, and witchy black suede, ankle-high boots with a small heel, and your hair for once came out perfect, and you're even wearing makeup, for God's sake, *then* you'll see homeless people. You'll trip over them. They'll hold their filthy hands out, nearly touching you, and ask for money. Or you'll pass one, asleep in a doorway, and for a long time afterward, you'll continue to smell the rancid odor of urine, wafting into your nostrils from your own clothes, which absorbed the stink as you passed it.

I knew it would take great luck to find Billy. It's not as if he had an address or a phone number. And even if I found him, it was doubtful he saw anything or could remember or relate what he saw if he had seen anything. Still, this, according to my mentor, Frank Petrie, was how you did investigative work. And since I didn't have a better idea at the moment, I figured I'd give it a shot.

Frank required a daily progress report that he could forward to the client so that, even when there was no progress, most days, you could outline where you went looking for it. According to Frank, the third law of investigation work is Look, kid, no one's paying you to sit on your ass and watch TV.

Dashiell liked the waterfront, and in nicer weather I did too. It was comforting to be near the river and expansive to let the eye rove far instead of being stopped every few feet by a building. There's more sky in the Village than there is uptown, because the buildings are lower here, more on a human scale than the skyscrapers in much of the rest of Manhattan, and at the waterfront you can see *really* far, to the Statue of Liberty if you looked to the southwest, to the twin towers of the World Trade Center south and slightly to the east. If you looked northeast, you'd see the Empire State Building, which to me is still the tallest building in the world. I'm always reluctant to edit the truths of my childhood.

I could see everything, including my breath, but I couldn't see Billy Pittsburgh.

We crossed West Street, walked a block to Washington, and headed uptown. A lot of homeless hang out in the meat district, a few blocks north from where we were. It was a long shot, but maybe someone would have seen Billy and might know where I could find him.

When we got as far as Gansevoort Street, we found a tattered woman slowly pushing her shopping cart full of possessions along the sidewalk. Poking out from inside her torn coat was the broad, striped face of a red tabby cat, and there were two small mixed-breed dogs, each wearing several sweaters, riding in the cart among her treasures. The homeless men usually collect deposit bottles. Many have become rather entrepreneurial, amassing large amounts of cans and bottles they can exchange for enough money for a meal. The street women seem far crazier than the men. Few talk to anyone. Many rave as they go. They seem more impaired than simply hideously down on their luck. At least, with this lady, her pets gave me a possible opening.

"Handsome cat," I said, the jowls telling me the cat was male, "what do you call him?"

She stopped, looked at Dashiell, then, to my surprise, looked at me. Perhaps Dash's presence signaled I was trustworthy.

"Tuna," she said. "Just use your nose, girlie. A

nose, by any other name, would smell a rat. Something's fishy in Denmark."

"I see," I said. "I mean, I sniff, therefore I am."

She tossed back her head and cackled.

"Sure would like some coffee," she said, lifting her head and air scenting, as if I might have some in my pocket.

"I'll get you a cup, um, what did you say your name was?"

"I smell, therefore I call myself Bo Peep."

"Wait here. I'll be a minute, okay?"

"No skin off my cat," she said, getting busy adjusting the parcels in her cart. The dogs sat perfectly still, staring down at Dashiell.

We were across the street from Florent, the wonderful little French bistro smack in the middle of the meat district on Gansevoort Street. I ordered a coffee to go, and while I waited, I figured out the name. It wasn't Bo Peep. It was B. O. Peep! Accurate, too.

When I got outside, B. O. was down the block. Dashiell and I ran to catch up with her. I handed her the bag with the coffee.

"B. O., do you know a homeless man called Billy Pittsburgh? He hangs around West Street sometimes."

She opened the bag, sniffing like a dog. "Coffee," she said, "I smell coffee." She closed her eyes and inhaled.

"Have you seen Billy around lately?" I asked.

"Billy *Pee*," she said. "Smells worse than Shithead here," she whispered. The little brown Chihuahua mix looked up at the sound of his name.

"He eats it," she said, her hand next to her mouth in a dramatic aside, dirty fingers poking out of her torn, gray woolen gloves.

"Has he been around? Billy?"

"He calls me Mary Perry," she said slowly to no one in particular. "Mary Perry. It rhymes. Mary Perry. Not my name, I tell him. My address."

She put the bag under Tuna's face, for him to smell the coffee. His eyes became slits and his lips retracted.

"Slow Black Billy," she said, laughing. "That's what I call *him*. He don't move too good."

She carefully took out the container of coffee and opened it, smelling it again for a long time.

"Do you know where I could find him?" I asked her one more time.

She began to push the heavy cart with one hand, and I could see the coffee sloshing out of the cup as she moved on. After going a few feet, she turned around.

"Haven't spotted him lately," she said. "But someone else sure did. Don't know who. Don't want to know." She was shaking her head as she began to make her way slowly down the block, still muttering. "Always making fun, that Billy. Always making jokes on *me*." She stopped, and it looked as if she were pointing to her chest. Slowly, the cart began to move forward again. "Now the joke's *on him*," she said, but then the wind came up and I could no longer hear her.

Dashiell and I walked uptown for a few blocks before heading back downtown, but I didn't see Billy or any other homeless people. It was dark by then, and the transvestite hookers were out, dot-ting the corners of Washington Street in the meat district like colorful birds, dancing in place, preening hopefully each time a car passed, singing to attract a mate, or at least the chance to earn a quick twenty.

When we finally arrived at home, the cottage seemed unusually warm, safe, and clean. I fed Dashiell, took a bath, and poured a glass of wine; then, remembering that the short version of the third law of private investigation says, At least *look* busy, I went upstairs to the office to play the other side of the tape I'd taken from Cliff's answering machine. As I waited for it to rewind, I hoped his messages wouldn't be as dull or annoying as most of mine. I hit play, then scrunched up against the pillows on the office daybed to drink the wine and listen.

"Baby, it's Imelda Marcos. I was wondering if you had time to go to Shoe Town today. I need pumps. Oooo. Call me, honey."

Beep.

"Clifford, it's Gil. I was wondering if I could enter Magritte in the Westchester County Kennel Club show in September. I just got the judging list, and I think our boy would do *very* well. Call me. The entry deadline is in two weeks. And, oh, thanks for the check."

Beep.

"Baby, it's Amy Fisher. I was wondering if you could recommend a good auto body mechanic. I need to get my dents pounded out. Oooo. Call me, honey."

"Oh, dear. CLIFFORD, IT'S MOTHER."

Beep.

"Osso buco tonight, you delicious thing. See you at seven, honey." It was the same voice as the Imelda Marcos and Amy Fisher calls. Louis?

Beep.

"Cliff, it's Dennis. Are you there? Cliff, pick up, damn it. Oh, shit."

Beep.

"Cliff, it's Mike. I can't take Magritte today. Sorry. Give me a call."

Beep.

"This is for Robert Sutherland. I'm at the Marriott, Bob. I'll be here through Monday. Oh, it's Stanley Salkin of Power Crest. Give me a call."

Beep.

These were among my favorites, wrong-number messages.

I've always wondered if I were morally obliged to call the people and tell them they didn't get who they thought they got. But I never did. I figure living with the consequences of your mistakes is part of being a grown-up.

"This is Margaret at Dr. Sobel's office. You have an appointment tomorrow at two. See you then. Have a good day, and don't forget to floss."

Beep.

"Cliff, it's Mike again. Are you there? Shit. Either you're fucking your brains out, or someone died. Jesus—I hope you're fucking your brains out. Okay—I can get him at four. Unless I hear from you."

Beep

When I woke up, I was still holding the tape recorder, but the tape had run all the way to the end.

I had dreamed I found Billy Pittsburgh and that he told me he had written down the license number of the car that had hit Clifford Cole, it should only happen.

But now that I was awake, I couldn't remember what it was.

11

Last Seen Flying West

THE FRIDAY *TIMES* had a large ad for the Cahill Gallery opening of Clifford Cole's work, white letters on a black field. Very dignified.

"A visual chronicle of the alienation of the nineties." Where do they *get* this bullshit?

I turned to the obits. Since I didn't find my name listed, I figured I better get my ass to work. I climbed onto the exercise bike, called Dash, and told him to find a ball. When he did, I tossed it out the door of the office, where it bounced off the wall and went noisily down the uncarpeted stairs to the living room, Dashiell in hot pursuit. Even after ten throws, there he was, eyes ablaze, ready to do it all over again.

I have days like that. Sisyphus minus the rock, but getting nowhere all the same. I was afraid today would be one of them. Nevertheless, by ten to eight, we were ready to begin another search for Billy Pittsburgh.

There was more of a chance he'd be in situ, asleep, if we hit the streets early, but then I might be waking up a lot of homeless men trying to find him. We headed for West Street, across from the waterfront, checking doorways and loading ramps, heat vents, alleys, any place where a person without a home might find some protection from the weather, which at this time of year was fierce.

It occurred to me that the only thing I knew about Billy was that he was black, but even if I had decided to let the Asian and Caucasian homeless men stay asleep, you couldn't tell who or what was under any particular pile of rags or which packing box was trash and which was someone's cardboard condo.

With the exception of an auto body shop, nothing was open yet on West Street. And I couldn't figure out where Billy might be, because the street got the full brunt of the wind off the Hudson. We turned up Christopher and found one crusty guy with a blanket draped around him holding out a paper cup from one of the ubiquitous Greek coffee shops, hoping for a handout. He was Caucasian, under a lot of crud. I dug into my pocket and pulled out a handful of change. Dropping it into the cup, I asked him if he knew Billy Pittsburgh.

"Not here," he said, shoving the cup in my direction, as if to ask for more.

"He doesn't hang out here?" I asked.

"No more," he said. He was shaking pretty badly.

I tucked a couple of singles into his cup.

"Do you know where he might be now?"

He shook his head. "Don't know much," he said. "God bless," and he walked away.

On the lamppost on the corner a handwritten sign with the word MISSING on it caught my eye. Underneath it said, "Blue and yellow macaw, last seen flying west on Christopher Street, answers (sometimes) to 'Arnie.' REWARD."

We started snaking around the streets between Washington and Greenwich, checking every doorway and pile of trash, but finding nothing. On Washington and Bank we saw two transvestites, probably left over from the night before. I could hear their deep voices as they walked by us. The taller of the two had done something wonderful with her scarf. I'd have to try that sometime. At least the morning wouldn't be a total loss.

Of course, I'd also have some news for Dennis, something other than that his friend was doing the outdoor version of being a toilet queen when he bought the farm. But I didn't think that the fact that I had looked for Billy Pittsburgh and failed to find him would make Dennis release balloons.

We spent about an hour walking around looking carefully at what seemed to be piles of garbage but which actually, sometimes, were someone's attempt to keep warm. I spoke to two other men. One began to rant and rave, making no sense at all. I think he was afraid of Dash, but I doubt he made sense when he wasn't frightened. The other guy, a much younger man than you usually see on the street, talked nonstop. He asked for money, for a job, for coffee. He told me how he lost his job and couldn't pay his rent. He said he got beaten up at the men's shelter and that it was worse than the street. He told me three places where he could get meals, but none of them were open on the weekend. He said he had never met a black man called Billy, but there was a black woman called Billie who slept in a loading area on Greenwich Street, near Charles. I thanked him, gave him a couple of dollars, and headed for Charles Street.

We found Billie asleep under a pile of filthy blankets and newspapers. I put Dash on a sit-stay off to the side so that she wouldn't wake up, see him, and get frightened. I called her name four or five times before she stirred. Slowly, a hand wrapped in rags pushed up a corner of the blanket, and I could barely see a face deep under the covers looking out at me.

"Are you Billie?" I asked.

There was no answer.

"I'm looking for the Billie who found a man lying on the pier a few weeks ago, the Billie who told the cops there was someone on the pier. Was that you?"

Still no answer. But the cover stayed up.

"You're not in any trouble. I can use your help if you know anything or if you know another Billy who might help me. It's worth a nice meal, if you can help."

The cover dropped.

By now I was freezing. I didn't know how these people survived outside in such cold weather. Of course, not all of them did.

I tucked a couple of bucks under the blanket, then stood there like an idiot waiting for a response.

Chilled and frustrated, Dash and I headed home,

stopping to pick up the photos I'd taken at the pier and at Cliff's loft on the way.

Why didn't homeless people flock together, like birds? Or sleep together for warmth? Then maybe someone would know Billy Pittsburgh's whereabouts. I felt stupid spending my time looking for him; I even began to wonder if Mary Perry really knew Billy.

Sometimes the homeless talk like the Alzheimer patients I worked with at the nursing home, stringing things together that they hear and talking about them as if they were real, adding parts of TV stories and overheard conversations to their own experiences.

I felt as if I were in a fog, too. So when I got home, I went straight up to my office, where I have an oversize blackboard I picked up at the flea market on Greenwich Avenue. I began to list the people in Clifford's life and to think about what each stood to gain from his death.

Dennis Mark Keaton, aka Dennis Mark Rosenberg.

Gain: one champion basenji, Magritte. Will he do anything Clifford didn't do, e.g., hire him out at stud? How much could you make doing that anyway? Find out. Loss: one best friend with whom he was possibly (hopelessly?) in love.

Louis Lane, aka Leonard Polski.

Inherits a previously worthless, now valuable art collection. Could there have been a long-term plan at work here? After all, Louis had hooked Cliff up with Veronica. Were there hard feelings, oops, between the lovers? A desire for revenge? A need for money? Loss: the love of his life? Or not.

Veronica Cahill.

Lots of SoHo galleries had closed and lots of others were in financial difficulties, so . . . Did Louis and Veronica, old buddies, team up? If yes, how could this connect with where the murder took place? If they planned to kill Cliff together, then use the murder to increase the value of his work, how did they know he'd be on the pier that night?

Why was I doing this? The man was killed at four in the morning on the Christopher Street pier, where he had gone with his dog to get lucky. Boy, did he not get lucky! The best I could hope for was a witness—talk about getting lucky—and one who was sane and sober enough to have gotten the license plate number. Fat fucking chance, as my grandmother would have said if there had been a Yiddish equivalent. Like on top of everything else, the guy would have had to have had a pencil and paper.

I added the next name.

Morgan Gilmore, Magritte's handler.

Gil and Cliff argued about whether or not to breed Magritte, but what could Gil gain from Cliff's death? *He* didn't inherit M. Did he think he would? Is there more to this picture? Would Dennis keep up M's career, or was Gil now out of a job?

Adrienne Wynton Cole, Cliff's mother.

She gets the dough. But it was probably hers in the first place, and she probably has a ton more. Mothers don't usually murder their children by running them over. They do it slowly, using guilt and disappointment. Even if she didn't accept her son or really know him (what else is new?), she lost her *son*.

Peter David Cole, Cliff's brother.

He would have gotten the dough if Adrienne had kicked off first. If Cliff was in his early thirties, his mother was probably somewhere in her fifties or sixties. Even if she would now leave everything *she* had to Peter, he'd have a pretty long wait. Not a terrific investment, killing your brother and waiting twenty-plus years for the payoff, unless she prefers a charity of some sort, other than her own son. That probably depends whether she approves of Peter David. Have to meet him. Maybe at the opening? Loss: his brother.

I began to think about Lillian and all the times I felt like strangling her. But I'd never actually *do* it. Even though you probably get angrier at your family than at anyone else, they're your history, too, the people who know every stupid story about you since day one.

Okay. Check out the lover. And the gallery owner. Hey, what they do is exploit artists, isn't it? Maybe murder comes under the heading of exploitation, furthering his career. After all, his stuff wasn't worth much when he was alive, was it? Check prices.

I tacked the photos onto the wall, lonely shots of the pier, Cliff's art, even his unmade bed, images to haunt me as I tried to make sense of what appeared to be a senseless crime.

I decided to check the main house before getting ready for the opening. Not bothering with a coat, I grabbed the keys off a hook in the kitchen and ran across the snow-covered garden, Dashiell leading the way straight to the Siegals' back door.

I unlocked both locks, stomped the snow off my boots, pulled the door open, and followed Dashiell inside. Once indoors, I signalled Dashiell to sit and watch me, then gave him the hand signal for go find, a flat, open hand first touching my right eye, then sweeping out forward as far as I could reach.

Dashiell headed for the front room. We always started downstairs and worked our way up. I followed along behind, making sure the doors were still locked, no windows had been broken, no gas was leaking, no pipes had burst. Dash made sure no one else was in the house.

Downstairs was where a burglar would be most likely to break in, even though some preferred access from above, coming from the roof of another building. In some places in the city, you could travel an entire block by running across the roofs.

In New York City, most accessible windows had bars on them. But Norma wouldn't hear of it. "They're ugly," she'd said when I suggested that window guards would help safeguard the house. "I will not live in a jail. That's why you're here." I was in no position to argue.

I followed Dashiell, telling him he was a good boy, checking to make sure the shutters were closed in the front of the house and open to let light in in the rear, those windows that faced the cottage. The thermostat was set at sixty so that the old house wouldn't take too bad a beating contracting and expanding as the weather changed.

We finished at the top without finding a single thief hiding under any of the beds or in the closets, double-checked the front door, shut off the lights, and let ourselves out the back.

Once, the first winter I was here, Dashiell had started to pace and whine, going to the living-room window that faced the main house and coming back to poke me with his muzzle and look into my eyes. I had taken my gun from the shoe box in the bedroom closet, and we had gone across the snowy garden in silence, my heart pounding as I opened the back door. Five minutes later we were face-to-face with the intruder, a homeless woman who had broken one of the front windows to get in from the cold. She was nestled under three blankets in the spare bedroom, trying to get warm.

This time, everything was as it should have been. By the time we got back to the cottage, stopping briefly to race around the big oak, it was time to get ready for the opening. I had planned to soak in the tub until I was as wrinkled as a shar-pei, but I couldn't. I was too excited about the thought of possibly meeting the killer in an hour or so and the question of whether or not I'd know him—or her— when I did.

In the Village, if your sweats are clean, you're dressed up. SoHo is another story. Not wanting to stick out like a bulldog at a field trial, I put on my long black coatdress with matching pants, wound my hair up, and clipped it at the back of my head. Then I stood by helplessly as most of it worked its way out of the barrette. Looking as if I'd just been Marlene Dietrich's stand-in in *Morocco*, I called my dog, and together we headed downtown to see if anyone smelled like a killer.

12

He Raised His Lovely Eyebrows

THE BIG BLACK dot was nowhere in sight, and the floor of the Cahill Gallery had been painted iridescent chartreuse. The walls, still white, were hung with Clifford Cole's paintings, which gave me the same kind of pang I got when I thought about my father not living long enough to see his grandchildren. Then again, who ever said life was fair.

Despite the fact that this was a posthumous show, the mood was festive. Artists turned out in great numbers, as they always do for openings—and the free food and booze—and there were an unusual number of collectors, especially for the shrinking art market of the nineties. There was press, too, so there would be, it seemed, even more articles in the papers and magazines about the young artist who died so tragically just as his tremendous talent was about to come to light.

God, did schmaltz sell. Then again, lurid sex crimes also sold. It was just a matter of time before the rest of the story came out, which would drive the prices even higher than the schmaltz had already done. Louis Lane was going to end up a rich man.

Dennis was in the back, with Magritte.

"Honey, *you* look sen-sa-tional!!"

"Yeah. Yeah." I leaned in as if to kiss his cheek. "What have you learned?" I whispered.

He leaned closer. "Well, apparently blue eye shadow is back!"

"Dog people," I explained.

He rolled his eyes. "And *Lois* is here." He indicated the location with a tilt of his head, and I turned to get a look at the new owner of the collection, prepared to loathe him on sight.

"She's doing an *interview*," he sang. "Does anyone ask *me*—" he began, but I cut him off.

"I'll see you in a bit," I said, leaving quickly and pushing through the crowd with Dashiell at my side.

Leonard Polski was a few feet away from where I had been standing with Dennis, talking to someone who was taking notes. I squeezed in close enough to hear some of the bull he was tossing around, sure I'd be hearing about his always having had faith in Cliff's ability, about how he encouraged him to try his last series of grayish, oversize paintings where images took several canvases to be completed, and richest of all, how pleased he was that Magritte was found and how much he loved the little dog.

What I heard surprised me. Even allowing for the distortion of the tape recording, this was clearly the same voice that left the warm and funny messages for Clifford that I had heard last night. That was as I had guessed. The rest was not.

Louis Lane was speaking softly about the rise of hate crimes, the resurgence of Nazism in the new/old unified Germany, the racial cleansing in Bosnia, and the rise in gay bashing here at home. Then he began to talk about Clifford, his painting as a kind of journal writing on canvas, the curiosity that drove him into his own psyche to troll for powerful material, his feeling that if he touched upon the things he felt deeply about, his paintings would touch others in some powerful way even though each person's history was unique and even though Clifford's own story was not fully expressed, just alluded to mysteriously. That, he said, the mysterious quality of Clifford's work, was what he, Louis, loved best.

"It was his way of expressing not only his own alienation and the alienation all gay men feel, but a far larger issue, the alienation of the nineties, the understanding that we never really know each other, and the question of whether or not many of us care for each other."

Of course, this made me wonder how well Louis Lane knew Clifford Cole, or why he thought this was a nineties concept. From the beginning of time, no one has ever known anyone. I mean, did Adam know Eve? I mean, *really* know her, beyond the biblical sense?

"He was very emotional," he continued, "yet in the translation to canvas, a kind of artistic flatness took over. I think without that, he couldn't have gone where he needed to go. The pain would have been too great. And in that, he was a strong voice for what is going on in the post-Bush era, the disappointment people feel resonating with the pain of childhood, as if Bush the father betrayed us just as our own fathers did."

In action, how like an angel! To coin a phrase.

The reporter nodded and kept writing. Behind him, there was a triptych I hadn't seen at the loft. In fact, looking around, I hadn't seen much of what was on display. I guess these were the paintings from the closet. Looking at the one behind Louis, this one *really* was from the closet; it was a middle-aged man in drag, but in each of the three pictures he had his back to the viewer. What was weird is that it looked like early TV, like Milton Berle in drag. It was even pained without color, in black and white and shades of gray. This was neither genderfuck, where there is a devil-may-care mix of male and female, say a guy with a beard smoking a cigar and wearing a strapless gown, his chest hair poking up from the bodice of the dress, nor was it cross-dressing, where the aim is to pass for the opposite sex. This was broad burlesque, but somehow creepy.

The dress was a cheap housedress. You should *see* what guys wear when they do drag. You should *have* the money they spend. But this was a somewhat heavy guy in a woman's cheap cotton housedress and a five-and-dime wig, ever so slightly askew, with a cigar in "her" hand. The cigar was the only thing to change in three paintings. That is, in the third canvas, the ash was dropping onto the carpet. Unlike all the other paintings I had seen, this one had no title on the last canvas. In fact, when Louis moved a little, I saw that the card on the wall read "untitled oil on canvas." It was dated this year. Perhaps it was the last series he had painted. Perhaps he never finished it.

I waited for the interview to end and introduced myself.

"Louis? Rachel Alexander. I understand Dennis told you he hired me to investigate Cliff's murder?" I put out my hand. "Can we talk for a moment? Perhaps we can duck out into the stairwell. It'll be more private there. And cooler."

He nodded, and Dashiell and I followed him out the side door of the gallery and into the hall in the stairwell. Unfortunately, others had gone out there to escape from the crowd and the heat, but we brushed by them and went up a flight, where we could be alone.

"You don't have a drink. May I fetch you one?" he asked in that lovely voice I had heard on the tape. "I guess I shouldn't say *fetch*. That must be his job," he said, indicating Dash with his wineglass. It seemed he had had a few before this glass. He stood a little too close, occupying some of the space I needed to have between me and any other being other than a baby, a lover, or a dog, but I didn't want to back up because I thought it would put him off.

"I'm fine, Louis, thank you. I wanted to offer my sympathy on your loss. I understand Cliff's family hasn't included you or any of Clifford's New York friends in their plans. I'm so sorry about that, but it's not an uncommon reaction, is it?"

He seemed taken aback at the abruptness and

the personal nature of my question. This is definitely a problem I have. I am only semiskilled at
beating about the bush.

"No. Unfortunately, it's more commonly the rule
than the exception."

"Are they here? His mother? His brother?"

"I expect not. We've never met, but I did get a
call from Peter yesterday saying the memorial service was this evening. In Virginia. I'd left a message
for him on Monday, to tell him about the opening.
So I don't expect them here. More importantly,
we won't be *there*. I assume that was the point. He
was very polite, of course. He said he'd come by
the gallery one evening next week, after he returns
from Frederick. Anyway, it's all water under the
bridge now, isn't it? The time to be supportive to
Clifford is gone.

"So *that* family can and will handle things any
way they like. I've talked to Dennis, and we're going to have our own service in New York after the
show closes, for Clifford's *real* family."

"What a good idea. So what's your take on this,
Louis? Do you agree with the police assessment of
what happened to Clifford?"

"It makes no sense to me at all. Oh, please understand, I am perfectly able to believe a gay man
would be mindlessly killed by a stranger for no reason other than that he appeared to be homosexual.
But I cannot fathom what Cliff was doing on the
pier at that hour. Or, to tell the truth, at any hour."

Have you ever noticed that people who interject
that expression, "to tell the truth," are often lying?

"What I was wondering about, mainly," I said,
"was the same thing. The night of the murder . . ."

He stiffened slightly at the sound of the word. "Where were you when Cliff left for the pier at three or four in the morning? Asleep? I mean, did he talk to you, say where he was going? Or why?"

"I told all this to the police," he said. "We weren't together that night. He stayed at his studio. He usually came to my place in the evening, and I'd cook for him or we'd go out, he'd almost always spend the night and then go back to the studio early in the morning, most of the time before I woke up. There's living space there—he was living there before we met. But we—I should say, I—never stayed there. I have a sensitivity to paint. And I'm allergic to dogs."

"Oh, I'm sorry, is he a problem?" I asked, looking down at Dashiell.

"Not unless I sleep with him," Louis said. He sighed, looked away, and then took a small sip of wine.

He was tall and slender, young, about twenty-eight, I guessed, with lovely olive skin, thick, dark hair, an angular face, almost but not quite too delicate, like a swarthy Montgomery Clift. His eyes were dark and intense. He was the kind of person that gave you chills when he looked at you. No wonder poor, pale, cloddy Dennis was jealous. I wish I looked half as pretty as Louis Lane.

"Was it unusual for Clifford to stay at the studio?" I asked after a moment of silence. "Had you had some sort of argument?"

"No, he was painting, he said, and he wanted to stay with it. He sometimes did that for several nights in a row, just went with it. But this time . . ."

"Yes?"

"He sounded tense that night, Rachel, not high."

When he said my name, it felt the way it does when a lover whispers your name during sex. He was good, this Louis Lane, a sort of work of art himself.

"When the painting was going so well that he couldn't stop working," Louis continued, "he'd be on a high, he'd sound wonderful, excited, energetic. But Tuesday night, he sounded, I don't know, funny, like there was something he wasn't telling me."

"And you didn't ask?"

"We tended to give each other a lot of room in that area, Rachel. I knew he'd tell me when he was ready. He always had."

I wondered what Leonard Polski had invented, besides his name. I wondered if he had murdered his lover.

Never assume, meaning never assume anyone is innocent until you're absolutely sure who's guilty. You could get killed that way.

"So you have no guess as to what happened, as to why he ended up on the pier?"

"Not a clue."

"Well, thanks, Louis." I took a card from my pocket. "Here's my number, in case you think of anything else you want to tell me, anything at all."

"Research. Interesting. I can't *imagine* how you do whatever it is you do do," he said. "I don't know what happened that night, and I wouldn't know where to begin to find out."

"What do you do?" I asked him.

"I teach high school Spanish."

Unless he had a *relativo rico*, there was no way

Louis Lane could afford his Gucci loafers on a teacher's salary. No fucking way.

"Well, *I* can't imagine how you—or anyone—does *that*. So I guess we're even."

He smiled and showed me his perfect, even white teeth.

"Dennis doesn't want to believe that this is a hate crime," he said. "But what else could it be?"

"That's what he hired me to find out," I said, looking up into Louis's fathomless dark eyes. "I was hoping to find a witness, actually."

He raised his lovely eyebrows. "Really?" he said.

As far as I was concerned, it was definitely a hate crime. The question was, personal hate or random hate?

At the foot of the stairs I stepped aside, and Louis walked ahead of me into the gallery, head high, posture perfect, his hair looking as if he had never even *heard* of a sandstorm.

I began to walk around and look at the paintings. I passed several of the ones I had seen at the loft. There were a few pieces of sculpture, too, painted wooden pieces. I stopped to look at one, a life-size Magritte, and found myself walking circles around it in the company of a woman my sister would describe as perky and a short-waisted, stocky man wearing gray sweats, red-faced and moist, as if he had just stopped in after a long run.

"Isn't this *divine*," the woman said. "God, it's sold!" I looked at the title card and saw she was right. Next to the price of $8,000 there was a red dot.

"Eight thousand," I said aloud, to no one in particular.

The guy in sweats whistled, one long, bright, clear note, and shook his head.

I turned to look at him, but all I saw were his broad shoulders and his back as he moved off into the crowd. Eight thousand, I thought, watching him disappear. He looked vaguely familiar, but I couldn't quite place him.

I looked back at the price and the red dot. Clifford must be rolling over in his grave. Actually, Dennis had said the body was cremated, and I wasn't sure one could still do that under those circumstances.

"What's your breed?" the perky woman asked. "Are you in basenjis?" And then she sort of squealed. She had apparently just noticed Dashiell. The funny thing about pit bulls is that sometimes they sort of disappear. Dashiell, who went everywhere with me, had a way of blending in so that, despite his formidable size, he often wasn't even seen, for example, lying next to the table at a restaurant. Until we got up to leave.

"I'm a collector," I told her.

I lied quickly and easily. Frank always assured me it was a useful skill, not a character flaw.

"Oh, I am too, in a way. I collect basenjis. I have eleven. Four are Magritte get," she said with great pride.

If I were a dog, my brow would have wrinkled and my ears would have gone up. A dog's get are his offspring. I had been told that Magritte had never been bred.

"Really," I said. "Did you get the dogs from Cliff?"

"Oh, I didn't *buy* the dogs. My Tiffany was bred to Magritte. She had a dog and three bitches."

"I see. Is this recently? I mean, are the puppies for sale now?"

"Oh, no. Are you looking for a basenji?" She looked down at Dashiell. Actually, she didn't have that far down to look. She was about five feet tall, sort of tightly packed, with the kind of hair and makeup I used to see on my Upper East Side dog-training clients. "They're wonderful with other breeds," she said, hoping to make a sale. Who's lying now? I thought. Most basenjis aren't even good with themselves. Magritte was a miracle of good temperament, partly good breeding and partly because Cliff had trained and socialized him so well. "Melisand is due in heat soon," she said, "and I was thinking of breeding her back to Magritte. She's his daughter, out of Windy Moment. That's Tiffany. I could put you on the wait list," she said, arching her neat eyebrows.

Exactly what I needed, an inbred basenji.

"Um, who have you dealt with for the breedings?" I asked.

"Gil, of course. I've known Gil for, what, seven years, ever since I got into basenjis. He's fabulous. I wish I could get him to handle one of my dogs, but he's much too expensive for me."

"Morgan Gilmore? I heard so much about him, uh, from Dashiell's handler, but I never met him. Is he here?"

She took another look at Dashiell, frowning. Of course, pit bulls are not AKC-registerable dogs, so if she knew the difference between a pit bull and an Am Staff, she would have wondered what the hell I was talking about. UKC handlers would be totally unlikely to also work at AKC shows, and if Dash had a handler, which he didn't, he probably would have no idea who Morgan Gilmore was.

"He's over there, see, red shirt, ponytail?"

"Great chatting with you," I said, and headed back to Dennis.

"Here," I said when I had squeezed through the crowd and arrived at his side. I handed him Dashiell's leash. "I'll be back soon and explain." I signaled Dashiell to wait, and began shoving my way to where Morgan Gilmore was standing.

When I got close enough to eavesdrop, I pretended to study *out, damned spot*, which hung starting to his left and continuing down that wall. He was talking to two men about Westminster, which was now only a few days away. It is always held on the second Monday and Tuesday of February, and the hound group goes up on Tuesday. Since Magritte had been found, he would, of course, be shown. I couldn't hear everything, only snippets. ". . . the best front of any dog on the circuit today." "Schedules are never a problem—" "—with *that* topline! Please!" "—very typey . . ." "—the epitome of his breed." All the usual dog show bullshit.

"Hi," I said when I could finally get his attention. I was now close enough to see that he was one of those guys who have five o'clock shadow by ten-thirty in the morning. He was oddly shaped, tall and thin, but you could see the bulge of a potbelly pushing out his shiny red shirt, as if he had swallowed a casaba melon whole. His hair was seriously receding, but he had let the back grow long, and he did indeed have a ponytail. And he wore a string tie and cowboy boots. My guess was that they were his signature.

"Uh, what's her name," I gestured into the center of the gallery, "Tiffany's mom—"

"Aggie?"

"Right! Aggie said you might be able to help me out. I have a basenji bitch," I said. Morgan Gilmore's smile cranked up to 150 watts, and he hunched his shoulders and head toward me in a mockery of sincerity and interest. "She's pointed, of course. She just needs one more major"—I bet he never heard *that* before, but man, if he could toss it, so could I—"but I think I'd like to breed her this spring"—I took an audible breath and let it out, the way you breathe when you're twelve if someone mentions the name of a rock star—"to Magritte. He's got the best front. Just perfect."

Morgan Gilmore beamed. "No problem," he said. He reached two bony fingers into his breast pocket and withdrew his card. The logo was a beagle puppy sitting next to a cowboy boot. Talk about non sequiturs!

"Do you specialize in the hound group?"

"I'll handle *anything*," he told me, and for once I thought he was telling the absolute truth. "So, little lady, just call me when your girl's cycle starts, and we'll arrange everything. *No* problem."

He had no questions to ask me. Not one. He didn't even ask for a recent brucellosis test, the very least thing you'd want before any breeding, since brucellosis causes sterility in both dogs and bitches and is nearly impossible to cure. But, hey, this is not to say the man wasn't careful. He probably only bred Magritte to "qualified bitches," as the ads always say, "qualified" meaning he'd get paid in advance.

"Well, what about his show schedule and all?" I

asked. "Will scheduling Crystal's breeding be a problem?"

"Well"—he paused and laughed intimately, since we were such good friends—"you know basenjis. They can be a handful, can't they? They don't always get along that well, even males and females. I'm sure your, um—"

"Crystal."

"I'm sure your Crystal is a dream girl, but I've seen some nasty bitches, and I can't take a chance my little boy will get hurt."

My little boy!

"So I just avoid the dangers of shipping, possible dogfights, or missed breedings because of Magritte's show schedule. None of this is a problem," he said smugly. "I bank his sperm."

Bingo! I thought. Morgan Gilmore had just moved up to number one on my hit parade.

13

We've Locked the Barn

IF YOU'VE NEVER turned on a date with a detailed description of how semen is collected and banked, and you think you might like to give it a try, just say, "I was thinking of using frozen semen to breed my dog. Less hassle." And when they ask the inevitable, just roll your eyes and say, "Don't ask." Human imagination always makes things more interesting than they actually are.

With Morgan Gilmore's card safely tucked into my purse, I pushed and shoved my way over to the bar, snagged a glass of white wine, then shoved and poked my way back to Dennis. Before I got there, to retrieve my dog and tell my client the news, I overheard a voice so condescending and full of authoritative ignorance that it could only belong to a gallery owner. Veronica Cahill was briefing the press.

"—a little steep for someone who's hardly sold, never had a show before, never been reviewed?"

"It might seem that way, but this is all there is of Clifford's art, all there's ever going to be." Dramatic pause. Eyes lowered. "Forty-seven paintings and five pieces of sculpture. This is it." She waved a careless hand to indicate the sweep of the gallery.

She was tall, about six feet one, what my grandmother Sonya would have called a long drink of water. But to an immigrant who lived where food was not plentiful, it would have been said with pity.

Veronica Cahill was anything but pitiful looking. She was stylishly slim and elegant, not poor and underfed. Her red hair, red from a bottle but nevertheless gorgeous, was cut short, boyish on someone else, but not on Veronica. Her features were slightly oversize—large eyes, long nose, wide mouth—giving her a dramatic look that the cropped hair, the makeup, the big jewelry, and the constant use of her large, long-fingered hands only emphasized. She had a ring on every finger, several bracelets that made noise as she moved, piercing hazel eyes that gave each and every one of us a turn. She was some piece of work, this Veronica Cahill.

"How did you discover Cliff?" someone asked.

"Oh, I've known Clifford for ages. I've been watching his art develop and waiting for a large enough body of work so that I could do this," she said, once again gesturing around the room. She smiled for someone's camera. She was wearing a short green silk dress to emphasize her legs, which, if she were lying down, would reach from here to Hoboken. And shoes I couldn't sit in, let alone walk in.

I had lost the drift of the interview for a moment, but something brought me sharply back.

"—saw it all, that poor, dear thing. It's lucky *he* didn't get killed, too. You can see, in Clifford's work of the last few years, how the image of Magritte, *our* Magritte, of course, not René, is used to express Clifford's emotional turmoil."

Shit. Dennis had told Louis, and Louis had told Veronica. Was that before he promised to watch his mouth or after?

"How do they know he was there? I had heard the dog was missing," a pretty woman in skintight jeans asked.

"Oh, it seems Clifford's friends have chipped in and hired a detective. A retired *police* detective. This is off the record, of course. It's all very hush-hush," she said to reporters from the *Times*, the *News*, the *Village Voice*, *People* magazine, and the *New Yorker*, according to the press badges I could see. "You know, so many of these cases go unsolved. Well, Clifford's friends would have none of that. At any rate, Magritte's collar and leash turned up at the pier. Poor thing. You know, it's most amazing, his recovery. It was because of a tattoo—"

The note taking had taken on a furious pace when I decided the only rational thing to do was to find Dennis and murder him. As I began to work my way out of the group that had gathered around Veronica, I could hear her finishing her botched story about how the National Dog Registry works and I heard her say, "The little darling is here, if you'd like photographs."

Somehow I knew it was Magritte she was referring to, not me, a retired *police* detective.

I decided to look at some more of the pieces, not wanting to find my face in Saturday's paper, even as part of the background. My only hope now was that my fucking name wouldn't appear along with the rest of the information I'd rather not have as public knowledge.

I decided to take a philosophical attitude.

A fuckup. How unusual.

The paintings were actually arranged intelligently, earliest to most recent. Unless you headed straight for the bar, you would see the few pre-Magritte paintings when you first came in. Next you'd see the beginnings of the flat technique, the texture of the canvas as part of the painting. The very early works looked more decorative, and though they were certainly beautiful, they didn't have the punch of the post-Magritte paintings, nor the humor of the Magritte pieces. *Our* Magritte, not René. I was surprised to see the small painting of Magritte as an angel, talk about oxymorons, because it had to have been one of Cliff's personal favorites, but then I noticed the "NFS"—not for sale—on the title card. That pleased me enormously. I loved the piece. It was as beautiful and perfect as an old miniature.

The alienation grew as you proceeded toward the later works, and then there was a sudden, harsh change with the appearance of the untitled "Uncle Miltie" painting and several other of these recent works, all in black, gray, and white or in grays with one startling touch of color. For example, there was one called *s.b.* that showed a street-tough boy, around twelve, in a dress. Everything else was typically male: dirty high-tops, one sock up and one halfway down, even the basketball steadied with one hand and poised on his hip. Everything was in shades of gray, except the basketball.

I looked around for *les and mor*. It should have been with this group of recent work, but it wasn't. I wondered if Veronica deemed it too weird to include it. But certainly others were equally disturbing.

When I glanced around for Dennis, I panicked. I had forgotten that Dashiell was with him. If Dashiell showed up in the papers, I might as well be there too. It would kill the chance for me to work undercover again. This was serious. Deception was not only essential in this work, it was one of my favorite parts, sort of like improvisational acting, only sometimes life-threatening.

The photographers had finished with Magritte, and I got over there as soon as I could get through the crowd. If Cliff had only lived to see this day. Then again, had he lived, he might have gotten one piece in a barely advertised group show during the slowest time of the year, and three people, all relatives of the other artists, would have shown up. He wouldn't have made a dime.

I got next to Dennis and looked around. Dash was nowhere in sight.

"*There* you are," Dennis said, before I had a chance to say a word. "My friend Roger took Dashiell for a walk. You were tied up with Gil, and Dash kept looking at pedestals as if they were fire hydrants. Maybe he was just too hot, I don't know. Rog should be back any minute. I hope that's okay?"

That's when it occurred to Dennis that it might not be okay. I could see the fear coming into his eyes.

"I did it again, right?"

But before I had a chance to describe the enormous knot in my stomach over the fear that a stranger had taken my dog and I'd never see him again (how could I be sure Rog wasn't the murderer!), I was thrown onto Dennis and nearly knocked him down. It was just Dashiell's way of telling me how happy he was to see me again. He often made his sentiments crystal clear with a head butt.

"Rog, this is—"

"Louise," I said, standing up and giving Dennis a look that if looks could kill it would have, "Louise Keaton. I'm Dennis's cousin." Seeing the look on Roger's face, I added, "Long lost. Which is why he may have never mentioned me." I was too distraught and angry to do a good job of this. I just shrugged, turned to Dennis, and said, "We have to talk, cuz."

"Roger, thanks." Then he turned to me. "You *know* Dr. Schwartzman said no more alcoholic beverages, Lou*ise*." And back to Rog. "I have to get her out into the air."

We retrieved our coats from the rack in the back room and headed for the stairs. Magritte jumped down each steep step, following Dashiell, who kept turning to see if he was coming. When we got to the street, I opened my mouth, and Dennis grasped the back of my coat collar and hoisted it, making me lose my train of thought.

"Not yet, Lou*ise*. We need a drink first."

I decided not to remind him that he had just finished telling Rog that I was under doctor's orders regarding alcoholic beverages.

We stopped at the first place we came to. I showed the waiter Dash's bright yellow Registered Service Dog tag. He didn't say anything about Magritte, so neither did I, and we were taken to a corner table.

"Two kir royales, please," Dennis said. "And keep them coming."

He turned to me, reached out, and covered one of my hands, covering his face with his other hand. "Give me a minute," he said. I decided to skip the several sarcastic things that popped into my head, and wait.

"Look. First of all, I'm sorry."

"You ought to be," I said angrily. "I don't make it a practice to lend my dog or my gun to strangers."

"You have a gun?"

"Do Hasidim have sheets with holes in them?"

Dennis rolled his eyes.

"Okay. I accept your apology."

"Except *that's* not what I was apologizing for. It was—the *other* thing. But I fucked up before you told me, uh, not to fuck up. Okay? I didn't think. I didn't know Louis Leaky would tell Veronica." He held up his hand. "Yes, yes, I know about it. And then for her to tell the press. God! At least she got it screwed up."

The kir royales arrived. The bubbles looked pretty rising through the raspberry-colored creme-de-cassis-spiked champagne. I lifted my glass, clinked Dennis's, which was sitting on the table, and took a sip.

"I spoke to Louis. He spoke to Veronica. We've, uh, locked the barn. I'm sorry." He picked up his glass and chugged half of it down. "Are you hungry?"

"Starved! Let's forgive each other and eat. But not until we have a few of these." I could feel the drink going to my head and warming my body, all at once and all lovely. The fact is, as long as my name and picture didn't appear in the paper, the rest was workable. I told Dennis. He leaned over and hugged me and finished his drink. The waiter brought two more. I hurried to catch up.

"Okay," I said, "there'll be a few articles about Cliff, they'll say thank God his lost dog was found, the prices of the paintings will go up, and"—I gave his glass another clink; this time it was in his hand—"Morgan Gilmore has been stealing sperm!"

"What?"

"Morgan Gilmore has been banking Magritte, for who knows how long. Evidently he refused to take no for an answer. So Magritte has sired pups, my guess is a *lot* of pups, and it looks as if Gil has been pocketing the stud fees."

"Good grief. Gil?"

"On Monday I'll go over to the American Kennel Club library and check the studbooks for the last few years and see if I can get an approximate count of Magritte's get. This could be big bucks, all stolen from Clifford."

"Rachel," Dennis said. He took a long drink of his kir. "*How* could I have forgotten! Well, I know how. I mean, it was *ages* ago, he never explained it, and, well, nothing happened. You know how it is, your own problems are at the fore, and you, well, you get caught up, oh God, I should have remembered. I should have told you."

"What? What are you babbling about?"

The waiter put two more drinks on the table. I felt something brush my leg, and suddenly a basenji was on my lap.

"About three months ago, Cliff came over looking really upset. It was in the evening, sevenish. I was having dinner. I asked him to join me, but he declined. He wouldn't even sit down. He was pacing. I hate it when people do that, don't you?"

"Dennis—"

"Right. He had left Magritte with me and gone out late in the afternoon, said he'd be gone a few hours, then come back for Magritte. I don't know where he was. He never said. He just said that he had found out something about someone and it had to be exposed, at any cost. I asked him what he had found out and who he was talking about, and he just said, 'Wait and see, old buddy. Wait and see.'

"Well, I was worried about him when it happened, but he never brought it up again. I was having this huge problem with my publisher, so I forgot about it. I wonder if he was talking about Gil, if he had discovered what Gil was doing. He was really upset, and God, he loved that little dog to pieces. He would have been wild, absolutely wild, if he had known what Gil had done. And Rachel, he was wild that night."

"But he never mentioned it again? He never said another word about finding out about something that had to be exposed?"

"Not a word."

"Does that strike you as unusual, I mean, to be so upset and then nothing?"

"Actually, no. I do it all the time, don't you?"

"Sure. But this is different. It's not like getting

dunned for a bill you paid. It's bigger. And ongoing. Why didn't it come up again, I mean, if it *was* about Gil?"

"Because of the way Cliff was. He'd get really angry, then he'd plot."

"Plot?"

"He'd let it simmer, and he'd figure out what to do to get even, to hurt the person who hurt him. He used to quote that saying, you know, revenge is a dish best served cold. I don't know if he ever actually *did* anything, but sometimes he liked to talk about what he *wanted* to do to someone he thought was an enemy, something sneaky, so they wouldn't know it was coming or, if they did, they still wouldn't be able to do anything to stop it."

"He wouldn't have been direct?"

"I don't think so. Even if he said something, he wouldn't necessarily have let it go, the hurt. You know what I mean?"

I nodded.

"You couldn't just apologize. You'd have to wait for him to get over it in his own time and his own way. Even if it was something trivial, like you forgot a date with him. Or you were late. He'd be friendly, then when you figured it was okay, he'd get real sarcastic. I feel so disloyal saying this to you, I mean, I . . . he was my *friend*."

Dennis was looking even paler than usual.

"The thing is, he was your friend despite his faults. That's nothing to feel bad about."

He nodded. "I guess."

"Here's something to feel bad about. You look like shit. Let's get some food, okay?"

"Sure, sure. You order for us," he said, and I did—osso buco, which I had been dying for since hearing Louis's voice on Clifford's old answering machine tape.

As soon as the waiter had taken the order, I put Magritte back on the floor. I was pretty sure that once the food arrived, he'd turn into a cat burglar, and I thought I might have a better shot at defending my dinner if the burglar weren't on my lap.

"Dennis," I said, tearing into a roll while we waited for the meal, "those paintings of that older guy in drag, the one with the flowered housedress?"

"What about them?"

"Have you ever seen them before?"

He shook his head.

"I was wondering about that one, because Cliff always put a title on the last panel, and that one doesn't have a title. It's the only one in the show that doesn't have one."

The waiter showed up with the food, which immediately captured the attention of all four animals at the table. But even though I was as hungry as the next omnivore, it's difficult for me to let go once I have a question on my mind. "And?"

"Probably just didn't finish it," he said, his mouth full of food. For a while, the only sound was the pitiful whining of a hopeful basenji. When I looked down to give Magritte the eye, the most powerful tool a dog trainer has, particularly when her mouth is otherwise occupied, I noticed that Dashiell, God bless him, was back asleep. He has this unshakable faith that if I have food with his name on it, I'll be sure to let him know.

When Dennis's plate was almost empty, he looked critically at mine.

"What?" I growled.

Getting raised by Beatrice Kaminsky is sort of like passing a car accident every day. You don't want to know, but your curiosity always gets the better of you. So even before he answered, I knew that asking had been a mistake.

"Eat your veal. Some little baby cow suffered so you wouldn't have to sate yourself on boring chicken."

"Yes, Beatrice."

"Beatrice?"

"My mother. You keep reminding me of her." I offered him my most insincere smile.

"Oh," he said, his hand to his bosom, "I like *that*. One little touch of guilt and criticism, and already it's getting testy with me. Eat, don't eat," he said, "it's all the same to me."

When the check came, Dennis and I had a brief battle over it, but not wanting to bruise the delicate male ego, I let him win.

"I'll walk you home," he said when we got outside.

"You don't have to do that. I'm a detective."

"Okay, then I'll walk you as far as Houston Street."

"Deal."

"Rachel, I have to go to Boston right after Westminster, to see my editor and meet with the art director. I'll be gone until midday Saturday. I could never get another good handler this close to the show. And Gil really brings Magritte out. But no matter what you find out this week, I don't want Magritte with Gil for one more minute after West-minster. You know, it wouldn't have been the money that would have bothered Cliff. It would have been the lying, for sure, but more than that, the loss of control of what happened with Magritte. He would have hated that. So I need a gigantic favor. Could you take Magritte for me until I get back from Boston? Gil said he'd keep him for me, but I definitely don't want to do that, and I can't bear to board him. He won't be any trouble at all. He's got wonderful manners. Unless you don't consider lick-ing his balls wonderful manners. Lucky mutt. I al-ways have to find someone else to lick mine."

"That can be very time-consuming," I said. "That aside, we'll take him. Dashiell loves to have friends sleep over." As a show dog, Magritte would be crate trained, so if I had to leave him home alone, I could still come home and find my possessions intact. And if he carried on, no one would hear him. Shelly and Norma Siegal wouldn't be back from Florida for at least another month. "I'll be at Westminster any-way. I'll just take Magritte home with me after Best in Show."

Dennis sighed. "Clifford sold more paintings to-night than in the entire time he was alive," he said. "Maybe he'll even get a posthumous cult following, like Frida Kahlo. Weird how things work, isn't it?"

The light was green as we approached Houston Street, so Dash and I ran to make it across Houston Street. When we reached the other side, I turned and waved to Dennis.

In a world where appearances are everything,

this proud oaf had loved a beautiful man. But now Beauty was dead, and the Beast was as lonely and miserable as ever. Sounds like one of the bedtime stories Lili used to make up for me when our parents were out and had left her in charge.

14

Let Sleeping Dogs Lie

WHEN I GOT home, I fed Dash, checked the answering machine, and got ready for bed, but I was as wide awake as if I had just run out of a sauna and jumped into a snowdrift.

There's a period in every case when I feel really confused. It's usually from right after I'm hired until I find out who did it.

Dog training is a lot easier. At least you know who the criminal is. Okay, *sometimes* it's the dog, but usually it only *seems* as if it's the dog. More often than not it's the owner, the so-called intelligent partner who thought it was cutesy-poo when little Killer growled for six months before he actually started putting his teeth into it.

The thing is, when you're called in to solve a dog problem, you get to meet all the players up front. You'd be surprised how clear things look when the dog is seen in the context of his pack. When a dog is an accident waiting to happen, you can see it, and when the problem is fixable, most of the time you can fix it.

With human beings, things are never so clear. Motives are more complex, behavior is more devious, and the histories are infinitely longer and more twisted.

Dogs live in the present. They're not capable of planned revenge. Alas, people are.

Had Morgan Gilmore been an accident waiting to happen? Was it only a matter of time before one of his clients found out what he was doing and confronted him? For surely, if he was doing this with Magritte, he could be doing it with any dog he was handling.

Did Gil murder Cliff because Cliff finally confronted him about the thefts? Had Clifford threatened to expose him? In that case, Gil would have lost more than a good client. He would have lost his occupation.

Still, the question remained, how did he know Cliff would be out on the pier so that he could try to pass off the killing as a gay bashing?

I was pacing now, the way Clifford did that night he told Dennis he had found out something and that someone had to be exposed. It went underground then, stewed and simmered in him. He couldn't rid himself of all the bad feeling, couldn't confront and forgive, or even if that's what he had decided to do, maybe Gil couldn't take the chance that people would find out what he had done.

The American Kennel Club library wouldn't be open until Monday. But I didn't have to wait to see if I could get more dirt on Gil. I had every Westminster catalog since I began studying dog training. I went into the study, pulled two recent catalogs off the shelf, opened the first, and found the list of basenjis. The catalog not only listed the name of each dog entered and the name of the handler showing him but listed the name of the sire, too. This wouldn't tell me how many litters Magritte had sired or how many stud fees Morgan Gilmore had pocketed. It would only tell me if any of Magritte's get had been entered in Westminster. It was only the tip of the iceberg, but it was the only thing I could do until I could get into those studbooks on Monday morning.

Two Magritte daughters had competed two years ago. By the dates of birth, as well as the names of the dams, they were not littermates. Last year, three of Magritte's get were entered, one of the same bitches from the year before and two dogs, not of the same litter as either the bitch or each other. Apparently the frozen semen business was brisk.

I thought about the message from Gil on Cliff's answering machine tape. He said nothing about needing Cliff to sign the entry form. I pulled out an events calendar from my pile of *Gazettes*, the magazine published by the American Kennel Club, and checked the form. It called for the name of the owner of the dog, printed, and his all-important AKC registration number, so of course Gil had to know that, but it could be signed by *either* the owner or his duly authorized agent. And Magritte's duly authorized agent was Gil.

But what about litter registrations? Those certainly needed the owner's signature. Then again, with thousands and thousands of litters registered every year, who was sitting around double-checking every signature to make sure it was the actual owner of the bitch or dog who had signed each form? Don't sweat it if you don't know the answer. It was a rhetorical question.

I had the feeling that even a false signature on a bank check would go undetected unless the amount was unusually large, in which case the bank might check the signature, or unless the owner of the account realized that a certain check had been written and signed by someone else when he or she got back a month's worth of canceled checks with the statement. As Joan Rivers would say, grow up. Stealing stud fees was no doubt even easier than collecting the sperm with which to steal them.

Dashiell was on top of the blankets with his head on my pillow, and being a devout believer in the adage Let sleeping dogs lie, I had no choice but to squeeze down under the covers from the top.

Clifford had told Dennis that he had discovered something that had to be exposed at all cost. Was the cost losing a top basenji handler? Was it losing someone he thought was a friend worthy of his trust?

It's a funny thing, trust. Like Humpty Dumpty, once it's been broken, you can never put it back together again.

15

I Have My Standards

DASHIELL'S WHIMPERING WOKE me. His feet were running in his sleep, his eyelids twitching. As I gently scratched the back of his neck to quiet him, I realized that I had been dreaming, too.

I was at a large table, a street map of the Village spread out before me, the twisty streets with their unexpected turns, the private mews, the alleys, all there, but without names.

I was trying to find my way somewhere, but each time I thought I had it, I looked again and found the map oriented a different way. Once again I'd find my starting place, and with my finger I'd trace the streets, trying to make my way to wherever it was I just had to go. And each time I thought I was there, I'd find myself more lost than the time before.

I got up, padded barefooted down to the kitchen,

put up the kettle, and opened the front door for Dashiell. There had been a fresh dusting of snow during the night. The yard was as still as a graveyard, everything silent and white.

I went back to the kitchen and made tea, still trying to shake the disturbing aftereffects of the dream. Dashiell came in, the *Times* in its cold plastic bag hanging out of his mouth, dropped it on my bare feet, and tossed himself onto the living-room rug with a sigh. I was feeling grumpy, too. I was coming down with a cold. The weather wasn't going to help, frigid winds coming down from Canada, chance of snow late in the day, high of twenty-two.

I started looking at the paper, just turning pages, barely seeing what was in front of me, until I got to the arts pages. Suddenly, I was on the qui vive.

There was Magritte, an incredible head shot, wrinkled forehead, manipulative dark eyes, to-die-for black gumdrop nose, head held on that slant dogs have perfected that can melt the hearts of statues. The title was short and to the point: WITNESS TO MURDER.

"A witness has been found in the murder of New York artist Clifford Cole, 32, who was found dead on the Christopher Street pier early on January 20th of this year in what the police are regarding as a random bias crime. The artist's dog, a champion basenji, the barkless African breed, who was reported missing the day of the crime, was recovered through an identifying tattoo on his inner right thigh."

It went on to say that it had been learned that the basenji dog, Ch. Ceci N'Est Pas un Chien, known to his friends as Magritte, had been a witness to the vehicular homicide of his master, whose opening last night at the Cahill Gallery in SoHo drew a record crowd. Veronica Cahill, who characterized Clifford's work as "William Wegman meets Diane Arbus," remembered to mention to the press that she had extended the run of the show from the usual three weeks to five weeks. And then came the good part.

The article quoted a couple of ersatz experts, the first a "dog psychologist" named Rick Shelbert who talked about "memory and trauma."

"If Magritte were in the presence of the killer," Dr. Shelbert stated, "there's no doubt he would react with fear. Because of the trauma," Dr. Shelbert had gone on to tell the *Times*, "Magritte would remember the scent of the killer forever."

Mobil, unleaded? It was doubtful the killer got out of his car.

"Magritte should be taken back to the scene of the crime," said Tracy Nevins, a local dog trainer.

Leave it to the *Times* to interview not one but *two* blowhards.

"With several visits to the area of the murder, he could be desensitized. Then nonfearful behavior could be shaped and reinforced with food treats, the most effective of which would be the freeze-dried liver tidbits with which handlers customarily bait the dogs in the show ring."

As to whether or not Magritte could finger his master's killer, Nevins was quoted as saying, "Definitely."

I read on.

"Magritte's new owner, Dennis Kenton, who writes

and illustrates books for children, said the plucky little dog 'seemed none the worse for wear.' "

Funny. That didn't sound a bit like the Dennis "Kenton" I knew.

" 'We are still planning on having Magritte compete at Westminster on Tuesday,' Kenton added. 'Clifford would have wanted him to be there.' The show, the second-oldest continuous sporting event in the country, second only to the Kentucky Derby, takes place Monday and Tuesday at Madison Square Garden. A representative of the Westminster Kennel Club said there was enormous interest in the show, particularly now that it was a champions-only event."

I decided not to call Dennis. What was there to say?

I felt a sneeze coming and put the paper down. A moment later, I heard a familiar *pop*. Then Dashiell showed up with a tissue hanging from his big mouth. I used the half he hadn't chewed on for the next sneeze. It made me wish one of my dog trainer friends were here to appreciate Dashiell's grand trick. But dog training is a loner's profession, and even when I was still part of it, I only got to see my trainer friends once a year, during Westminster and all the posh award dinners that preceded it.

When I first got into training, I got a kick out of crashing the Ken-L Ration dinner. It was an invitation-only black-tie event and considered the big ticket of the weekend. So it was a coup to be seen there. No matter how you got in.

It was at the Waldorf then, and for years this other dog trainer, Chip Pressman, and I used to meet there and sneak in together. Like basenjis, we wanted to be precisely where we weren't allowed.

The raison d'être for the dinner is to honor the top show dogs of the year and their owners and handlers, and, of course, get all sorts of nice publicity for the product. There's always a guest speaker, usually someone funny to warm up the audience before the long, repetitive award ceremony, and lots of opportunities for schmoozing up new contacts and work possibilities.

Gil would be at the dinner. Shouldn't I be to? It would be a good way to hear a little helpful gossip, and it might be fun to try my hand at crashing the dinner, because now you had to do more than just sign in. Now you had to present your invitation to the guardians at the door. Difficult, true, but this was New York, where everything is possible.

Some people think New York is only a great place to visit, but take it from me, it's also a great place to live and work. For example, if you ever get a craving for Glatt kosher take-out for a long, hungry stakeout or you're dying to see a Broadway show you can't afford and don't mind missing the first act, you'd really appreciate this town.

For the first yen, try Lou Siegal's Glatt Kosher Restaurant on West Thirty-eighth Street. They deliver, but for a stakeout you should pick up. Law number four says, Don't call undue attention to yourself.

You used to be able to get kosher Chinese at Bernstein on Essex on the Lower East Side or Moishe Peking in the thirties, and kosher Japanese, yet, at Shalom Japan in SoHo, except of course on

Shabbos, but they're all gone now. Like it or not, things change.

Anyway, as to the play, simply walk in with the smokers after the intermission. The stories aren't that complicated, and they always save the best stuff for the second half.

You can also crash almost any large celebratory dinner, such as the Ken-L Ration award banquet, which I was now planning to crash, by waiting until it begins and entering as if you belong after the invitation collectors have closed up shop. You have to figure that with two to three hundred people there, someone didn't make it. So there will be an empty seat for you. But be sure you dress as if you've been invited, or you'll stick out like a Great Dane at a cat show.

If this method would make you so tense you'd feel as if you were digesting a piano, opt for the second one.

Don't go an hour late. Go an hour early. Begin the evening by crashing the press hour that precedes the cocktail hour. Simply walk in carrying an expensive camera—I use my Nikon—and be prepared with the name of a magazine or newspaper, particularly one that usually doesn't cover dog events. In that way, you're less likely to run into the reporter or photographer the magazine *actually* sent, and you won't be questioned, because who would want to offend, say, the *New Yorker*? You can even disarm them by complaining that you just heard about their event yesterday and would they *kindly* give you a little more notice in the future. Using this method, you don't miss the free drinks, and there's much more chance to circulate and eavesdrop.

I heard the familiar nasal twang the moment I entered the cocktail hour for the winners and the press.

"Kaminsky, you bitch, where have you been keeping yourself?"

I turned around to see Susan Samuelson, who writes about the fancy for *Dog World* magazine. The fancy refers not to people who fancy dogs, such as myself, but to people who show dogs, such as the people being honored at the Ken-L Ration dinner.

"On the coast," I lied.

"Miss New York?" she asked, raising her plucked eyebrows. She was a sixtyish elf in velvet leggings, ballet slippers, and a tux jacket, her hair in a pixie cut.

"For sure."

"Back to stay?"

"Think so. I missed the humidity."

"Yeah. So where can I reach you when I need a quote? Are you listed or un?"

I wrote my number on the back of her press notes. Susan used to call me all the time for quotes when I was working as a trainer, which helped my reputation and the accuracy of her articles, making for a very serendipitous symbiosis.

"Susan, *I* need a little info. A client of mine got an unbeatable offer, sort of a half-price deal, for breeding to a top show dog—for cash. From the *handler*."

"Naughty, naughty. Who?"

"Confidential?"

"Always. Unless you tell me otherwise. Cough it up, kiddo."

"Morgan Gilmore."

"Uh—no surprise."

"How come?"

"You don't read the secretary's pages anymore?" She scraped her pointers at me, just like in grade school. "Reprimanded by the AKC, once for disorderly conduct, twice that I know of for registration violations."

"And he's still handling? He wasn't suspended? How the hell does he get away with it?"

"Grow up, my dear. They don't call him the Teflon handler for nothing. And anyway, if we tossed out the people who cheat, there might not be enough people left to run a dog show, and I'd be out of a job. We'll talk?"

"Definitely."

"Great. Hey, Kaminsk, where's your tan?"

"Sunblock. I used a shitload of sunblock."

She nodded and turned away. A moment later, there was a hand on my shoulder.

"Where have you *been*, bitch?"

It was Mike Chapman, a dog trainer who wrote a newspaper column for the *Bergen Record*, a Jersey paper. I guess I should explain that, as a dog trainer, I never considered "bitch" a criticism, merely the proper nomenclature for the female of the species.

"The coast," I said. "L.A."

"Are you back for the show or back back?"

I always wondered how Mike did the work. He was about my height and as wide as a doorway, big belly hanging over his belt so that he could never button his jacket, hands and face red, and he wheezed when he spoke.

"Back back," I told him, "I missed the snow."

The waiter came by with skewers of chicken basted in ginger and soy sauce. We each took two.

"So, you're going to be training in Manhattan again? Or what? Were you working out on the coast?"

"Sort of. Got married and divorced since I saw you."

"Heavy!" he said. "You okay?"

"I'm great."

"Hey, I heard about Bernie. Sorry, kid. What are you working with these days, another Golden?"

My mouth was full of chicken. "Pit bull," I said as soon as I could. "And I have a nice little basenji bitch, pointed, I want to breed."

"Basenji? Rachel—"

"I know. I know. Anyway, I was thinking of breeding her to Magritte. I got this swell offer from Morgan Gilmore, his handler—"

"Morgan *Gil*more! Shit!"

"What?"

"Six, eight months ago, that SOB tripped another handler in the ring, guy from the coast, maybe you know him, Ted Stickley?"

I shook my head.

"Fucker fell and broke his left arm, got up, punched Gilmore right in the snout with his right. Got a round of applause, too. Don't deal with Gilmore, Rachel. He's a snake."

"I wouldn't have to send my bitch to him. He banks Magritte." I took the last bite of chicken and waited.

"All the more reason to be careful. He could be sending you *anything*. His *own* sperm, for all you'd know."

I made a face. "Thanks for warning me."

I walked over to the bar, asked for a glass of white wine, and stood watching everyone talk while I sipped it. Being called Kaminsky had instantly drawn me back to the suffocating bosom of my hypercritical family. Beatrice had been dead for over five years, but the memories lingered on.

"Where are you going?" she used to ask me.

"Out."

"Yes, but with your hair like that?"

Gotcha.

People were starting to head out, and when I looked at my watch, I saw it was time for the regular cocktail hour. The award winners and press moved to a larger ballroom, actually two rooms with several bars, tables full of raw vegetables, cheeses, and dips, and several hundred people who knew what and where a hock joint was.

Morgan Gilmore was a few feet from where I was standing, his neat ponytail resting on the satin collar of his tuxedo jacket, a glass of wine in one hand and a cigar in the other. He wore his string tie instead of a bow tie and cowboy boots. Black lizard. How fitting! He was as classy as a bowling trophy.

I intended to stick as close to Gilmore as gum on his shoe, but I was back in my old milieu, and every time I tried to eavesdrop, someone else had another story to tell me. When the dinner hour arrived, I trailed behind Gil, ever hopeful, and managed to sit at the table next to his. But once again the animated conversation close at hand precluded hearing anything from his table. So while I ate my steak dinner, I ended up listening to how many points everyone's dog had accumulated during the last year. Just when my eyes were about to roll permanently up into my head, the ceremony began. I angled my chair so that I could watch Gil watch the proceedings.

The fifth law of investigation work says, Don't jump to conclusions. I began to wonder if I had. Just because Morgan Gilmore was a thief and a distasteful, repugnant human being did not make him a murderer.

In fact, I was only dead sure that he was distasteful and repugnant. I didn't even know for sure that he *was* a thief.

Suppose Cliff had lied to Dennis. Dennis thought Cliff was close to broke. Was it part of Clifford's southern manners to hide yet another easy source of income from his hardworking friend?

How did I know that Gil wasn't giving the stud fees or some agreed-upon percentage of them to Cliff after all? What if he was just a tasteless slime, and not a thief at all, let alone a killer?

Suddenly all I could think about was Clifford Cole's cozy little den, where, among his other papers, he kept his bank records. A peek in there might let me know if Gil was sharing those hefty stud fees or not. I figured the stud fee for a good-quality champion basenji sush as Magritte would be five hundred at the lowest, and up to maybe one thousand if Gil had a real sucker interested. I didn't know if I'd find anything that might possibly mean Gil was sending checks to Cliff, but whether or not he was became the loose thread of the moment.

I decided it would be too rude, even for me, to leave in the middle of the speeches. So I waited until the bitter end before air-kissing my table companions and then running off to beat them to the coat check. I have my standards. They may be low, but they're there.

16

Nowhere in Sight

I TOOK A cab to the cottage, changed clothes, draped Dashiell's leash around my neck, and headed for Greene Street. Twenty minutes later I was sitting at Cliff's desk, the small green shaded desk light making a warm, bright circle on the open file folder with Clifford's bank records.

One large deposit was credited to Cliff's account every month, probably from some trust fund. It was done automatically—there were no deposit slips for those amounts. In fact, there were no deposit slips, period. Unless Gil was paying Cliff cash, unlikely with a deductible expense, he was indeed pocketing Magritte's stud fees.

I returned the file folder to its place in the lower left-hand drawer and opened the other drawers again to see if something would register that didn't the first time around. The more you learn on a case,

the more you can understand the possible impor-
tance of what you see, the significance of something
ordinary that normally might not catch your eye.

I was looking at the odds and ends in the middle
drawer, the place where people keep pens, paper
clips, rubber bands, and loose change. First I
found a receipt for slides from B & H Photo. I put
it in my pocket. There can be nothing more heart-
wrenching than looking at the last photographs
someone took. It's like getting mail from someone
after they've died. But I thought Dennis or Louis
would want them anyway.

Next I spotted a penlight and remembered that I
had wanted to look at the paintings in the storage
closet, but the light hadn't been working. I wondered if there'd be anything left to look at, or if,
like the rest of the loft, the closet too would be de-
pressingly denuded of Clifford's art.

I flicked on the penlight, shut off the lamp, and
walked across the hall. The closet door opened with
a slight creak, releasing the musty smell of a place
too jammed with stuff to have been cleaned. There
was also a faint odor like that of raw wood in lumber-
yards, probably from the unfinished floor. I walked
in, the penlight making the tiniest imaginable circle
of light in the nearly empty closet.

Dashiell followed me into the closet and started
sniffing the floor as I sent the small circle of light
slowly around the walls, looking to see if any painting had been left by accident or design. After revealing nothing but the bare closet on three of the
four sides, the light hit three stretchers that were
leaning on the wall to my right. I walked farther
into the closet to take a better look.

Each of the three was as empty as a gaping, toothless mouth. It was my impression that stretchers were made and canvas stretched onto them only when the artist was ready to use them. Materials were expensive, and if someone other than Cliff were making the frames and stretching the canvas, then it was likely one would be made at a time. When I looked closer, I saw that these weren't new stretchers at all. They were dirty, splattered with drops of paint, and there were staples and threads on the back of each, as if canvas had been in place, used, and then removed.

I was leaning them back against the closet wall when I heard a key in the front-door lock.

I hadn't ever put on the light in the front room, and when I left the study, I had turned off the lamp, good training from my grandmother, who had lived through the Depression. So except for the small light from the penlight, the loft was dark.

For the briefest moment, I thought of Dennis, coming to check the answering machine.

I heard the door open, there was a silence, then the door closed.

If someone had entered the loft, they were wearing sneakers. Or they were barefooted. I tried to stop breathing so that I could hear them, but the loft was silent. I slid my finger off the button of the flashlight. Then I remembered Dashiell. I could no longer see him in the pitch-black closet, and my own breathing seemed so loud now that I couldn't hear his.

Suddenly there was light coming from the front room. I looked behind me and then stepped back into the far corner of the closet. When I turned, I saw Dashiell at the closet door, standing absolutely still, his head cocked to one side. I could see his nose twitching, trolling for a scent. It would come toward him in the shape of a cone, strong and narrow where it left the person, wider and fainter the farther it traveled. I needed to get Dashiell's attention so that I could signal him to come closer to me and stay quiet, but a sick feeling in my gut told me it wasn't Dennis, and I was reluctant to speak. Instead I reached behind me to scratch my nails on the wall so that Dash would turn and look at me.

I heard a drawer open and close in the front room and some clicking noises, and then there was silence except for the small whoosh of Dashiell blowing air out of his nose, the way dogs do when they ride with their heads flying out of car windows, to clear the way for an interesting new scent. Then, just as my hand found the wall, I heard Dash sneeze, and I knew he had the scent he was after. Faster than you could say *Gesundheit*, he was, as they say in my neighborhood, out of the closet.

For a few seconds I heard only the sound of Dashiell's nails on the hardwood floor. He was walking slowly, as if he were going to meet an old friend.

Was I being too paranoid, even for New York? If Dashiell wasn't worried, it *must* be Dennis who came in to check the answering machine.

Of course. That's what the clicking must have been. The answering machine.

Dashiell sneezed again. This time it was the kind that could blow your house down. Someone inhaled audibly—okay, gasped—and then I heard the crash. The front door opened and, a moment later, slammed shut. I bolted out of the closet and ran like hell toward the front room.

The odor hit me first, a sickly sweet cloud of after-shave or perfume. Lately, they all seemed the same. A sort of nasal androgyny has taken over the scent business. Whatever it was, it made me sneeze, too.

I rounded the corner and saw Dashiell. He was standing in the light of the lamp near the front door, just wagging his tail. Next to him, lying broken on the floor, was Clifford Cole's answering machine. When I picked it up and popped open the cover, I saw that the spool on the left was empty. I looked around on the floor, but the message tape was nowhere in sight.

17

If the Shoe Fits

LILLIAN TRIED TO get her arms around me as I
debused, but couldn't make it. Both my arms were
wrapped around her bulky birthday present, and
Dash was pulling me in the opposite direction, doing a great imitation of an untrained dog.

"How are you?" she asked.

I sort of nodded and grunted. I had arrived more
in body than in spirit.

I had gone to the huge windows in the front of
Clifford's loft, struggled to open one, and then hung
out, despite my fear of heights, as far as I could,
just short of what would make me tip forward a
trifle too far, lose my grip on the frame, and plum-
met screaming to the street, where my head would
split open like a ripe melon dropped from the roof.
I tried like hell to see who was leaving the building,
but the gallery, Haber's, had these colorful flags

out front with their current artist's name on them, so all I saw was a glimpse of a tall man in a camel-colored coat, black beret, and white scarf quickly turning right and disappearing.

How many people had keys to the loft anyway?

"I said, 'Are you working?' " I heard Lillian say. She had taken Dashiell's leash, and we were heading for her Jeep Cherokee. Dashiell jumped up onto the backseat, and Lili helped me place Mr. Present next to him.

"Feels expensive."

"I don't want to think about that part."

"You must *really* love me," she said, pulling out of the parking lot. She was beaming.

"I got work," I told her. Then I gave her the bare bones of the case, skipping my visit to the loft late last evening. Hey, I was alone at a murdered man's residence in the middle of the night, and a tall man in sneakers, cheap aftershave, and a camel coat came in, broke the answering machine, and stole the message tape. What's the big deal? But my family has a low threshold of irrationality, forcing me to edit everything I tell them.

"You think this handler with the ponytail killed him?"

"Too soon to say."

Ted came out to meet us, wearing his white chef's apron with a wooden spoon in his left hand, and gave me a long bear hug. "Rachel has a new case," Lili told him excitedly. Then she frowned. "Is this one going to be dangerous?"

Lili filled Ted in on her version of my version of the case as we walked inside.

"Would this artist have threatened the handler

over the money?" Ted asked. "How much is involved in these stud fees?"

"Could be a lot. Thousands, anyway. But I don't think it would have been the money. He would have been livid about losing a choice as significant as whether or not his dog should be bred. At least, that's how Dennis sees it."

"And you? What do you see?" Ted asked.

"I'm still collecting data," I told him.

"But tell me, Rachel," he said, "how did this Gil person get Clifford out onto the pier?"

"Don't get technical," I told him. It was a Beatrice favorite when she was caught in an inconsistency.

"So this we don't know yet," Ted said. He was bending over, reaching into the oven, so I could see his bald spot.

"Roast chicken! I don't know about you, but I'm starving."

"So," Lillian said, "she's starving. What else is new?"

Had the intruder followed me? I wondered. But he had a key. What was he after on the message tape? Was it a message he himself had left and didn't want anyone else to hear?

"So, are you seeing anyone?" Ted asked. He was taking baked potatoes out of the oven one by one with a long-handled fork.

"No one special," I said.

"Well, we've met this young man, a single man, very nice. He sells woolens, imported fabric from Scotland, it's his own company, and—"

I wondered if he wore those plaid skirts.

"—we thought you and he could come to dinner sometime. You might like him."

"I don't know, Ted—"

Half the guys in my neighborhood wore skirts. Why would I have to come here for that?

"We hate to see you—" His voice trailed off, leaving the obvious unsaid. My family *is* subtle. You've got to give them that.

"What about all those good-looking policemen at the Sixth?" Lili chimed in. "Aren't any of them single?"

"Probably."

"So? A man in uniform? With good medical benefits?"

I sighed. "Cops leave the toilet set up."

"Rachel, don't you get tired of—"

"I'm not alone," I said, skipping the part where she told me I would be forever and ever if I didn't learn to compromise. "I have Dashiell."

"Mea culpa," Ted said. "I'm sorry I mentioned it."

Lili called the kids and opened a bottle of white wine.

We gathered around the big round table in the open kitchen, which was a huge balcony overlooking the living room below, the spectacular view of the Hudson River ahead. For a while the only sounds were of platters being picked up and put down on the bare, round oak table and Lillian asking her children why they weren't taking vegetables onto their plates. As if it were the first time this was happening.

Don't talk about yourself, she'd told me more than once. Give the man a chance.

When would I get the message and stop coming to dinner on the lost continent, where time stopped in

1952? I was surprised my sister wasn't wearing a circle skirt with a poodle on it.

I tuned them all out and began to think about my case. Sometimes I'd get a message I wanted to save for one reason or another. I'd flip the tape, or if I *really* wanted to save it, I'd take the tape out of the answering machine and put it away, putting a new tape in the machine. But what could be on Clifford's tape *now*? Didn't everyone know he was dead? After all, it had been in the *New York* fucking *Times*.

"Ma!" It was Daisy.

"Stop teasing your sister," Lili said without even looking. She had probably said it a million times. "And don't fill up on bread," she added.

"My God, Lili, they've turned into us!"

"Zachery, use a fork. What do you mean?" she asked me, looking at me with her large hazel eyes.

I just shrugged. People not only dislike it when you make suggestions about their kids and dogs, they don't like it when you criticize the behavior of said offspring, unless that's what you're getting paid to do. At least that's what my shrink used to say as she criticized my behavior without the least inhibition.

"I've got this case now," I began to tell Daisy, who was seated across from me, "where half the people have changed their names."

"Maybe the other half have, too, but you just haven't found that out yet," Zack said.

"You may be right," I said. He was the older of the two, fifteen, and used to look like a cherub. Now his feet looked five sizes too big, and he had zits.

"Lots of people, in my day, changed their names for business reasons," Ted said.

"Yeah. Yeah. You mean they got rid of Jewish-sounding names so they could blend in."

"Did you ever think of doing that, Dad?" Daisy asked Ted.

"In *my* business? Hardly!"

"Did the people on your case change their names so that no one would know they were Jewish, Aunt Rachel?" Daisy asked.

"I don't know."

Lili got up to clear the table. My family are all graduates of the Evelyn Wood speed-eating course.

Had Dennis and Louis wanted to appear to be more mainstream? Or less like pushovers? Except for the Israelis, Jews were often characterized as wimps.

Had I thought Alexander sounded more game than Kaminsky?

I looked out over the living room and beyond to the river. It had gotten dark already, and the bridge lights were on. You could see the traffic slowly snaking its way to and from Westchester County, across the Hudson. I took Dashiell out, and we walked up to the crest of the mountain. Despite the quiet and the beauty around me, all I could think about was the case.

Maybe Clifford Cole's death *was* the result of random hate. Louis thought it was. It was easy enough, wasn't it? You just got a few friends together, took some sticks or bats and drove through the tunnel, then headed for the Village. The latest trick was to stop the car, ask directions to a gay bar, and if the stranger you had stopped gave them to you, everyone would jump out of the car and beat him to a pulp, justifying the action with the belief that no one but a lousy faggot would know how to get to the Monster or Sneakers. It's sort of a modern-day Cinderella story, a bunch of Jersey princes going around looking for a princess, or, in this fairy tale, a queen. And when they think the shoe fits, wham.

But what about the man in the camel coat? Could there have been a ponytail under that scarf or stuffed into that beret?

When we got back to the house, Ted was sitting in front of the fireplace, a fire burning and the brandy out, picking up the glow of the flames. I sat next to him, and for a while neither of us felt the need to talk.

"Stay over," he said after a while. "You can drive in with me in the morning."

The brandy was burning in my stomach. I leaned against his shoulder and sighed. "I can't," I said, the warmth of the fire on my face.

"You don't have to work tonight, do you, little sister?"

"No. But it's too quiet here. If not for Dashiell's snoring, I'd think I was dead."

He reached behind him, but I jumped up and out of the way. Then, due to my extensive professional training and a quick wit, I managed to get the brandy snifter off to the side before the couch pillow came sailing at me and hit me square in the chest.

"You're lucky my pit bull is such a sound sleeper," I said.

But Dashiell had awakened. He ambled over and was licking up the drops of brandy that had splashed out of my snifter when I got hit. Lili joined us then, and we talked for a couple of hours before they loaded me up with leftovers and drove me back to Nyack to catch the late bus home.

18

He Barked Twice

I HAD JUST stepped out of the shower when the phone rang. It was someone from Bailey House, the AIDS hospice at the foot of Christopher Street, saying they had heard about me and Dashiell from a caseworker who visited the Village Nursing Home, and they had both agreed that Dashiell would be an absolute godsend for their indigent AIDS patients. Since their social worker was in that morning and had a terribly tight schedule, they wondered if I could come over with Dash, say, in an hour, for a walk-through and a discussion about my adding Bailey House to Dashiell's schedule.

It was nine-thirty. I had to get over to the AKC library, check the studbooks to see if I could get some idea of how big a business Morgan Gilmore was conducting with Magritte's frozen semen, drop Dashiell off at home, hightail it over to the Garden, and see what else I could dig up about Gil from his fellow handlers. I told the person on the phone I'd be there in half an hour.

Bailey House is on the southeast corner of Christopher and West, across the highway from the Christopher Street pier. The building that houses Bailey House used to be the River Hotel. The whole top floor, with its sweeping, spectacular river views, belonged to the expensive, chic La Grande Corniche restaurant. You can still see both signs, but now homeless men and women occupy the whole building, people dying of AIDS who have nowhere else to do it.

I approached with the mixed feelings I always had doing this work. Why the hell was I here? How could I say no? Perhaps that's why Zachery says I'm only a medium-boiled detective.

Mr. Sabotini said he'd like to watch me with a few patients and see what Dashiell did, and then we could talk about the feasibility of regular visits. He was short and small with annoying little hands that fluttered constantly as he spoke, and he did that—speaking—slowly and carefully, exaggerating the enunciation of each and every syllable as if I were retarded or perhaps suffering from dementia. He was bald across the crown but had cleverly combed some long hair from the side of his head over the top and glued it down with something that made it look wet and stiff, so that of course no one could tell. And he was one of those self-important prigs who often end up working in institutions, people whose personalities are so offensive that they could never make it in any sort of private practice or in any situation where people feel they have any choice.

I was ready to split when one of the patients walked into the office where we were talking and noticed Dashiell.

"Oh, God, it's Petey," he said, falling onto his knees and embracing Dashiell without asking anything. Lots of people called Dash Petey, the pit bull with the line drawn around his eye that was in the *Our Gang* comedies.

"Hi," I said. He didn't look up. His head was bent down against Dashiell's neck, and his arms reached way around, squeezing as tight as he could.

"He's won-der-ful," he said, his face so thin it was barely more than a skull, his eyes shining with the look some people get shortly before they die.

"His name is Dash."

"I'm Ronald," he said, taking his arm from around Dashiell and pointing to himself. "Will he be coming here regular?" He sat back on his heels and tightened the belt on his robe. "I like him so much."

"Ms. Alexander and Dashiell are here to discuss that today, Ronald," Mr. Sabotini said.

"Rachel," I said. "Can we walk you back to your room, Ronald?"

"Sure. Really?"

I handed him the leash and told him how to get Dashiell to heel.

Ronald was beaming. "Can I do this? Yes, I can do this. This is the most fun I ever had here."

"Me, too," I said. Mr. Sabotini was taking notes on a very little pad as we walked Ronald to the elevator, and seemed to miss the joke that Ronald and I were sharing.

I will say this for Robert Sabotini. He hung back

and let me and Dashiell do our thing. Ronald, not Sabotini, became my guide, taking me from room to room, filling me in on names and bringing me up to date on each person's latest opportunistic illness, which Ronald referred to as an OI. He held Dash's leash and then passed it on to those who wanted to walk the big dog, too. Anyone who could, did.

I was surprised at how much I was enjoying myself, even though that's a funny term to use about a place like this. But each time we entered a room, the occupants would light up, and though their evident pleasure was because of Dashiell's presence, not mine, I still got to bask in the results. After we had visited nearly a dozen patients, Sabotini said he had seen enough and we could go downstairs and talk.

"No, wait. She di'n't meet John yet," he said. "Gotta show John Petey, okay, pleeze, Mr. Sabotini, it'll just take a minute. You go. I'll bring her down. I know the way."

"Well, if Ms. Alexander has the time, Ronald," Mr. Sabotini said.

"It's fine," I said. "We'll be down in five minutes."

"If you're quite sure," he said, smoothing down a hair that had come unstuck.

"She is. She's quite sure," Ronald said.

We watched Sabotini leaving like two little kids watching the teacher leave the room. Ronald took my hand and pulled me down the hall to a room at the end, near the window.

"This is John's room. I love him, John. He's so funny. He could always cheer you up, no matter what he has." Then he put his hand at the side of his mouth and in a dramatic aside told me, "He has KS. Kaposi's sarcoma," he said, enunciating carefully in a witty parody of Sabotini. "That's *cancer*," he explained. "Don't say nothin'. It makes bumps and dark spots, you know, on your skin, and John's real self-conscious about looking ugly."

"Okay," I told him, "I'll be cool."

We entered the small, sunny room with only one of the beds occupied, the other stripped, meaning John's roommate had recently died. Here you checked in, but you didn't check out.

Even though he was under the covers, I could see that John was unusually tall. He was also unusually thin, a not quite gaunt mocha-colored man with a bad case of KS, his face as lumpy as a flophouse mattress. He wasn't as thin as Ronald, who had wasting syndrome, but he was no Refrigerator Perry either. When he spoke, I heard the unclear, raspy voice that meant he had severe thrush, another sign of a system going down.

"Who you brings, man? You brother?" he said to Ronald. Then he began coughing into a small towel that had been lying next to him on the bed.

Ronald lit up. "See, Rachel, I told you. Isn't he funny? No, John, it's *your* brother. Only kidding. It's Petey. From *Our Gang*."

"Yeah. And who I be? Buckwheat?" he said, coughing again.

"This is Dash. And I'm Rachel." I put out my hand, but he brushed at the air instead of taking it.

"You wanna walk him? He walks real nice," Ronald said, holding out Dashiell's leash. But I could see that John was not up to getting out of bed.

" 'Nother time," John said. "I takes him next

time. Shows him where I use t'live. He like it they. Be real spacious." Then he began to cough again. I began to feel he was beyond where a visit from a dog could interest him, but a moment later, he asked if Dash knew how to bark. I told him yes and he asked me if I would show him.

"You can do it yourself, John. Just tell him *speak*."

"Will he?"

"Yes. Try him."

He shook his head, then lay back and closed his eyes. "I'n wants to'*do* it. I needs t'*hear* it."

I said Dashiell's name and asked him to speak. He barked twice, a booming, deep roar, his front legs coming off the floor, his ears flying up, then flapping back down like a bird's wings at takeoff.

John's eyes stayed shut, his lips spreading wide into a smile.

" 'S true, what I hears," he asked, eyes still closed, "a barking dog don't bite?"

I opened my mouth to disappoint him with the answer, but I didn't get the chance.

"Wunt touch 'at sucker wit no ten-foot pole. Wunt bark no how."

"He just did," I said. I was about to signal Dash to bark again when John spoke again.

"You comes back. This dog I likes."

"I will," I promised.

"I will," he repeated, smiling.

Ronald and I headed downstairs to Sabotini's office to cut a deal. A few minutes later Dashiell and I were in a taxi heading uptown to Madison Avenue and the American Kennel Club library. Dashiell spent the ride making nose prints on the right-side passenger window as I watched the city pull by us on the other side.

Sabotini had given me a list of patient names and room numbers as well as a batch of forms so that I could take some brief notes for him, but I had only glanced at the pages before folding them and putting them into my purse. For now, I had to see what I could find out about the illegal activities of one Morgan "No Problem" Gilmore.

The American Kennel Club library is a place where no librarian would ever have to say *Shhh*; from what I have always been able to see, it's one of the best-kept secrets in New York. The only other person I've ever seen there is the librarian.

The studbooks register the pedigree, that is, the sire and dam, of a dog or bitch that has been used at stud or has whelped a litter for the first time. They also contain the name of the owner of each dog listed and the breeder of that dog. What I would be looking for would be Magritte's name, Ch. Ceci N'Est Pas un Chien, as a sire, to get an idea of how many of his offspring had been bred last year.

Not all the dogs Magritte sired would be on this list. Some would never be bred, some would still be too young to breed, or, if they had been bred before, wouldn't show up because the list was for first-time parents only. Still, it would give me an idea of what Gil was doing, and it was also the best way of complying with laws one and three.

I made careful notes whenever Magritte's name showed up. In fact, by poring carefully over the register for the previous year, I found the listing of when Magritte was first used at stud. It appeared that Morgan Gilmore had been using Magritte at stud and stealing the fees for a little better than two years. With a bitch, that wouldn't mean much. But in the case of a dog, whose work didn't take much time at all, even less when his sperm was banked, it could mean a lot of puppies sired and a lot of money paid in stud fees.

When I had finished with the studbook registers, I opened my bag to put in the notes I had taken and took out the papers Robert Sabotini had given me. The forms to fill out for each patient were fairly predictable, mostly things to check off such as: patient was up and about, patient remained in bed, patient responded to dog, patient did not respond to dog. There was a small space for any comment I wanted to make, and supposedly these notes and comments would be used by Sabotini and the staff to make the patients I visited more comfortable or happier. In some places that was so. In others, the forms got filed unread. But either way, on some visits Dash might make the patients forget about their illness for a few minutes; on others he might help them talk about it, if that's what they needed to do. I was sure at least two of them were already looking forward to his next visit.

I put the pages one behind the other as I looked them over until I got to the list of patients Sabotini wanted me to see. There were only six names on the list, those, it seemed from my visit today, who were responding least to other stimuli. He was sending us to the most depressed patients at the hospice, even though the place was small enough for me to visit everyone. Ronald's name was not on the list, but I was sure he'd want to escort me again. John's name was given as John W. Doe. Very original, they gave

him a middle initial. Perhaps they kept track of
their John Does by coding them alphabetically, the
way busy dog breeders code their litters, never mix-
ing the Ivy, Iris, and Irving puppies with the Jack,
Jake, and Jessica ones. That theory would make
John the twenty-third John Doe, unless it was the
second or third time around the alphabet.

Of the other five patients on Sabotini's list, only
one was female, Sivonia LeBlanc. I hadn't met her
yet. I wondered which of these names, if any, were
real, if any of these people even remembered the
names they had been given when they were young,
healthy, and had homes of their own.

Sivonia LeBlanc. Yeah. Yeah.

I checked my watch. If I moved fast, I could be at
the Garden by two, in plenty of time to ogle my favorite breeds. Then, after most of the dogs had
been judged, the handlers would be available for
dishing, rumormongering, and the purveying of
vicious gossip. For this case, the world of pure-
bred dogs might turn out to be just what the doctor
ordered!

19

I Never Knew It Could
Be Like This

IT HIT ME as soon as I entered, even before I
showed my ticket to the uniformed guardians of
the gates to dog-person heaven, hit the way the flu
does, gradually, but all at once too. In no time I was
trembling, sweating, anxious, no longer in control,
my legs like overcooked spaghetti. I could hardly
navigate, but the crowd moved me along, swept me
into the tunnel under the stands, on toward the
benching area, my pulse rapid, my temperature
rising like smoke on a clear day, until I felt like
screaming, screaming out until I had lost my voice,
yes, yes, yes, I never knew it could be like this.

Westminster! It's better than sex. And the way
my life's been, more frequent too.

I took the escalator up a tier above the floor
where the rings were, an old habit from my training
days. I always liked to start out high up in the

cheap seats, watching the rings from above. It was an interesting perspective on movement and gave one an overall look at all the rings at once. Amazingly, considering how vast the crowd was, I could usually spot my old friends, even from that lofty, distant perch. It wasn't difficult. Captain Haggerty towered head and shoulders above the crowd, his head shaved bald. And the other person I wanted to see was also head and shoulders above the crowd. In his own way.

I looked down at the rings, both in them and around them. Inside the rings, the breeds were being judged, the judge assessing the dogs to see which of each breed came closest to that breed's standard, to see which the nearly perfect Platonic pointer, puli, or poodle was. They looked at the dogs stacked—standing in standardized positions according to breed—and checked the angulation of their legs, the line of their backs, the width of chest, the breadth of skull, their proportions, balance, overall beauty of form. Then the dogs were gaited, running one at a time with their handlers in a pattern set by the judge or all or many at a time, circling the ring, some breeds at what seemed like breakneck speed.

It had taken me a while to understand movement, thinking it was different for each breed. It is. And it isn't. Though a saluki and a Westie move very differently, in each case you're looking for the dog to move like a beautifully made, well-oiled machine.

From the movement, which is different with different structure, you can see if the dog would be able to work at the task he was bred for, rousting a rodent from its nest, moving the sheep, treeing the raccoon, finding the fox, bringing the shot-down bird to hand, whatever. At least, that's the theory.

In practice, much of the breeding for the ring was producing empty-headed beauty queens who wouldn't last half an hour doing the work that breed was originally bred to perform.

I watched some of the dogs gaiting, heard some cheers from the far left corner as the judge there made her selection, and then began to scan around the rings, finally spotting someone I knew.

His head was tilted just a tad to the left, as if he were listening to something very important that was difficult to hear. He still needed a haircut. His shaggy brown hair covered half his collar. And he was wearing the same damn Harris tweed jacket he always wore to the Garden. That meant he'd wear a blue blazer and a red tie tomorrow, for Best in Show. Some things never change.

I watched him for a while and thought about coming up behind him and grabbing his cute ass, just the way I always used to, asserting my right to be just as vulgar as any man, but when I got up to walk down the stands, I reminded myself that I had work to do. So I went straight to the Am Staff ring, not to the bull-mastiff ring where Chip Pressman stood, his arms folded across his chest, his catalog dangling from his right hand.

American Staffordshire terriers are sort of elegant pit bulls, the differences minor enough that some dogs have dual registration. That, however, was no reason for the people in either camp to like or respect each other's dogs. Deep in their hearts, Am Staff people tend to think of pit bulls as scrappy, unpredictable, badly bred mongrels. And pit bull people regard Am Staffs as beauty queens, dogs no longer up to scratch. A dog who wouldn't face his opponent by approaching the line scratched in the dirt of the pit lost the fight. Worse to some, he was considered a coward: If you said a pit dog turned, it meant he had turned back from the line, that he wasn't game. But if you said a Doberman turned, it meant something entirely different. It meant he turned on his master. He wasn't a coward. He was an ingrate.

The handlers were stacking their dogs, lifting each leg, one at a time, and placing the paw carefully down in just the spot that would make the dog look best. The more confident handlers let their dogs free-stack, holding their attention with bits of dried liver or bait, which the handler might even place in his own mouth and soak with his own saliva to make it all the more appealing. Or appalling, depending upon your personal taste.

The bait gets the dogs to lean forward, making them look elegant rather than clunky, bringing them up on their toes, making their necks seem longer, giving the proper angle to their shoulder assembly and a nice extension to their rear legs.

The dogs focused on the liver. The handlers watched the judge. After walking down the line of stacked dogs, dogs always between the handler and the judge so that the handlers did not obstruct the judge's view, she gave the signal to move the dogs around the ring. The muscular beauties ran with their handlers. The judge watched carefully, occasionally whispering to the steward, who made notes in his book.

I left before the Best in Breed was selected. I'd

see that dog tonight, when the groups were judged. It was seldom what I cared about. It is the behavior of a dog that interests me. To some people I've met over the years, behavior equals obedience. But while some compliance is necessary for the safety of the dog and the sanity of the owner, it is the delicious peeks inside a dog's mind that excite me, understanding how dogs learn, crack jokes, communicate, even how they pick up the rules of a game and then change them, just as their human opponents can.

I headed for the benching area, stopping, as I always did, to buy a present for Dashiell, this time a new Flying Man because his old one was falling apart. It always amazed me to see a powerful adult animal playing with a faux-sheepskin gingerbread man with a squeaker in his belly, acting as silly and thrilled to pieces as any three-month-old. Dashiell would never find himself in therapy searching for his inner puppy.

I checked my catalog to make sure I wasn't about to bother anyone who was yet to go up and began to schmooze with handlers, first about their breed; then, if things went well, I'd progress to frozen semen and Morgan Gilmore.

There were two people sitting in the Akita area, and I knew the Akitas had gone up in the morning, so I admired one of the dogs, who was immediately removed from his crate and stacked for me in the crowded aisle. I guess I sounded like a potential puppy buyer and had found an owner. Her companion, a no-nonsense woman in the de rigueur ring outfit—longish A-line skirt, blazer, and thick-soled, clunky oxfords—I suspected was a handler. My suspicion was confirmed when she gave me her card, so that when the Akita puppy I was about to buy from her friend got old enough, she could handle it for me and make it a champion. Hey, if you want people to open up to you, you have to ingratiate yourself with a few appropriate lies.

As soon as I could, I slipped in my usual fable about a neat little basenji bitch—this time I said she belonged to my sister—and the wonderful deal we were offered. I tried to look as if I had just arrived from a farm in Kansas instead of a lair in Greenwich Village. The women passed a look between them, a combination of pity and alarm.

"Tell your sister that's not a good idea," Trish, the handler, said.

"Why not?"

"Well, uh, you should be dealing with the owner?" Margaret, the Akita breeder said, looking again at Trish.

"I think like the guy who owns the dog has the handler take care of the breedings. Anyway, he said the dog was banked, you know, like a sperm bank, so—"

"Look," Trish said, "it sounds fishy. You know what I'm saying?"

"You mean—"

"Right." She looked all around to see who was within earshot. "The guy's a slime," she whispered. "Never did anything in an upright way in his life."

"Oh," I said.

"Trish knows. She sees him at all the shows. I don't usually travel with Bomber," Margaret said. "Trish shows for me. But of course, for Westminster, I mean, I wouldn't miss this for anything."

"How'd he do?" I asked.

"*He* did fine. The judge prefers another type."

"There's more than one type?" I said. Gee, and here I thought there was only one AKC standard.

"She likes a finer-boned dog. Bomber is heavy boned."

Trish snapped the leash up and took a piece of liver from her pocket, and Bomber snapped to attention. "See?"

"Heavy boned," I said. "Well, about the sperm thing. Are you sure? I mean, what sort of stuff were you referring to?" I whispered after looking around, not that *I* would know who to watch out for.

Margaret slid over, and I squeezed in next to her.

"I understand he gets real close with some of the judges," she said.

"How close?" I asked.

"*Real* close," Trish said, rubbing her forefinger back and forth along the ball of her thumb.

I clapped a hand over my mouth to express my astonishment.

I thanked Trish and Margaret, made a point of carefully putting their cards into my purse, then headed over to see the miniature bull terriers.

I began to chat with a stocky guy, mid-forties, male pattern balding, flat nose, drive-in pores, small, pale eyes, named Larry Benton, "but my friends call me Speed." He showed me his dental implants, canines and all, and I hoped, for his sake, those friends weren't referring to his sexual pacing. At least he was eager to talk.

"They call him Liver Lips," he said when I mentioned I was thinking of having Gil handle for me since he was so good with basenjis, "because what he does, see, he holds the liver in his mouth and makes it real juicy. Then he holds it here," he said, pointing to the middle of his bottom lip, "and then spits it to the dog, see, and the dog catches it. Makes the dog look at his face, at Gilmore's face. The judges, they eat it up. They think it's rapport. Think the dogs actually *like* him. Act like he's fucking Jim Moses or somebody who can *really* bond with a dog. But get this, he also spits the pieces of liver as he runs, see, so it'll distract the other dogs, get them to break their gait trying to grab the treats. Going in the ring with him is a handler's nightmare."

"Is that *legal*?"

"Legal, schmegal. Boy, are you naive. You like minis?"

"Love'em," I said. It felt weird to say something true.

"Willy Boy here's got the best head I've seen in the breed. You know they're a head breed?"

I nodded. "Who doesn't?"

He referred, of course, to shape, not content. A dog with the IQ of cement could still win Best in Show.

I looked beyond Speed to Willy Boy's crate and saw his blue ribbon proudly displayed. Apparently someone else agreed that Willy had a beautiful head, a funny thing to say about a bull terrier, if you think about it.

I took Speed's card: "Larry 'Speed' Benton, Professional Handler, when you care enough to get the very best." Original!

I needed to get out of the intense crowding of the benching area for a while, so I went back upstairs, high up, bought a soda and a hot dog, and went back to the cheap seats to observe from above, where at least there was some air. It was canned, but still it was air.

Looking down at the rings below, I watched the tail end of the judging, the bichon frises in ring one, the rotties in ring five, the giant schnauzers in ring six. The dignity of the Giants could be seen even from above, but from high up, the rottweilers moving looked like black pillowcases full of bricks being mysteriously thrust forward. The bichons were circling, too, just about ready for the final pick. I closed my eyes and waited for the screams.

I nearly jumped a foot when a hand touched my shoulder.

"Kaminsky! Is it you?"

"Hey, Pressman. Nice jacket. Is it new? How the fuck you been?"

"What's it your fucking business?" he answered.

We both started laughing, and he slid into the seat next to mine.

"Where've you been keeping yourself?"

"Um, the coast, mostly."

"Yeah. Someone told me you were in California for a while," he said.

"Did you say something?" I asked, after killing some time concentrating on the rottweiler judging.

"I asked if you'd been on the coast." He was talking slowly and too loud now, as if he were talking to one of the inmates at the old folks home.

"I guess so."

"You *guess* so? You guess L.A. or S.F.?"

"NYC."

"NYC?"

"Yeah. The *East* Coast."

"You mean you *weren't* in California?"

"Nah. I can't seem to tear myself away from the theater."

"Not to mention the museums."

"I didn't."

"What?"

"Mention the museums."

"How true. Well, glad you're back, so to speak."

"Me, too. Glad to *be* back. As it were."

"So, tell me, is it true? What I heard?"

"Was it something negative?" I asked, unscrunching myself from the orange plastic seat. "Then it was probably true. More than likely true, I'd say. Well, definitely true." I grabbed his shirt and pulled him into my face. "What did you hear?"

"That you're divorced."

I let go of his shirt and slouched back down into the seat. "Oh, that," I said, brushing away an imaginary insect with the back of my hand. "Who isn't?"

"Not me," he said. He was sitting next to me, making the kind of direct eye contact only the most confident dogs make, only his eyes were green, not blue or brown.

I wanted to say something, to comment or respond in either a cheeky or compassionate way, but the thought came to me that I may have completely forgotten how to speak in English, and that if I dared open my mouth, I might find myself speaking in Chinese.

Chip didn't speak either.

Anyway, the screaming from the bichon ring was so loud we would have had trouble hearing each other if either of us *had* spoken.

I could smell his musky aftershave, or was that

just him? I had the urge to sniff him, the way Dashiell would have, but I decided to hold off. At least for the time being.

"So, what are you up to? Still training?" he asked, reaching for my soda and taking a sip.

"I wouldn't want to lose my hand," I said, putting my arms on top of the back of the seat in front of me, resting my chin on the back of the top hand, and looking down at the rotties being stacked.

"You mean, at *training*?"

"Among other things. A woman's got to know how to take care of herself these days. What with all the divorce going around."

"I noticed your ad is no longer in the Yellow Pages."

I sat back up and looked at him, but said nothing. He had those little flecks of reddish brown in the green of his eyes.

"Have you finally found an occupation more in keeping with the delicacy of your gender?" he asked, draining the drink and letting an ice cube fall into his mouth. "No. Don't tell me. Let me guess. You've opened a yarn shoppe."

I smiled. Inscrutable as a chow chow.

"Did I ever tell you—" Then he began to laugh. "Same old Kaminsky."

"It's a family thing," I said. "It's genetic. None of us ever change. You might say I'm just a chip off the old block."

I thought he was going to put an ice cube down my shirt or something equally immature, but he didn't. He just sat there looking down at the rings. The rottie people were going wild. One of the pillow-cases had won.

"I woke up too late to save the marriage," he said, still watching the dogs. "I hope to hell it's not too late to save fatherhood. You'd be surprised how difficult it is to accept the fact that you're not the kid anymore. You're the parent."

I exhaled for the first time since Lincoln was shot and waited.

"We're doing joint custody. Ellen says I spend more time with the kids now than I ever did when we were married."

I nodded.

He nodded back.

We both looked down at the rottie ring and watched the winning dog getting his picture taken.

"How'd you know I was here?"

"Saw you walking up the stands. I'd know your— walk anywhere."

"Horse shit, Pressman."

"No, it's true. You have one of the great walks. I've always thought so."

"Be that as it may," I said, but then I shut up. I could feel my face getting hot.

The thing is, if you've been attracted to someone when he wasn't available, that fact could have made him more attractive then he really was. And because you knew you wouldn't let anything happen, because who wants to always celebrate holidays on the wrong day and just sit by the telephone with nothing to keep you company but your low self-esteem, you never looked at him as a viable mate. So you just have this tantalizing impression. Which has zero to do with reality.

"Just when it's getting interesting, I have to meet a client," he said. "But I—"

"Yeah. Yeah. I've got to get back to work myself."

"I tried to call you, Rachel. You're not in the book anymore? Not even in the white pages?"

"Not listed."

He raised his eyebrows in unison and waited.

"Jesus! What do you need to find an old friend, a fucking private detective?"

I thought from there I could cleverly segue into the story of my life but I didn't. Instead, I took out a pen, slid his catalog off his lap, and on the inside back cover wrote my name and my unlisted phone number. He leaned toward me just as I was looking down to put away my pen. His lips landed on my nose.

"Was that as good for you as it was for me?" He was grinning.

"I never knew it could be like this," I told him. His eyes were the color of moss.

"Same old Kaminsky," he said, pulling out his wallet, fiddling with its contents, and finally extracting his business card.

"We're not at the same number either."

"We?"

He handed me a photo of a shepherd.

"Betty," he said.

"Davis?"

"Boop."

She had a dark saddle, a red chest, piercing, intelligent eyes.

Okay, so I only trust people who carry a picture of their dog in their wallet. But the photo alone wasn't enough reason to run out to Condomania and stock up. Was it?

The good part of sleeping with your dog is that he

never, ever gets out of bed, looks back at you, and says, "You, know, babe, you'd have a great body if only you'd lose ten pounds."

And he never goes back to his wife.

I thought I should tell Chip that my new career required Zenlike concentration and that I couldn't afford the distraction of a sexual liaison at this time, or just make some childish, offputting, hostile remark to cover up how nervous he had made me, but before I got the chance to do either, he left.

I watched him making his way down the crowded stands, then crossing the Garden floor. His gait was strong and smooth, with no sideways movement or wasted effort, as if he were a beautifully made, well-oiled machine.

The river of dogs was still moving in circles in ring six. The crowd near ring two cheered. I watched, waiting for my heart to start beating at its normal pace again. When it did, I felt so drained I could have curled up among the empty soda containers on the sticky floor and taken a nap.

I've always had trouble dealing with more than one thing at a time. And right now, I reminded myself, my time was bought and paid for.

The day's breed judging was over, and they were starting to tear down the rings and sweep in preparation for the group judging that came in the evening: the working, terrier, nonsporting, and herding groups on Monday night, the sporting, hounds, and toy groups, then Best in Show, on Tuesday night. People were clearing out now to go for dinner and many to change to formal clothes for the evening judging. I stayed. I loved the Garden when it was empty.

I had once come with Art Haggerty to interview the three families who had dog acts in Ringling Bros. Barnum and Bailey Circus. We had come in the morning, interviewed and watched the acts all day and all evening, and then were invited to stay late, after midnight, to watch a new dog act being trained for the next season. We waited in the stands, whispering to each other. It would have seemed disrespectful somehow to speak out loud. After a while a young boy, his hair wet and slicked neatly back, came out and walked to the center of the center ring. The only light in the whole place shone down on him as he played the trumpet, which in this cavernous, empty space sounded so mournful and moving we could barely breathe. When he finished and left, a very tall blond woman came out, bowed to the empty stands, and then blew a whistle. With that the dogs appeared, one by one, running into the ring and jumping onto small, high stools, then turning around to face her with rapt attention. These were the Daring Dobermans. As we watched her put the six male dogs through their paces, we figured out and whispered to each other the separate commands that, when seamed together, made up each routine.

The circus families trained dogs the same way they trained wild animals, not the way dog trainers trained, and so Letitia swung a kind of small fake whip over her head as she cued the dogs to work, a reminder of the fruits of disobedience.

We had watched the acts during the day and evening from the floor, but from close up we could see things we would not have been able to see even from the first row. We could see the size and strength of the flat metal collars used to contain the chimps, the pain and anger in their eyes too. We could see the sharp hooks on the rods that seemed to merely tap-tap at the elephants to keep them moving, and we could see the scars all over their bodies. Backstage, chained in a long line, they rocked and rocked, the way people in mental institutions sometimes do. We could see something so frightening in the eyes of the big cats, it defied description. We could see the scars they had left on their trainer, too.

From the floor, we had seen everything. I hadn't been to a circus since.

The Garden was quiet now. I opened my bag and took out the list I had made at the AKC library. Or at least that's what I thought I was taking out. Instead, it was the list of names Sabotini had given me. I began to read it. James T. McEllroy, Michael Smith, John W. Doe.

I shoved everything back into my bag and ran like hell for the pay phones.

20

You Can't Play This

HERBIE SUSSMAN AND two of his cousins were lined up at the curb on the other side of the street with their penises out. One at a time, they urinated into the street to see whose stream could reach the farthest.

Lili and I wanted to play, too.

You can't play this, Herbie said. You're girls.

Can, too, my sister Lillian sang, chin up, eyes defiant.

She pushed me up to the curb, told me not to move, and came back a minute later pulling the garden hose behind her. She put the nozzle between my legs.

Hold tight, she ordered. Then she turned the nozzle.

The hose sputtered. Then the arc of water sprayed

far into the street, almost to where the boys were standing.

We win, Lili shouted, head cocked, hands on her hips.

The cold water dripped into my sandals.

No fair, Herbie yelled.

He stood alone now, his pinkie of a penis pale and flaccid at the opening in his pants. His cousins had already turned around, shaken their members back into their pants, and were running for home.

I was only six at the time, but I learned two valuable lessons. First, if you really want to do something, don't waste your time waiting for someone else's permission. Boys always say "You can't play this." If you believe them, you'll end up a teacher or a nurse when what you really want to be is a dog trainer or a detective.

Second, sometimes you have the edge. Sometimes you don't. Either way, life's unfair.

It was the second lesson I was reminded of when I heard the voice on the other end of the phone say, "Bailey House. Can I help you?"

I had gone to the bank of pay phones on the higher tier, the ones hardly anyone used, and listening to the phone ringing on the other end, I had wondered who I'd ask for, but the moment someone answered I knew. I asked for Ronald.

Patients didn't have bedside phones, but Ronald was ambulatory and had no trouble coming to the phone.

"Ronald, it's Rachel. Listen, the list Sabotini gave me of patients to visit, it had John down as John W. Doe."

"Yeah. They do that when guys come in all

drugged out from the street. He was, you know, a user. He couldn'ta said his name if he knew it. So they give him one."

"Does he know his name now? Does he at least remember his street name?"

"Now? Yeah, sure. But they ain't going to change the record. I mean, it's not like he's getting family or anyone visiting him, you know. And like we all got used to calling him John before he got cleaned up, so, you know, it's hard to change, Rachel. How's Petey?"

"He's fine, Ronald. I'll bring him by again soon if you like, to see you and John. But tell me now"—I closed my eyes and inhaled—"Ronald, what name does John remember?"

"His name that he had when he was a little kid. You know, when he was growing up. But he don't care if you call him John. He don't get upset or nothing."

"So, Ronald, when John was a little kid, what was his name?"

"Oh, I thought I said. It was William. Willy was what his mama called him. That's what he told me, Rachel. You know, when he could."

"Did he say *where* he grew up, Ronald? Do you know where he lived when he was little?"

"Yeah. Sure. He likes me, John. He tells me everything."

"So, where was it?"

"Oh, right. Pittsburgh."

My heart flopped.

"You know," Ronald added. "In P.A."

I was hyperventilating. He hadn't parroted me, saying "Will he?" He was telling me his name! And he had seen Magritte. That was why he wanted to hear Dashiell bark. Magritte couldn't, so he thought that meant he'd bite.

"Ronald, you're the best. I'll be there in the morning. What can I bring you?"

"A milk shake. Chocolate, Rachel. If you would."

"I would." Then I fairly shouted into the phone, "I will."

I *Will*. I had found Billy fucking Pittsburgh.

I made one more call, to my friend Marty Shapiro, at the Sixth. The Sixth is home to the bomb squad, and Marty handles Elwood, the yellow Lab whom Dash adores, which is how we met. Billy had been in such bad shape when he had come in, the guys had gotten him a bed at Bailey House. No way they were going to let him back onto the street like that, Marty told me, no fucking way.

Small wonder I hadn't found him, waking up the homeless in the dead of winter, talking to crazy people so I could feel justified I was earning my fee.

On the other hand, for all the good it had done me, Mary Perry *had* seen him, saw him with KS, *spotted* him. Wasn't her, she said. But someone sure had. Someone who had been kind enough to offer him the use of a needle most likely.

I sat with Dennis for the evening judging, but I had trouble keeping my mind on the show.

"Where's Magritte?" I asked Dennis after the last group was judged.

"At home. Why?"

"When and how does Gil get him, for the show tomorrow?"

"I bring him in the morning. I'm meeting Gil at the benching area at eight-thirty."

"What time does he go up?" The damn catalog was sitting right on my lap, and I had already looked it up at least twice, and now I couldn't remember the ring or the time.

"Eleven-thirty. Ring three."

"Look, I know this is going to be tight, but I need you to meet me at Bailey House on the corner of Christopher and West streets—do you know it?" He nodded. "With Magritte, before you bring him here."

"Rachel—you know the dogs have to be benched all day!"

"No, no, look!" I was paging through the catalog. "Here it is, 'Benching hours,' " I read aloud, " 'eleven-thirty to eight P.M.' See?" I shoved it in his face. "Dennis, this is *really* important. Eight A.M. In the lobby. We'll be at the Garden before nine, by eight-thirty if we're lucky. Trust me."

"Okay," he said. I must have been ranting, because he looked at me as if I was. "Eight A.M. Bailey House. In the lobby. And you're not going to explain this, right?"

"Right," I said, grabbing my coat. "Not just yet."

And like a husky let off leash, I was gone.

21

You Can Recommend Me

RONALD WAS IN the lobby waiting. I handed him the milk shake.

"It's all set," he said, holding the shake with both hands. "To, you know, go upstairs and see John."

Dennis arrived on time with Magritte tucked under his arm. We headed for the elevator.

I walked into John's room alone. He appeared to be asleep.

"Will?"

He opened his eyes. "Oh, it the dog lady. Where he at?" He picked his head up to look beyond me.

"He's not here today, Will, but I have to ask you some questions about another dog, the one you saw on the Christopher Street pier. The one who frightened you because he didn't bark. Remember?"

"I'n't remember nothin' from then," he said, looking suspicious. "Why you aks?"

"Well, there was a young man murdered that night."

He looked away, toward the window.

"Billy?"

"Yeah, a young man murder'd."

"And you were the one who told the police that there was a body on the pier. Remember?"

"A body. Yeah."

"Billy, did you see the young man before he got killed? Did you see him walking with the little dog onto the pier? Think hard, Bill, it's so important."

"No," he said, "Ah di'n't see tha'."

"I have the little dog here, Bill. The one you saw. The one you were afraid of because he didn't bark, remember? The one you saw on the Christopher Street pier."

"Oh shit," he said.

"Now listen to me, Bill, this dog does not bite. He doesn't bark because he can't. Did you hear him make some other sounds that night, like cries?"

I ducked back into the hall where Dennis, Magritte, and Ronald were standing and lifted Magritte into my arms. I stepped back into the room but stayed right at the door. Billy didn't move. I bent and kissed Magritte on top of his head, and he lifted his muzzle and licked my mouth. I could feel the heat of his body where I held him against my side.

"He's a very gentle dog, Bill, or I wouldn't have brought him. I thought if you saw him again, it might help you to remember what you saw."

"I never forget what I sees tha' time."

"How come?"

"Be a hard night." Billy Pittsburgh squeezed his eyes shut. A single tear rolled down one cheek.

"Bill, was the young man already dead when you first saw him?"

Billy Pittsburgh sat bolt upright in his bed. "Does I look like a doctor? Hey, I'm not a doctor. I'm a fucking *dope* addict. How'm I s'posed to know if he alive or dead?" He shook his head. "No sir. I don't know nothin' about that. What you aksing me that fo'?" He fell back against his pillow, all his energy gone as suddenly as it came.

"Billy?"

"Okay. Okay. I hears you." He pulled the cover up to his neck, his hands shaking badly. "He 'live."

"But you said you didn't see him walking onto the pier with his dog, with this dog?"

"You aks me if I sees th' man goin' wit th' dawg. I di'n't. He go alone."

"Alone? Are you sure?"

"I sure. Man, I sure I do not wanna *do* this."

"Please, Bill. Please help us out."

"Okay. You aks me. I goin' tell it." He held up one trembling finger. "Car comes." Then a second finger. "A white man take th' dawg an' drag 'im out th' pier, t' th' end. He tie him they." A third finger, his thumb, the nail bitten short. "He go back t' th' car and he sit they."

His hand was shaking so badly he put it under the blanket.

"Th' young white man come," he continued. "Th' dawg, th' one you got, he carryin' on, somethin' awful. The young 'un, he hears 'im an he start t' run t' 'im."

Billy's eyes are now full, and tears, one after the other, slide down his cheeks.

"And th' first man, th' man in th' car, he start up

the motor, he put the lights on and he drive after th' second man."

He lifts his hands and covers his face.

"He knock 'im down. He back out an' leave 'im they. He leave th' dawg they an' the dawg cry out for 'ours 'n I di'n't go look 'til he gots 'imself out o' th' collar and runs away, because I always hears if a dawg don't bark, it bite. Tha's what my mama tol' me. Yes, sir."

I felt a tear run into my neck and realized that I was crying, too.

I walked over and sat on the side of Billy's bed. Magritte was as still as cold water. Slowly, Billy Pittsburgh reached out his hand and let Magritte lick his long, thin, trembling fingers.

"Billy," I said, "did you tell this story to the police?"

"No," he said. "I di'n't."

"Why not?"

"They di'n't aks me nuthin'. I's on drugs 'n they figure I di'n't know nothin'."

I turned toward the door. Dennis and Ronald had moved into the doorway.

"This is Dennis, Bill. The young man was his best friend."

"I sorry, man," Billy said, "I so sorry 'bout you friend."

"Bill," Dennis said. He seemed unable to say anything else.

"One more thing, Bill. Do you remember anything about the car, anything at all?"

He shook his head.

"Thank you, Bill. We want to find this man.

You've helped us a lot. Can I come back soon with Dash, you know, Petey?"

He nodded. I squeezed his arm and turned to leave.

"Black," he said.

I turned around and looked at him.

"New."

I nodded.

" 'Merican. Th's all I see."

He shrugged and turned back toward the window. There was a pigeon on the sill, its head down, its wings tight to its sides, like an old man with his hand stuffed into his pockets.

"I di'n't know 't was goin' happen. Cunna stop 't 't nohow. Not nohow."

"Nobody thinks you could have," I said. "This wasn't your fault, Bill."

He turned his lumpy face toward me.

"Then why'm I bein' punish?" he asked.

In the taxi on the way to the Garden, the little basenji curled up on the seat between us, and Dennis was nearly rigid.

"He got Cliff out there with Magritte," he said.

"What do you want to do?" I asked.

"Kill him," Dennis said.

"Dennis, that's not your job. And we're not positive it was Gil. Let's take this a step at a time. First, what do you want to do now, about Westminster and Magritte? Should we even be going?"

"Oh God, Rachel, we have to. Clifford wanted this more than anything. Magritte has to go up today. But how can I give him to Gil?"

"Look, Dennis, even if what we suspect is true

and Gil committed the murder, we have no reason to think he'd hurt Magritte. If that's what he had wanted to do, he had the opportunity the night of the murder. Besides, he's been doing pretty well with Magritte and he might just think things will continue along as they were, only with you the one he's cheating instead of Cliff. Let him think that. Be charming. For God's sake, Dennis, just act dumb. Okay?"

"Yes, but—"

"No buts. Here's what I want you to do. Just give Magritte to Gil, no problem, okay? Tell him you've changed your plans, the trip got canceled, and you're taking Magritte home right after the show. Eight-thirty, on the button, you'll get Magritte from the benching area and bring him to your box. Unless, of course, he takes the breed. In that case, you'll be able to keep your eye on him because he'll be in the group, right in front of your face.

"The rest is up to me. I'm going to hang out in the benching area. I'm a big fan of Magritte's, remember? Gil knows all about my precious Crystal. He's already offered to cut me a deal. So he won't find it weird to see me there. I'll ask a lot of questions. I'll even tag along when he goes to the grooming area. When he's with Magritte, I'll stick to him like peanut butter on the roof of his lying mouth.

"I'll be ringside when he goes up at eleven-thirty. I'll see you there, but I can't sit with you. I can't sit with you tonight either. Gil can't know that we know each other. Okay? Then, after tonight, we'll figure out where to go with the case, okay? I still have to *prove* he did it, Dennis, *if* he did it. So far, the evidence is all circumstantial—mounting, but circumstantial.

"You still have your trip tomorrow. But I'll have Magritte. You'll give him to me tonight, just as we planned. And if I work my can off and we're really lucky, maybe I'll have something more concrete by the time you get back from Boston. So are you with me on this?"

The cab had stopped at Eighth Avenue and Thirty-second Street. Dennis just sat there.

"Dennis?"

He nodded, then reached for his wallet. "Sorry," he said, coming back to life. He handed the driver a ten and then turned to look at me.

"Rachel, what would I do without you? You're the greatest."

"Yeah. Yeah," I said, lifting Magritte and making sure I had a good grip on his lead before I opened the door, "if any of your other friends have a loved one killed, you can recommend me."

22

Take Your Time,
I Told Him

WE SHOWED OUR tickets, then Dennis and I began to bulldoze our way into the benching area, passing and being passed by a sea of handlers with dogs of every size, color, and possible shape, Afghans and salukis sporting silver-lamé snoods to keep their long, feathered ears clean and dry, drooly dogs wearing bibs to catch the saliva that would periodically stream down from their loose flews, Yorkies and silkies, their long coats sectioned, wrapped in paper, and rolled in curlers to keep it from getting damaged, let down only on the grooming table and in the ring.

Dogs of astonishing size were carried, some on the hip or high up over the shoulder, like babies, and just as passive. Some were so docile they allowed themselves to be cradled, back down, feet up, or just held close to the chest. They were amazingly pliable, having stood on a grooming table and been manipulated into position from the time they were weaned.

There were photographers, too, nearly one per dog it seemed, shooting everything, dogs sitting not in but on their crates, dogs with teddy bears, dogs that were all coat, resembling mops, and dogs that had no coat, hairless dogs, so vulnerable looking they made you want to cry.

Even before we got to row six, Dennis and I separated. He headed directly for Magritte's spot, and I turned the other way, meandering past the rows of benched dogs on one side and concessions on the other. The benching area, raised platforms covered in sturdy green outdoor carpeting where the dogs are assigned to stay when not in the doggy bathrooms, the grooming area, or the ring, was surrounded by booths selling books, magazines, food, jewelry, all for dogs or dog related. Going around the long way, I'd eventually come to the area where the basenjis were benched from the opposite side.

From that moment on, whether Morgan Gilmore liked it or not, everywhere he looked, for the rest of the day, at least, I'd be in his face.

By the time I had worked my way to Magritte's assigned spot, Dennis was gone and Magritte was asleep in his crate, his chin resting on one hind leg, his white-tipped tail uncurled. Photos of him taking the breed at other shows were propped on top of the crate, and alongside, a stack of Morgan Gilmore's business cards.

"Do you think he'll ask to win today?" I asked Gil's ponytail.

He turned, scowled, and raised his eyebrows. My face was becoming for him like so many had been for me all the years I'd gone to dog shows, someone you see at every event but have trouble remembering exactly who they are, where you met them, or why they're there. We had talked at Cliff's opening, and he had probably seen me at the Ken-L Ration award banquet, but he couldn't place me. He was one of those people who didn't really pay attention to anyone he deemed less important than he was, which in Gil's case was nearly everyone. I wondered what he was hiding under all that arrogance.

"Crystal's mom," I said. With considerable pride.

He nodded. "She's not—?"

"In heat? No, April, I think."

"No, I was wondering if she was *entered*?"

I hadn't given him a registered name, just a call name, and since he didn't know my name, he'd have slim chance of knowing if any of the bitches being shown in the Best in Breed competition were my precious angel. Unless he knew all the dogs, which, with only ten entries, was certainly possible.

"No," I said, looking down at the vicinity of his cowboy boots. "She needs one more major."

Gil nodded, looking vaguely bored and annoyed. He needed me hanging around like he needed Lyme disease.

"So, do you think Magritte is up for this today? Does he have that I-want-to-win attitude he's so famous for?"

"Always," Gil said. "Dog's never had a bad day in his life."

"I guess he had one or two," I said.

Gil smoothed back his hair and, holding on to his ponytail, pushed up the band that held it. He tightened his string tie, too. "I guess you're right. I guess he has had a couple of bad days at that. But today he's going to have a good day. An excellent day. You know," he added, "when you show your little girl next time out, don't be thinking about her bad days. Makes for bad karma. You people, you're all alike. Think you can do the job of a professional. Always looking to save a little money. And what does it get you? The dog picks up all your negativity and you find yourself with a self-fulfilling prophecy on your hands."

He leaned toward me, his back to Magritte's crate and one boot up on the bench.

"That might be Crystal's whole problem. What I'm saying is, *you* might be her whole problem."

"You mean—"

"Little lady," he said, standing straight now to show me his full magnificence, "I can *guarantee* you that major Crystal is missing. No problem. We even can get that out of the way, if you like, before she comes into season so that you'll be breeding not just a dog but a champion. Think about your advertising. Champion sire and dam. Sounds pretty good, doesn't it? You've got to learn to think ahead, think about marketing." He lowered his voice to a stage whisper. "You get some of these serious show folk won't touch a pup unless both parents have proven themselves in the ring. Now you know that's the good Lord's honest truth, don't you?"

"Well, I don't know, it's awfully expensive to have a dog campaigned, isn't it?"

"If you're interested, I feel sure, as reasonable people, that we could work something out. After all, you're talking short term here. Unless of course she turns out to be so good you want to special her. Then we're talking a whole 'nother story."

"Could you do it, like, if I met you at the shows? Or would you have to actually *take* her?"

"In order to give you that guarantee, I'd take her south, young lady. Where the winning is easy. A month. Two months at the outside."

"Well, how much would that be? I mean, exactly."

He leaned close enough now that I could smell the coffee he had had earlier that morning and the spicy smell of the pomade he used to slick back his thinning hair. "Twelve a month. Plus expenses, of course. Much less than you thought, am I right?"

I nodded.

"I can bring in that championship for under five for you. Do you believe that?"

"Why wouldn't I?" I said. Too harsh, Kaminsky, I warned myself. "I mean, that's incredible! Truly."

I walked around him, bent to look into Magritte's crate, and saw his lovely, almond-shaped brown eyes looking back at me. His paws were crossed, left over right, and he was calmly surveying the scene. When I straightened up, I picked up a picture of him taking the breed in Monmouth County. Gil, in cowboy boots and a light blue jacket, was holding the leash taut and looking proudly down at Magritte, who stood, as in all these pictures, perpendicular to the photographer, showing off his level topline, his lovely wedge head, his wonderful double-curled tail, and his burnished copper coat, which shone like silk in the sunshine. I put the photo back carefully among the others and picked up one of Gil's cards.

"I sure would love to see a picture of Crystal like

that. Taking the group. And I sure would love to see her *here* next year." Now I stood on my toes and whispered into his ear. "That's my *dream*. Westminster."

It's not hard to intone *Westminster* as if you were in church. For die-hard dog people, it *was* church.

"You really gave me something to think about," I said, feeling smug. I had successfully established my presence in his face for the day. Magritte was safe.

Or so I thought.

"Look, if you want to go for coffee or something, I'll stay with Magritte. There's nothing else I want to do today but think over your, uh, offer, and watch Magritte take the breed." I held up both hands with my fingers crossed.

Gil brightened up. "Are you sure you wouldn't mind?" he asked. "Well, if you're planning on sticking around anyway—"

"Absolutely. There's nothing I'd rather do than be near Magritte."

"Okay, okay," he said, "if you're sure. I could use a coffee and a run by the rings."

Good, I thought, time to snoop.

"Take your time," I told him, and he took off without saying another word.

I peeked inside the crate. Magritte was asleep. I suddenly realized how vulnerable he was, left by his duly authorized agent with a complete stranger who could easily lift him out of his crate, carry him to the escalator, ride down, and leave the Garden without anyone noticing or saying a word.

Who the fuck was I that he could leave the dog in his charge in my care!

Dogs were stolen all the time, not all of them from backyards, cars, or where they had been left for just a half a moment while the owner ducked into a store to buy a Boston lettuce.

But in fact I hadn't taken the time to ingratiate myself with Magritte's handler in order to steal Magritte, not that that made this Morgan Gilmore's lucky day. Quite the contrary. I had weaseled my way here to protect Magritte, and while I was at it, see if I could find something that would make the evidence against his handler more concrete than speculative.

I looked behind Magritte's crate to see if there was a camel coat neatly folded and tucked back there, and noticed, right at the side of the crate, in plain sight, that Gil had left, in a small heap, a pile of change, his liver pouch, his calendar, and his card case.

I opened the calendar first to January 19, the day Magritte had been stolen. There was no notation. Nor was there any under the 20th, the day Clifford was killed.

Well, how unusual. It didn't say, "Tuesday, January 19. Call Clifford Cole and find out when he'll be out without his dog. Kidnap Magritte."

Nor did it say, "Wednesday, January 20. Murder Clifford Cole."

I put the calendar back where I had found it and picked up the card case, flipped it open, and found not only Gil's business cards but his credit cards as well. It was a wonder to me that someone so dishonest could trust in the honesty of so many strangers and leave his valuables lying around where anyone could take them. Or did he have the poor judgment to trust that I would protect his valuables for him?

There was only a raincoat behind the crate. Bummer. Not even a beret or a white scarf tucked into the sleeve. I reached into his coat pockets and, underneath a handkerchief and an extra show lead, found his key ring. After a quick peek around during which I discovered that no one was paying the least bit of attention to me and that Gil had not returned to find me with my hand in his pocket, I pulled out my own keys and checked the loft keys Dennis had given me against Gil's ring.

I slipped the keys back into the bottom of Gil's pocket and put the raincoat back behind Magritte's crate.

There would have had to have been times when Gil had to pick up or drop off Magritte when Cliff couldn't have been there. So Cliff did the only practical thing he could.

He made Gil his own set.

23

You'd Have to Wonder

"HERE'S OUR BOY!" I heard, close enough to startle me and loud enough for several aisles of people to hear.

I turned to see Veronica Cahill, stunning in a double-breasted black pantsuit with gold buttons, bending from the waist to look Magritte in the eye.

"You better win, you little *vantz*," she told him. "You're costing me a fortune."

I got a wad of pretty good-looking tissues out just in time to catch a sneeze. Magritte sneezed back, as if I were playing his favorite game.

Just behind Veronica, Louis Lane was standing and waiting, but clearly not waiting his turn to greet Magritte. He spotted me and opened his mouth, but I shook my head in time to close it for him.

Veronica straightened up, making me feel like a troll. She was even taller than Louis.

"He looks wonderful, darling," she said, her hand on Louis's chest. "There's not another to equal him. I never get tired of looking at Magritte." She winked at Louis, whose neck reddened.

Perhaps it was his allergy acting up.

"Come on, Veronica. Oughtn't we try to get ringside now so we don't miss anything?"

"No, no. I want to see the others, the ones he's up against, those scruffy little interlopers." She turned down the aisle to check out the other basenjis, leaving Louis to follow or not.

Louis's mouth opened, then closed. Neither of us said a word.

He was wearing a white sweater with a charcoal-gray jacket over it, a long white silk scarf draped around his neck. I wondered exactly what kind of game he was playing with Veronica. I wondered if, at least on this occasion, he had stretched a point and considered the virtues of bisexuality. For business purposes.

"Naturally she'd be interested in what happens here with Magritte today. Considering"—he paused, but didn't take his eyes off mine—"her investment."

I heard Magritte resettle in the crate and, without looking, poked my fingers in for him to sniff.

"It can only help Clifford's name. If Magritte wins. And"—he got his handkerchief out just in time to catch a triple sneeze—"you know what this would have meant to Clifford."

"You don't have to explain anything to me, Louis," I said. "I'm only the hired help."

"Life is for the living, Rachel," he said. Then he turned and made his way down the aisle to Veronica.

Lots of people were making their way up and back

in the benching area, and whatever their reason for being at Westminster, they didn't want to miss the chance to see Magritte. Some thought a barkless dog would be perfect for apartment living. No complaints from the neighbors about noise. Others were just attracted to anyone or anything important enough to be written about in the papers.

Most of them just stopped by quickly, checked their catalog, poked their fingers at Magritte, then headed for the concessions or down the next aisle. Short-attention-span disease was rampantly on display. I was sneezing back and forth with Magritte to keep him amused when I became aware that yet another spectator had stopped in front of us. I looked up.

"Pardon, is this Magritte?" His voice sounded hoarse.

"Yes, it is," I said.

It was the stocky man from Cliff's opening, now spiffed up in a navy suit, white shirt, and maroon tie. He bent to look into the crate.

I wondered if he was a reporter. I looked for a press ribbon, de rigueur at Westminster, but there was none. Nor was there a Nikon or a Hasselblad hanging from his shoulder. Not a reporter.

Maybe he was a dog trainer. He had a ruddy, used-up sort of face. Working outdoors, training dogs, can do that to you.

Especially if when you finally come indoors, you do a shitload of drinking.

"Is he going to win?" he whispered in his raspy voice. "He really got some fabulous press, didn't he?" He hiked his tan leather backpack higher onto one shoulder.

"Maybe he'll get the sympathy vote."

"Oh," he said. "Maybe he will. Are you—?"

"A friend."

"A friend of *his*?" he asked.

I merely smiled.

Most dog shows attract serious dog people, professionals who earn their living training or showing dogs and breeders who need to prove their stock and see what the competition is producing. This one, because of its location and the fabulous press it gets, even when none of the dogs competing have recently murdered owners, attracts a broader audience, families dragging their kids through the crowded aisles, hoping by looking and asking questions to select the perfect breed, the curious, the lonely. Rich or poor, the bored take in Westminster. They come to see Nanook, Rin Tin Tin, and Lassie, for a once-a-year lively alternative to the museum or the movies.

He bent and looked at Magritte again, putting his face close to the cage. His dark hair was so even in tone, I wondered if it was natural.

"He's so quiet," he said. "Is he always this quiet?" He straightened up. "Funny, isn't it? It's so hard to tell them apart. I wonder how the judges know which is which."

A detective listens, Bruce Petrie used to tell me. I thought this might be a good time to practice keeping my sarcastic mouth shut.

"Unless, of course, the color is different."

I nodded.

I wondered if he had used that stuff on his hair you comb in and no one's supposed to notice that in three days your hair is suddenly the color of a desk.

"I'm enjoying the show," he volunteered.

I nodded. I figured it might seem rude to ask. The whole idea is to fool people, isn't it? I mean, even if you're in your eighties and your hair is solid black, like enamel paint, or if, like Tony Bennett, you have a hairline considerably lower on your brow than it was when you were younger, no one's supposed to know it's not a result of Mother Nature's glorious and perfect design.

I checked my watch. "He's going up at eleven-thirty," I said. "Are you going to watch him in the ring?"

"Eleven-thirty," he repeated to himself. "I wasn't going to stay, but I guess I shouldn't miss that. Where would I go?"

Despite the fact that he had a catalog and could have looked it up himself, I told him the ring number.

He nodded, then turned and made his way through the folds of humanity clogging the aisle, stopping and squatting low to look inside the other basenji crates as he had done with Magritte.

"Here he is. So what's the big deal!"

There were two women in front of Magritte's crate now, one tall and thick, built like a tree, hair shorn short in front, the rest pulled back and tied with a scarf, the other short and soft and round with breasts that began under her chin and ended somewhere around her pillowlike stomach. The tall one clutched her catalog to her chest. The other kept methodically pulling pieces of rice cake from her pocket and putting them into her mouth.

"This *is* Magritte, isn't it?" the short one said.

I nodded. I was going to have a neck like a nose tackle by the end of the show.

"The *News* says he's a shoo-in," she said, a real edge in her voice. There was a thin mustache on her upper lip that she apparently hadn't had time to wax or bleach.

The tall woman checked her catalog and then bent to look into Magritte's crate.

"Orion has a better ear set," she said to no one in particular.

"They say he'll take Best in Show," the short woman said.

Her skin was doughy and pale, with small scabs on her cheeks. Her short, curly hair was dyed aubergine. I've always thought that color looked better where it belonged, on an eggplant.

"Well, he hasn't taken the breed yet," I said. "There are lots of other good dogs here today."

"But none as brave and *famous* as this one," she said, sarcasm dripping off her tongue along with a fine spray of rice cake.

In 1984 rumor had it that the Newfoundland Ch. Seaward's Blackbeard would take Best in Show before he had even drooled and rolled his way into the Garden to compete in the breed. And he did. But that kind of successful second-guessing was rare, and even though some people assumed BIS was already a done deal at this show, I wasn't one of them. I refused to make assumptions about Magritte's chances.

I supposed they had a basenji entered and didn't care for the edge Magritte had picked up when he lost his owner and gained Veronica Cahill's publicist. I was going to ask which dog was theirs, but

not wanting another rice cake shower, I decided not
to. Instead I picked up Gil's catalog, hoping they'd
take the hint and go away.

You wouldn't have to be a detective to figure
out which dog was theirs. Ch. Turkon's Heavenly
Hunter, a male, four years old. That would make
them Poppy O'Neal and Addie Turkle. But which
was which I couldn't say.

Once they had moved on, Poppy or Addie leaving
a trail of puffed rice, like Hansel and Gretel in the
woods, I got up to stretch, then stood up on the
bench where I had been sitting to see if I could spot
Gil. It was getting close to the time for Magritte to
go get brushed, go potty, and present himself ringside. But Gil was not to be seen.

I remembered a story Chip had once told me
about a famous handler. She had arranged to show
a boxer the owner thought had great potential
but was herself unable to win a major with. The
handler met the owner and dog outside the ring
the very moment the dogs were called. The owner
had been standing and waiting, afraid the handler
wouldn't show. The dog, absorbing all her anxiety,
stood next to her, his head low, his tail down. As the
handler took the leash, not saying a word to either
of them, the dog's head came up, giving his neck an
elegant arch, his dark eyes danced, his tiny, docked
tail shot straight up and began beating rapidly from
side to side. He won the breed, finishing his championship, and later on, with the same handler holding the leash, all know-how and confidence, he took
the group.

If Magritte took the breed today, wouldn't it be a
bittersweet victory? Like Clifford's soaring career,

you'd have to wonder if all the great press, the sympathy, the sheer drama of recent events, would have made for a win that in the normal course of events wouldn't have happened.

I saw Gil approaching from the opposite way he had left. He was walking with another man, who was small and thin, his hair and skin the same dead-looking steely gray, a cigarette apparently stuck onto his dry lower lip despite the fact that there was no smoking allowed and that this was announced over loudspeakers with predictable regularity.

"—should go up. After today," the little man said in his gravelly voice as they got near enough for me to hear them.

"Without a doubt," Gil said. "You can bank on it." He smiled at me but didn't bother to introduce me to the little man, who ignored me so completely at first that I thought perhaps he hadn't seen me sitting next to Magritte's crate. When he finally took notice of me, he merely tossed me a hard stare, then turned back to Gil.

Gil reached in and took Magritte out of his crate, tucked him snugly under his arm, picked up his tack box, checked his other pocket for a show lead and his armband with Magritte's number on it, pulling them each out and then carefully replacing them, and headed for the grooming area, the little man at his side, me trailing behind like an obedient puppy.

"The chances are good. Is that what you're saying?" the gray man said, one eye closed to let the smoke drift by.

"Excellent," Gil answered. He found his spot,

put Magritte up on the table, and, taking a brush out of the tack box, began to brush him. "You just leave it to me, Doc."

Doc reflected on what he had heard, standing next to the grooming table and puffing on the stub of his cigarette. When it finally got too small to smoke, he held it between two dry yellow fingers, took another from his pocket, popped it into his mouth, lit it with the stub, and despite the fact that there were dogs all over the place, dropped the stub on the floor without bothering to step on it. "I'll be ringside," he said.

After Doc had left, Gil reached into the tack box and took out an electric nail grinder. Magritte backed up a step, but the noose on the grooming table kept him from retreating any farther. Like every other dog I've ever met, he hated having his nails done. Gil plugged in the grinder, reached into his jacket pocket, felt around, and came up with a piece of dried liver. Magritte's tail began to wag, but to his dismay, the treat went not toward his own mouth but into Gil's. Liver Lips began to make a series of revolting slurping sounds, making me wonder if in another incarnation he had been a construction worker. He turned on the grinder and, lifting one paw at a time, began to work on Magritte's nails. When he finished the last foot, he leaned his face right into Magritte's and let the dog ever so gently take the moistened piece of liver from between his lips. Here was a man who truly lived up to his nickname.

That finished, Gil went on with the rest of Magritte's grooming routine, wiping him down briskly with a mitt to bring out the shine in his coat, powdering and wiping off his paws, and finally, spraying Show Foot paw tack on his pads to prevent him from slipping in the ring.

"Make yourself useful," he said, handing me the tack box. He hoisted Magritte and headed for the nearest exercise pen, the doggy bathroom, where we silently waited our turn on line, standing in the red cedar chips that spilled out as each satisfied customer emerged. The chain-link pens were hung with plastic sheeting, not for privacy, though an occasional dog *did* care, but to protect passersby from getting what in my neighborhood is called a golden shower.

When Magritte had finished, Gil lifted him again. The crowds were much too formidable to walk a small dog through the benching area and onto the floor where the judging took place.

Gil pushed his way through a constantly reappearing wall of people, me following along behind as usual. We stopped at Magritte's bench, where I dropped off the tack box and Gil handed me Magritte long enough to strap on his bait pouch and secure his armband with a single rubber band around the middle. After pushing and shoving for another two minutes, we were finally ringside.

24

For No Apparent Reason

GIL WENT AROUND to the side just below the stands, where only handlers with their dogs were allowed. We had arrived ringside just as the basset hounds were finishing up, so, having manners more suitable for the IRT than any place above-ground, I elbowed and kneed my way around to the far side, where there was a single row of padded red folding chairs, and snagged one. Of course, there were plenty of seats in the stands, but those didn't place viewers nearly as close as they'd be sitting or standing ringside on the Garden floor.

Within moments, the basset people were replaced by basenji fanciers, catalogs open, ready to mark the wins.

Poppy and Addie were on the end of the row, to my left, funereal expressions on their faces. Beyond them, down the left side, I spotted Dennis. He was standing against the lavender velvet rope that de-marcated the parameters of the ring, staring straight ahead.

When I turned to scan the opposite side, I saw the object of Dennis's gaze: Louis Lane, standing so close to his companion you'd have trouble slipping a foil-wrapped latex condom between them.

Veronica was whispering in his ear. From where I was sitting, her features looked too big after all.

Especially her nose.

Doc was up in the stands. He looked as de-hydrated and gray as if he had died ages ago but no one had bothered to bury him.

I spotted Aggie too, standing ringside, near where the handlers entered. She was wearing a fuzzy aqua sweater with little faux pearls sewn all over it, per-haps to coordinate with her faux hair color. Even from where I was sitting, it seemed she had put on her makeup with a steam shovel.

The judge, ready to begin, nodded to the stew-ard, who signaled the handlers. Gil placed Magritte down onto the floor, gave ever so small a pop to the lead, and that quickly, Magritte came to life. The ten basenji contenders, led by their handlers, en-tered the ring to great applause from the ringside fanciers and lined up inches from where I sat, to be stacked in show pose as a group and then exam-ined, one at a time, by the judge.

Watching Am Staffs, Goldens, shelties, or Chi-nese cresteds does not prepare you for the basenji ring. Wherever basenjis are, they need to be else-where. It's just their nature.

Three of the ten dogs simply tried not stopping when they got to the far side of the ring. Two con-

tinued on under the velvet rope until they were
pulled back by their handlers. One put its paws
on the rope, perhaps contemplating trying out for
the circus that would be back at the Garden come
spring.

After stretching like cats, deep into their backs,
two of the dogs, a brindle and a tri, began bat-
ting at each other with their front paws. A lot of the
dogs stood up against their handlers' legs, begging
for food, and were simply pushed off with a small
movement of the knee. But one, a black-and-white,
added humping to the routine and annoyed his handler enough to get a smack on his rump.

Gil knelt next to Magritte, reaching into his jacket
pocket and placing a piece of dried liver at the ready
between his teeth, then lifting each of Magritte's
freshly powdered white feet and replacing it carefully in just the position necessary to show off the
dog's conformation as its best—level topline, straight
forelegs with well-developed sinews, straight flexible
pasterns, moderately well bent stifles, hocks well let
down. Magritte did not move. Head high, tightly
curled tail quivering with excitement, his farseeing
dark eyes looking straight ahead, he remained poised
and still, his wrinkled forehead giving him the
intense, intelligent, brightly curious expression so
characteristic of the breed.

After the judge walked down the group and back,
stopping to study each dog in turn, she motioned
for the handlers to take them around, and the
merry-go-round began, handlers and dogs trotting
swiftly around the ring. The judge's forehead became as wrinkled-looking as any basenji's as she

studied the dogs in motion, looking for the quick, tireless gait deemed desirable in the breed.

Despite the fact that the basenjis were held so tight they were just short of choking, the fine little entrant two tricolor dogs behind Magritte still managed to pull sharply into the center of the ring, breaking stride in the process. His handler gave him a sharp pop with the show lead, quickly getting his attention back. No matter. The damage had been done.

While I didn't actually *see* Gil flip or spit a piece of bait as he was moving Magritte nicely along, I couldn't swear he hadn't done just that.

I looked to the left and saw that Addie or Poppy's pasty complexion had turned even less healthy looking, and she was popping rice cakes into her mouth double-time. I checked the number on the handler's armband against the catalog listing. It had been Orion who had fallen for Gil's trick. And what an effective piece of work it was! Basenjis hunt by sight *and* scent. If Orion hadn't seen precisely where the liver had landed, he certainly could have found it by its odor, a property Gil always augmented by rehydrating the liver with his own saliva.

Gil had his back to me for the moment, but I noticed that right after the tri broke, his hand went fishing around in his jacket pocket and, finding nothing there, went into the small leather pouch he had fastened onto his belt only moments earlier in the benching area, the pouch in which he kept his supply of liver treats.

The judge signaled the handlers to stop. Once again, each knelt on the mat and fussed with his or her dog, stacking, brushing, baiting, trying to get each to show at his best.

Gil pulled out the small brush that was sticking out of his back pocket and ran it over Magritte's back. Then he stood and dramatically took a few strokes with the same brush in his own hair, showing oneness with his little charge.

He stacked Magritte and stood again to face him, a piece of bait held shoulder height in his hand, seizing Magritte's attention with it, teasing him into leaning forward so that his shoulder assembly would be bent rather than straight, so that he'd be literally and figuratively up on his toes, so that his neck would look graceful, so that he might even look good enough to win. Gil kept smacking his lips to remind the little dog precisely how yummy the treat would taste when he had finally earned it.

Finally the judge asked each handler in turn to take the dog around once more in the prescribed pattern while the rest of the handlers kept their dogs in line, pretty, stacked, and waiting, some letting them chew on the bait as they held it in their fingers, others moving the bait in a mesmerizing pattern as if to say, See what you'll get if you do this right.

Gil was third in line. I watched him look back and forth between the dog-and-handler team moving across the ring and Magritte, making sure his own dog's attention was still crisp. Gil's face was shining with perspiration, and I noticed that twice he swapped Magritte's lead back and forth so that he could wipe his hands on a handkerchief. Finally, it was their turn. I felt something small as a bit of paper flutter and rise in my chest.

First the judge examined Magritte on the table,

feeling his body, making sure there were two testicles, both fully descended into the scrotum, checking his bite, and looking carefully at his quizzical expression. Afterward, he was placed back on the mat and Gil was asked to take him around.

Gil began gaiting Magritte down the far side of the ring, going quickly at first in a well-practiced lope, his eyes on Magritte as he ran. When he got to the side opposite the judge, he turned, as the two handlers before him had, crossing in front of where Addie and Poppy sat, Magritte trotting beautifully between Gil and the judge.

With all eyes on him and Magritte, Gil approached the final turn that would have taken him diagonally back toward the judge, whose body language revealed her keen interest. (This, after all, was serious *business*.)

Gil never made the turn.

Instead, face flushed pink, he slowed his pace. And stopped. For no apparent reason, or so it seemed, he lost his balance, going down hard onto his right knee, the knuckles of his right hand bracing him on the floor.

There was a gasp from the crowd and, almost immediately, the nervous laughter of people grateful that what has happened to someone else hasn't happened to them.

We sat waiting for Gil to get up, grin sheepishly, put a crease back in his pants, put a snap into the lead, and continue like a trooper. After all, Morgan Gilmore wasn't the first handler to slip and fall in the ring. Nor would he be the last.

But he didn't stand up.

He lifted his right hand to his collar and scratched at it, as if he were a dog. It was almost comical, until his left leg skidded sideways and, with all the grace of a forty-pound sack of Eukanuba tipping over, Morgan Gilmore, now the color of skim milk, pitched forward, facedown, onto the mat.

25

Everyone Wants to Win, You See

THERE WAS AN enormous cry from the crowd, people who had been seated standing up. I felt my catalog slide off my lap and heard it land with a dull thud at my feet.

Then it was all movement again, not dogs and handlers going around, but the judge, the steward, and a rush of uniformed security guards, all surrounding Gil so densely that in a moment he was no longer visible to the crowd. One of the security guards stood on the outside of the circle, speaking urgently into his walkie-talkie.

Magritte was outside the circle, too, the end of his leash apparently still in Gilmore's hand, because twice he pulled to get away—basenjis do not take interruptions lightly—and twice he failed. He sat instead, a major no-no in the ring, his back to where his handler was down and surrounded by noisy strangers.

I heard the walkie-talkie crackle.

Magritte was frantic. He wasn't looking anxiously from side to side the way a German shepherd or a Dobie would. He was in an almost Zenlike trance, staring straight ahead. Except for one pretty white paw raised and doing the dog paddle in a heart-wrenching gesture of supplication, he was still. But I could see that his sides moved in and out too rapidly, and he was opening and closing his mouth as if biting the air.

Two men in white came running into the ring with a stretcher. Between the judge's legs and the steward's, I saw one of the technicians bend and take Gil's pulse at the neck. They closed ranks even more after that, moving quickly and efficiently while we all stood and waited to hear what had happened, having somehow forgotten the basics of breathing.

An elegant man, tall, thin, in his sixties, a flush across his cheeks as if he'd been running, appeared center ring. He lifted his hands and rode them down once, then twice, through the air, signaling us to sit, which we did, as tractable as the dogs in the ring, still frozen in show pose as they had been before Gil fell. Poised, calm, and eloquent, he began to speak.

"There's no reason at all to be alarmed. Mr.—"

He paused, and the steward whispered in his ear.

"Mr. Gilmore has fainted."

He smiled and looked down at his expensive, polished shoes. "As many of you know, and others can guess, this is tense, hard work."

He smiled again.

"Everyone wants to win, you see."

There was the laughter of recognition from a dozen or so in the audience.

With one long-fingered hand, the gentleman in center ring smoothed his trim, white mustache, his starched white collar, his red silk tie.

"There's absolutely nothing to be concerned about."

Again, his hands rode down the air in front of him.

I turned to look at Dennis, who was whispering with the steward, right at the place where the handlers enter the ring.

"Please," the man with white hair said. "Keep your seats, ladies and gentlemen, so that we may continue with the judging."

I looked up in the stands in time to see Doc's back as he tore up the steps to the third tier.

When the speaker's hands returned to his sides, I could see they were trembling. Yet he soothed us with his voice, jollied us with gentle dog show humor, and when he had finished speaking and had nodded to the judge, we saw that Gil was no longer lying there. He had been circled, hidden, and spirited away.

I saw the judge nod and gesture for the handlers to take the dogs around. And there was Aggie, in her aqua sweater and thick-soled dog show shoes, standing in third place, Magritte at the end of the lead, high-collared and nearly choking. The ten handlers popped the ten leads and, along with ten basenjis, just as before, began to run around the ring.

I turned to my left, then my right. People had opened their catalogs to the hound group, to the basenjis. They sat quietly, pens poised to mark the

win, as if Morgan Gilmore had never been there,
had never teased and baited his client's dog into
posing for the judge, had never gaited him across
the garish green indoor-outdoor carpet, praying
for a win, had never fallen, face pale, struggling for
air, and then been carried away, as if he were an in-
jured player at a football game.

Morgan Gilmore, in his cowboy boots and
string tie.

Was I the only one wondering if he was alive
or dead?

I practically knocked over my chair getting out of
it, pushing my way to get into the aisle where I
could move. I was going to go get Dennis, but decided against it. Instead, I ran for the medical office, which was tucked away deep under the stands
across from the basenji ring.

I moved as quickly as I could, sideswiping several
people and spilling at least one woman's bathtub-
size soda, but never stopping to apologize. This was
New York. I didn't have to.

The security guard standing in the exit tunnel
tried to stop me, but when I told him the man who
had just been carried past him on a stretcher was
my handler, reluctantly he let me go by.

I know. I know. I just wish to hell I knew what a
handbasket was.

Cheering and screaming echoed down the tunnel
after me from one of the larger rings. Perhaps one of
the harriers or an Ibizan had just taken the breed,
making everyone but his owner and handler absolutely positive the judge was as blind as a mole.

Good sportsmanship, like chivalry, had gone the
way of fins on Buicks.

Even before I got to the medical office, I heard the engine of the ambulance and turned to run for the ramp where it stayed parked and ready for emergencies. I saw the back of it going down the dank, dark ramp, where smokers more law-abiding than Doc gathered periodically to turn the area into a gigantic ashtray.

I heard the faint wail of the siren as the ambulance hit the street and listened to that lonely sound until it was out of earshot, and other noises, the closer sounds of the Garden, were all I could distinguish.

When I turned around, I saw the security guard with the walkie-talkie who had called for the stretcher.

"He's my handler. Where are they taking him?"

I lied so emotionally, I almost believed myself.

"They go to St. Vincent's, lady. You can call there later."

He turned away and, hands linked behind his back, rocked a little on his heels.

"Was he conscious, awake?"

"I couldn't say, lady. They had an oxygen mask on him, so he wasn't saying nothing to nobody." He looked around, stepped closer, took a meaty hand, and patted his chest. "Looks to me like it was his heart," he whispered. "All that running, all that tension. Don't you worry now," he said, patting my arm lightly. "They'll fix him up, your friend."

I headed back to ring three, to find Dennis.

Orion was stacked on the table the judge used to examine the basenjis individually, and she was baiting him herself, to see his expression. He was a beautifully made little boy, but not as flashy as Magritte.

"How'd Magritte do?" I asked. When in Rome. The only heart problems at a dog show are the breaks and tears you get from losing. There's no world news here. No family obligations, holiday blues, overdue bills. There are only dogs, and the question of who will win and who will lose.

"Not so hot," he said. "Aggie had him choked so short his front feet barely skimmed the ground. How's Gil?"

"They took him to St. Vincent's. The security guard said it looked like a heart attack. I don't know how bad it is. Maybe you can call later. How did Aggie come to take Magritte?"

"You know these show people. All that counts is that the dog gets his shot. They don't care *what* happened to Gil. Well, neither do I," he said. "Anyway, she volunteered. I went to get him, and she was already talking to the steward. I figured, oh"— he sighed—"let him have his chance."

We stayed ringside, standing across from Louis and Veronica, watching each of the basenjis in turn get examined on the table and then gait in the pattern Gil had nearly completed before he fell. I tugged at Dennis's sleeve and told him to bring Magritte after the judging and meet me back in the benching area. His mouth opened, I guess to ask me why I was leaving, but then he turned back to the ring, figuring I probably wouldn't tell him anyway.

Gilmore's coat was still behind Magritte's crate, his calendar beneath it. I opened it to the front, where compulsive people fill in the lines under "In

case of emergency, call." He had: "Marjorie Gilmore," and an address the same as the one above. I
checked my watch. It was still too soon to call and
find out my husband's condition.

I took Gil's stuff, including the crate, to the medical office and signed Dennis's name on the receipt
they gave me. I went to the pay phones and left a
message for Marty Shapiro to make sure he'd remember to walk Dashiell. Then I got a huge Coke.
Since I had miles to go before I'd sleep, caffeine
seemed a good idea.

Dennis looked downcast coming down the aisle,
carrying Magritte under one arm. "He made the
cut, but he didn't win," he said. "Aggie can't handle the way Gil can."

Maybe Gil was right. Leave the showing to
the pros.

"Where's the crate and all Gil's stuff?"

"I turned everything in to the medical office. I
figured it was only a matter of time before they'd
think to come for it. I looked in his calendar first
and got his wife's name. I can use that to call the
hospital, try to find out how he is."

"Magritte is supposed to stay until eight-thirty.
Where are you going to keep him?"

I patted my lap.

Dennis sat next to me, but he held on to Magritte.

"Do you think I should call Marjorie and tell her?"

"Maybe we should call the hospital first, see how
he's doing."

He nodded, glad, I figured, not to have to do
anything.

We sat quietly, Magritte asleep on Dennis's lap.
After a while I went to call St. Vincent's, and on the

way to the pay phones I decided that instead of making things more complicated, I would simply tell the truth.

"I'm sorry, Ms. Alexander," the attending from the ER said, in a voice more weary than sad. "He arrested in the ambulance, on the way here. Everything was done that could have been done. We weren't able to get him back."

He paused, but I said nothing.

"Would you like us to try to contact Mrs. Gilmore, or would Mr. Keaton prefer to do that?"

"Thank you, but we'll take care of it," I said.

I headed back to the benching area to tell Dennis.

26

You'll Only Have Yourself to Blame

"WHAT WAS IT? His heart?" Dennis asked, his pale complexion looking gray under the harsh lights.

"I guess. He just said he arrested in the ambulance and they weren't able to resuscitate him."

"Well, that's that," he said. "You know, it's difficult to feel happy, even satisfied. I wanted to kill him myself, Rachel. Now that he's dead, I just feel, well, nothing. Empty. I'll go call Marjorie."

We slid Magritte onto my lap. He barely opened his eyes. His tail curled partly and then relaxed again. He was back to sleep before Dennis was out of sight.

Dennis came back, carrying a five-pound bag of Nutro Max kibble.

"He really loves this shit. You'll still take him, Rachel, won't you? It's too late for me to make other plans."

"Of course. Did you get Marjorie?"

"Thank God, I got Chris, the kennel manager. She's going to tell Marjorie. This way Marjorie won't be alone when she hears. I gave Chris the number of the hospital, and the number here. She has my number at home, of course, in case there's anything I can do. I said that. In spite of everything. I mean, Marjorie didn't do anything wrong. Except marry badly."

I barely listened as Dennis told me how much food to give Magritte, and when. He gave me his hotel number in Boston, just in case I had a problem with Magritte. At the dinner break, I insisted he go out and sit someplace nice for dinner and eat something other than a greasy hot dog. After he left, I walked around the benching area with Magritte, got myself a greasy hot dog, and went back to Magritte's bench to eat.

As it got closer to the groups, people began coming in who had been at home or in their cars when they had heard about Gil on the news. The story spread quickly around the benching area. I was glad I had finished my hot dog before hearing all that talk about heart attacks and everyone's theory on why.

"He was a smoker, you know," a short guy with thick glasses said.

"Weight's not everything," a really fat man said, "it has more to do with how many high-density lipids you have, whatever a lipid is anyway."

"All that running in the ring," a young man with long, blond hair holding a black-and-white whippet said, "you'd think heart disease would be the *last* thing a handler would get."

A woman in red said that *Live at Five* had reported that Gil had fallen in the ring at 12:11 and had arrested at 12:14, in the ambulance. They mentioned Clifford, of course, and went on to dub Ch. Ceci N'Est Pas un Chien "the bad luck dog." They had showed his picture, but hadn't had one of Gil. Now when people passed where I sat with Magritte, they did so silently, shaking their heads. Or they were careful to look anywhere but at us. Poor Ceci!

At eight Dennis and I went to his box seats to watch the evening judging, Magritte with us. I had gotten my coat from the coat check on the way so that after Best in Show I could make a hasty exit. I draped the coat over Magritte so that he could curl up on my lap and still be out of sight. Too many people were staring. Besides, there were TV cameras and press photographers everywhere, and I didn't want to see my own face on TV or in the paper. They'd probably dub me the bad luck bitch and report that I had once married outside the species.

As if they were perfect!

I wasn't sure why we were staying. We no longer cared who'd win, and considering the circumstances, Magritte could have gotten excused, but leaving would require energy, and energy was something neither of us had.

Dennis finally left right before Best in Show. I stayed; I was there already, and it seemed as good a place to be as any. With Magritte asleep under my coat on Dennis's vacated seat, I watched Mark Threlfall handle the springer spaniel Ch. Salilyn's Condor to the win.

I even stayed in my place to watch all the reporters and photographers rushing out onto the floor to take pictures of the pretty springer with his huge blue ribbon and sterling silver Tiffany trophy, his humans behind him, beaming.

For just a moment, I let myself think about how much Dennis would have loved to have stood there with Magritte, and I got so sad, I nearly cried.

The Garden was half empty by the time I woke Magritte and walked him toward the ladies' room. Crates full of dogs, stacked three high on dollies like doggy apartment houses, were being wheeled out by grim-faced handlers. Better luck next time, I wanted to say. But I didn't say anything. I thought they were pretty lucky already. *They* were still alive.

I was only paying enough attention to where I was going not to step in some dog's "accident" and not to trip over a leash, an empty dolly, or a very short dog, when something in front of me slapped my brain awake.

I saw him from the back, only his shoulders were too narrow, his feet too slim.

It wasn't a him. It was a her.

She was wearing a long camel coat, her hair tucked neatly into a black beret so that I couldn't tell what color it was or if it was long or short.

She took a step and turned toward me so that I could see not only her profile but her companion as well.

It was Veronica Cahill, bending her long, graceful neck so that Louis Lane could take the white silk scarf he had been carrying for her around his neck and put it around her own.

Too bad the case was closed, I thought as Magritte and I continued on our way to the ladies' room. It would have been deliciously satisfying to pin something on those two.

I still had questions I couldn't answer. There was one less now. It had been Veronica Cahill who had come to the loft to remove the tape from Clifford Cole's answering machine. Her perfume had made me sneeze a second time when she had come to see Magritte in the benching area. And one more. Why?

Suddenly I found myself thinking about Beatrice and the time I had gotten stitches on my arm right after getting my first two-wheeler.

"Don't touch those," she'd said as I poked around under the bandage. "Leave well enough alone."

"They're my stitches," I told her, "and I'll do as I please with them."

"In that case," she said, turning her back toward the sink and away from me, "whatever happens, you'll only have yourself to blame."

Maybe the case was closed for Dennis, but I never had learned to leave well enough alone.

27

You Can Send Your Dog

THE CRUCIFORM LADIES' room, swinging doors on two sides, was nearly empty when I walked in, schlepping my heavy coat, Magritte, and Magritte's Nutro Max. Two handlers, armbands still in place, were at the sinks washing their hands. The aisle where the stalls were was deserted. There was no line of patient, chatting women, making friends while waiting their turn, no purses visible on the floor of the stippled gray stalls, no ugly crepe-soled, laced-up dog show shoes, facing forward, visible under the doors, no cries for toilet paper, hands fishing around in the neighboring stall, no toilets flushing, no one humming, laughing, or sobbing because their dog hadn't taken Best, no nothing. When the handlers left, Magritte and I were alone.

I went two-thirds of the way down the aisle, hoping for a cleaner stall that way, took Magritte in with me, hung my coat on the hook, and propped the bag of dog food against the front left pilaster. The moment I sat, Magritte on my lap and licking at my face, I heard the door open, the one on the side that led to the benching area, the one I had used.

I was doing nothing but wishing I had thought to use the handicapped stall at the far end of the aisle, where I could have put Magritte on the floor and peed in peace, when I heard the sound of stall doors opening and closing, one, then the next, then the next, coming toward me.

I wondered if they were about to close the Garden and wanted to make sure they weren't locking anyone in the john, but I checked my watch and it was much too early. I was sure the cleaning staff would be here for hours.

Maybe the first few stalls were out of toilet paper. It was late in the day, after all.

Two more doors opened and closed, getting closer to me.

Maybe she had inadvertently left her coat on the hook behind the door and was looking for it.

I don't know why, but I leaned carefully forward and picked up the bag of dog food, squeezing it onto my lap in front of Magritte. I lifted my legs, too, stretching them straight out in front of me and bracing myself with my feet against the door.

Then the oddest thing happened. The doors stopped banging open and everything was very quiet. Too quiet. Until the lady began to whistle, a sweet, clear little tune, just four notes, a pause, then those same four notes again.

As if she were calling a dog.

And again, four notes, a pause, the same four

notes, only an octave higher now, the sound echoing off the tiles, reminding me just how empty this place was so late in the day, and how isolated.

Magritte stiffened, his hackles going up. And he growled, a low rumble in his throat I could feel as I quickly hooked his collar with two fingers just in time to prevent him from jumping down and disappearing under the door.

When he discovered he wasn't free to do as he pleased, he began to whine.

Suddenly the bathroom doors opened again, this time from the side that led to the passageway under the stands. I heard a woman's voice.

"God, it's late. Even the bathroom's deserted."

Immediately the door to the stall next to me opened and closed. Only this time, the lady who had lost her coat was in the stall.

"Do you have a comb? Dotty, a comb? Thanks."

I leaned down and away from that side, careful not to dislodge Magritte and his food, until I could see the shoes of the lady who had finally found a stall to her liking.

I saw white leather sneakers.

Big white leather sneakers.

Facing the wrong way.

Unless she was about to throw up, the lady next to me was not using the john in the usual way.

I waited hopefully for the sound of retching.

No such luck. She was using the stall as a place to hide.

"So, where to next?" I heard from the area where the sinks were.

"I'm off to a cluster. The South, thank you. Isn't

this New York weather something? How do they live here?"

I took another peek at those shoes.

My sister Lillian wears a size eleven, and these feet could make her look as if she were Cinderella.

In my neighborhood, no matter *what* someone is wearing, feet that big can mean only one thing. The person in the stall next to me was no lady.

A chill went through me that precluded nearly all bodily functions, including the one I was there for.

The sixth law of investigation work says, Don't get caught with your pants down.

Quietly putting Magritte and the food down for a moment on the side opposite Big Foot, in one move I covered my ass, literally at least, slipped into my coat, and, hoisting Magritte but ditching the bag of Nutro Max kibble in the stall, bolted out of the ladies' room, almost knocking down Dotty and her friend.

"What's *your* problem?" I heard behind me before the swinging door closed.

But I never stopped to answer. I ran down the moving escalator, Magritte now under my coat and snug against my chest, and kept running until I was on Seventh Avenue.

There were people everywhere, all waving frantically for cabs. Not wanting to stand around vying with the crowd for too few taxis while whoever had been in the bathroom got the chance to catch up, if indeed that was his agenda, I headed for Thirty-second Street.

Carrying Magritte, exhaustion pressing against the backs of my eyes, I turned the corner and began walking rapidly toward Eighth Avenue.

As I walked west, I was more and more alone. Except for a sense of peril I couldn't shake.

I stopped once and pretended to check my pockets, but I didn't see anyone else stop and wait, nor did I spot a particular person behind me or across the street that I remembered seeing near me earlier.

Still, I couldn't shed that funny feeling, one that made the hair on my arms stand up. I began to run.

When I reached Eighth Avenue, the wind was whipping around, blowing dirt off the street into my eyes. I stepped off the curb into the street, one hand on the outside of my coat propping up Magritte, who by now felt as heavy as a semi, the other up and out like a flagpole, hoping to attract a vacant cab.

Watching the empty street in front of me, I found myself wishing I had my attack-trained pit bull at my side so that I could feel smugly safe instead of terrified.

My imagination can really get out of hand when I'm this tired.

Why would I be followed if the man who had killed Clifford Cole was dead?

Hey, relax, I told myself. It was probably just a pervert in the john. New York is full of them.

Or some guy who couldn't read English, made a natural mistake.

"Not to worry," I said out loud, to Magritte. "This case is closed as tight as a Brittany's lips."

But the feeling of being followed stayed with me. Even when it's baseless, it can be more frightening than being followed.

When you are sure you are being followed, you

can do something about it, step into a store, jump on a bus, get lost in a sea of humanity or traffic.

Except it was nearly midnight in a deserted part of the city. There were no open stores, no buses, no sea of humanity. There wasn't even a fucking cab.

Okay, still.

You can draw a gun. (Mine was home.)

You can turn around and shout, "I see you, you cowardly scumbag, hiding in the shadow of that building. What are you doing there, jerking off and thinking about your mother?"

You can pretend you're going home and lead him to the Sixth Precinct.

And, if there's absolutely no other choice, you can send your dog to talk some sense into the bastard.

Unless the only dog you happen to have with you at the time is a lousy basenji.

In which case you're nuked.

That's when I turned around again, just in time to catch the man who was hanging back partway down the block step quickly closer to the building line where he'd be less likely to be seen. I could see the fronts of his white sneakers shining in the moonlight.

I was just about to succumb to the most hideous feeling of helplessness, a feeling I loathe because it's always easier when you can actually do something, when a cab pulled up.

I wrenched open the door and told the driver my address.

And had I not looked out the back window as my cab pulled out into the street and seen the man who had been standing in the shadows run to the curb with *his* arm up like a flagpole and immediately get a cab, the creep, I would have thought I was okay.

Safe.

But now I knew I wasn't. The signs were in place that someone wanted to know where I was going. As clearly as the toilet paper that might be stuck to the bottom of his sneakers would have told the world where he'd just been.

All I could think of was how good it would feel to be home with the door double-locked and my own dog at my side.

There was only one thing to do. I offered my driver an extra five if he'd get me home in five minutes, and he nearly left my head on Eighth Avenue making the turn on West Thirty-third Street, past the north side of the main post office, to go downtown.

And all the way home, all I could do was hope that the man who had been following me hadn't thought to make a similar offer to his driver.

28

Who Wouldn't Make
a Face?

WHEN I WAS putting the key in the front-door lock, I heard the phone and nearly broke the key in half trying to get inside.

"Rachel, thank God you're okay."

Magritte had run in. Dashiell had run out. Now they were both in the garden, the door open, the warm air flowing out and the frigid night air coming in.

"Dennis?"

The dogs came barreling in and headed for the food bowls.

"Hang on a sec," I said, slipping off my coat and tossing the Flying Man into the living room.

"Hey, where were you raised," I asked Dashiell, "a kennel? Close that door."

He came from behind it, butted it once with his cinder block of a head, and then did a neat paws-up. The door slammed so hard, the house shook. I turned the lock and put on the chain.

"That's better." He and Magritte were tugging on the new toy.

"I'm back," I said into the phone, "what's up?"

"Thank God you're okay. I've been worried sick."

"What's wrong? What happened?"

"You're not going to believe this. Gil didn't die of a heart attack. He was poisoned!"

"What? How do you know?"

"When I got home, there was a message from Marjorie, saying it was urgent she speak to me as soon as possible, even if it was in the middle of the night. So of course I called."

"And?"

"A technician was moving the body, you know, Gil, because the ME has to autopsy to determine cause of death, and when he was getting him onto a rolling stretcher, he smelled bitter almond."

"Cyanide."

"Right. It wasn't a heart attack. It looks as if Gil was *murdered*."

"Have they done the autopsy yet?"

"Hey, we're talking New York here. There's a major backup in autopsy. But get this, the technician starts checking everything, you know, really looking at the body carefully and checking all the clothes, the pockets, whatever, and finally he opens the pouch. Well, as you might imagine, it stinks to high heaven."

"Of course, that's what liver's supposed to do," I cut in. "That's why it works so well as bait."

"But this liver smelled like bitter almond. This is where the smell was coming from."

"So how come Gil didn't smell it?"

"Maybe because he was working, you know, concentrating really hard on what he was doing with Magritte. Anyway, he was a smoker. Cigars. Dulls your sense of smell."

"And taste," I added. "Not only that, once he popped it in his mouth, by the time he might have realized anything, it might have been too late. Cyanide is fast. You don't get an awful lot of time to react."

"Rachel, doesn't that mean Gil put the poisoned liver in his mouth while he was in the ring? Right in front of us!"

"Yes. And not only that, it means not all the liver was tainted."

"How do you know?"

"Because I'm pretty sure he spit a piece to trip up the tri. So he would have died then if it was all laced with cyanide. And so would the tri if he'd spit it out before he went down."

"But the toxicology lab said all the liver in the pouch was poisoned."

"It was. But the liver in his pocket wasn't. That's how this was done, Dennis. Someone swapped the liver in the bait pouch for the doctored liver."

"How? When?"

"While Magritte was being groomed."

"You're kidding!"

"I'm not. Look, the pouch was where Gil kept his supply of liver, but he took some and put it into his jacket pocket so that he wouldn't have to wear the pouch until he was in the ring. He left the pouch with his stuff, in back of Magritte's crate. It was there, unattended, when we all trooped off to the grooming area. In fact, Doc left before we did. He also beat it away from the ring when Gil went down."

"Who's Doc?"

"This hideous little man Gil was talking to when he came back to get Magritte ready for the ring."

"Do you think *he* switched the liver?"

"All I'm saying is he *could* have. Dennis, *I* could have. Gil left all his things there when he went for coffee. But he had some liver in his jacket pocket, untainted liver, because he gave some to Magritte when he cut his nails. So, that means—"

"Magritte. Oh, God, you mean he could have—"

"No, Dennis, it went into his own mouth first, for a while, too. He kept swishing it around in his saliva to get it all juicy, and he teased Magritte to distract him from the indignity of getting his nails cut. That means the liver in his pocket was okay. That explains why the tri is okay, and why Gil wasn't poisoned in the group run."

"So you're saying that when he took liver earlier from his pouch, it was okay. And when he used liver later, from the pouch, it wasn't."

"Right. In fact, a moment after I saw him fish around in his pocket and then go into the bait pouch, I saw him make this awful face. I figured, shit, who wouldn't make a face, putting liver in his mouth. But, you know something, he didn't make a face in the grooming area, and he practically *ate* the fucking liver while he was grooming Magritte."

"But when he got a piece with cyanide, he did notice it was bitter."

"Apparently."

"My mother used to make me eat liver when I was a kid, you know, for the iron, and I still remember that some of it was sort of sweet and some of it was really bitter."

"So Gil could have thought he had just gotten a normally bitter piece. It's not like he had time to taste-test the whole pouch. He was in the ring, working. And anyway, he didn't have time for another reason."

"The cyanide. It's too fast."

"Exactly."

"Do you think the killer planned it so that it would happen in the *ring*, right in front of everyone?"

"I don't know. But if he did, it would mean that whether or not he was there, he'd hear the results of his handiwork on the news that night. There's no way something this dramatic would go unreported."

"Damn clever of him."

"Or her. What else did Marjorie tell you?"

"That the technician sent the pouch to the lab for testing. Once there's suspicion of murder, there's no delay, and two hours later the toxicology results were in and, big surprise, the liver had been laced with enough sodium cyanide to fell a fucking horse. That's what they told Marjorie."

Something was nagging at me, holding a part of my attention captive, but I couldn't get a grasp on what it was.

"They're sure it was cyanide poisoning?" I asked him.

"Pending autopsy results. But the doctor was sure enough of the cause of death to call Marjorie. Not his heart, he said. *Cyanide.*"

"Dennis, you said you hardly knew Marjorie. Why did she call *you* right away?"

"I told her to call if she needed me, Rachel. She asked me if I would talk to the police, see what I could find out. She said she'd given them my number, and she hoped that was okay. I mean, she's so far away."

"Is she coming up?"

"I don't think so. You know how most people are. They figure if you just set foot in New York, next thing you know, you'll be murdered."

"Where could people get an idea like that?"

I thought about Big Foot in the ladies' room.

"Dennis, I—"

"I guess *he's* off the hook," he said.

"What did you say?"

"Well, if someone killed him, doesn't that let him off the hook?"

"We don't know for sure the two murders are connected, do we?"

"What do you mean?"

"Suppose someone killed Gil, and it had nothing to do with Cliff's death?"

"Who would want to kill Gil? Well, except me?"

"How about anyone who had been in the ring with him? Didn't you see what he did to the little tri? There was also this handler he tripped in the ring. Ted Stickley. He fell and broke his arm. You can't handle dogs with a broken arm. Dennis, I wonder if he was at Westminster. Maybe he was biding his time, waiting for a way to get back at Gil. Did you save your catalog?"

"Of course."

"Check it for me."

"Hang on. Stickley, Stickley, Stickley. Yes. Ted Stickley. He handled a saluki."

"Well!" I said, as if handling a saluki were proof of his guilt. "There are a lot of people who hated Gil. Everyone knew his habits, Dennis, I mean everyone knew that liver went into his mouth."

"So you're saying maybe the person who hated him enough to kill him had nothing to do with Clifford's death?"

"Dennis, Gil's death doesn't *solve* this case. There's too much we can't explain."

"What next?"

"Sleep. It's been a long day. I'll call you tomorrow, in Boston. Everything changed today. I need some time to think."

"Be careful, Rachel."

"Yeah. Yeah," I told him.

But I hadn't even looked down the block when I'd gotten out of the cab, carrying Magritte, my keys ready in my right hand. I was just so happy to be home. Was I kidding myself to think we had really lost Big Foot?

When I hung up, I looked over at Magritte. He'd had three close calls, two the night of Clifford's murder when he could have been intentionally killed by whoever killed Cliff or accidentally killed crossing West Street after he'd gotten free of his collar. And another at Westminster, had Gil had the time to spit the tainted liver to him before he went down. That he hadn't may not have been an accident. Most show people care much more about dogs than they do about people.

Three close calls. Yet here he was. The *good* luck dog.

Magritte began washing himself, like a cat. Perhaps he had nine lives, too. If so, he was going through them mighty fast.

I poured a glass of wine and began to think about the loft and those three empty stretchers. Had Clifford changed his mind about three paintings, ditching them because they weren't good enough? I'd read that Picasso worked that way, painting quickly, creating many works, and keeping only the ones he liked.

Or was there some other reason those canvases were gone?

Who was Mike? *He* must have had a key to the loft, too, since he had left a message about picking up Magritte.

More important, who was Big Foot?

It had been easy to assume that Morgan Gilmore had been the killer. He had the motive and the opportunity. He had keys to the loft. He knew Cliff would do anything to get Magritte back.

My head was aching, the questions I couldn't answer eating at me. I picked up Marty's note, which, as usual, was on the green marble table, just outside the kitchen.

Rach,
Dash played with Elwood and had dinner at the precinct, two slices of pizza, a burger without the bun, and a cinnamon doughnut. Sorry. You know how the guys are with dogs.
Marty

I stroked my hand over Dashiell's big, round belly, then scratched the base of Magritte's tail. They were heaped in a pile, sound asleep, Dashiell's head on the Flying Man, as if it were a pillow. Suddenly sleep seemed the perfect idea.

29

Tunnel Vision

I NEVER MADE it upstairs. I woke up at seven-fifteen, covered with my coat, the grayish light of winter slipping through the shutters, making stripes on everything.

I let the dogs out and watched them chase each other around, taking turns being hunter and prey.

Now that I knew it had been Veronica Cahill at the loft, I didn't need to check the *Young Detective's Handbook* to figure out why. But law seven says, Confirm your hunches.

I decided to catch Louis Lane before he left for school. That I most certainly did. He worked the late session and didn't have to be in until ten forty-five.

"Louis," I said, not bothering to apologize for waking him, "I was at Clifford's loft one night, and someone in a camel coat, black beret, and white scarf came in and took the tape from the answering machine."

Ba da boom. I never beat about the bush before I've had my first cup of tea.

"Oh, that was Veronica. She's so paranoid about people trying to cheat her out of her commission."

"But—"

"I told her that it couldn't happen because *I* own the art now, and of course *I* wouldn't cheat her, but she still had to go and get the damn tape. I guess it means she doesn't even trust *me*."

"She told you about going?"

"Of course. But only *after* she did it. She said there was some man-eating *beast* there and it nearly scared her to death, and I—oh! *You!*"

"Right. We scared each other."

There are always people who try to get around the gallery commission by buying directly from the artist, and few people, if any, would know that Louis, not the Cole family, now owned the art. Perhaps Veronica was right to worry—some people will do anything for money.

I wondered what else Veronica Cahill and Louis Lane might have done for it.

"Louis, there's something else, it's about Cliff's art and the way he worked. Did he sketch on paper before he painted?"

"Sometimes. But not always. Oh, he'd scribble on napkins in restaurants and stuff them in his pocket, on matchbook covers, anything at all when he got an idea, just little quick reminders. Then he'd sketch right on the canvas. In fact, when he got into his noir period, those gray paintings, a lot of the way he worked changed. *He* changed."

"How so?"

"He began working long, long hours. Sometimes he wouldn't even take Magritte out in the afternoon. He'd ask Dennis to do it. Or he'd use a dog walker. He just kept at it, painting until late at night, not coming here for days at a time."

"Did you worry? Did you think something was wrong?"

"Not *really*. He'd done it other times, I mean, get on a streak and paint almost around the clock. But never quite like this—"

"Louis, what about the piece at the show without a title?"

"He probably didn't get a chance to do the last panel."

"That's what I thought," I said quietly. "But wouldn't there be a partial fourth panel? A sketch on canvas? Something? The first three are clearly completed paintings. Is that how he worked when he did a multiple-panel piece? One at a time?"

"Actually, no. He worked on all the panels at once."

"Even so, you think the last panel never got done?"

"I don't know. Does it mean something?"

"It could. Louis, by any chance, do you know the name of the dog walker Cliff used?"

"Mike. I don't remember hearing his last name."

"Great. Thanks."

"I heard about Gil," he said.

I waited.

"Rachel? Are you getting anywhere?"

"It's too soon to say," I told him, wondering what

his shoe size was and if he ever wore anything but Gucci loafers. "But I'll keep you posted," I lied.

I opened the door. The dogs were digging and burrowing in the snow. I let Magritte in and sent Dash back to the passageway for the *Times*.

The piece about Gil was in the sports section, adjacent to Walter Feltcher's piece about the springer's win, not with the obituaries. It was small, but dramatic.

Death at the Dog Show

Morgan Gilmore, handling the basenji Ch. Ceci N'Est Pas un Chien, whose owner, Clifford Cole, had been found dead on the Christopher Street pier late last month, fell in the ring and died just minutes later in the ambulance on the way to St. Vincent's Hospital, a representative of the Westminster Kennel Club said. Pending autopsy, the presumed cause of death was heart failure.

Mr. Gilmore, 47, of Greensboro, North Carolina, had been a professional handler for twenty-three years. He is survived by his wife, Marjorie, and his parents, Lloyd and Ellen Gilmore of Charlotte.

I called Marty.

"Shapiro. How goes it?"

"Could be worse. How's your case coming? I was going to give you a buzz, Rach, about that question you asked me, whether or not the victim had semen in his anus."

"And?"

"He didn't."

I knew I'd be looking for clues there one day!

"I saw in the paper Magritte's handler died of a heart attack. Bummer. Was he heavy?"

"This is why I'm calling, Marty. I got a call from the client, late last night. It wasn't as the papers reported it."

"So what else is new?"

"Marty, it was cyanide. He was murdered."

"No shit. Is this connected to your case, you think, or coincidental?"

"I thought he was our man until I heard how he bought it."

I told Marty what I had found out about Gil and the frozen semen business, and about all the loose threads that were driving me crazy.

"Be careful, Rachel."

"Hey, listen to you, playing with bombs day in and day out, the man tells *me* to be careful."

"You know something, kid, I feel much safer the seven years I've been doing this than I ever did the eleven I was on the street in uniform. At least no one's taking potshots at me now. Say, how's my boy Dashiell? He do okay on yesterday's menu?"

"Dog has a cast-iron stomach, Marty. Thanks for helping out."

"Hey, anytime, Rach. You know, the article upset a few of the guys. The heart thing. We fucking *live* on doughnuts around here. They're pretty high in cholesterol, aren't they?"

"What am I, a fucking nutritionist? Read the box. It's all there, in black and white."

When I hung up, I remembered one time when I was talking to Marty and he was gesturing with a powdered doughnut in his hand, the sugar falling everywhere, quietly, like snow. Dashiell's head followed the doughnut's every move, as if he were watching the ball at a tennis match.

Exactly the way the dogs in the ring watch the bait.

Now I knew what wouldn't stop tugging at a corner of my mind, like a terrier peeling a tennis ball. I ran upstairs to my desk and started leafing through the Cole file. They had even called the piece "Witness to Murder." Magritte's picture accompanied it, his brow wrinkled, his dark eyes so alert.

I read through the article quickly—artist dead, witness found, artist's dog, undiscovered genius, Dr. Shelbert, Tracy Nevins, bingo!

"As to whether or not Magritte could finger his master's killer, Nevins was quoted as saying, 'Definitely,' " giving the killer his motive.

" 'We are still planning on having Magritte compete at Westminster on Tuesday,' Kenton added. 'Clifford would have wanted him to be there.' "

The poison was in the *bait*.

I was so blinded by what I knew that I hadn't seen the simple truth.

Morgan Gilmore had been murdered by accident.

The poison had been meant for Magritte!

The article even included the whereabouts of the potential victim, giving the murderer a perfect blueprint from which to work.

If Magritte was the intended victim, whoever had tried to kill him knew by now he had failed. Gil's death, though the cause was misreported, had been all over the news last night and was in all the papers this morning.

That was no pervert in the john. It was the killer.

He was out to try again, and now he knew Magritte was with me.

It was tunnel vision, thinking the cyanide was meant for Gil. Just because *we* knew the practices at dog shows, it was the only way we were able to see the crime.

But the most logical and obvious conclusion, which we never thought of, was that if you want to kill a dog, you poison something he's going to eat. A five-year-old could have seen this clearly.

I added Mike's name to the blackboard. He had the key. Here was someone else who knew how Cliff felt about his dog. Maybe he had a motive, too. I'd have to call him. His number would be in Clifford's address book, which I had copied.

There were too many people I hadn't spoken to. Now was the time to change all that. I ran back downstairs, double-locked the door, and came back up to the desk where I could take notes. It was time to see broadly, to check every little detail out again, to consider every possibility and to avoid jumping to conclusions.

As Ida, my therapist, used to say, pushing up her sleeves and making two lines between her eyes, *finally* we're getting started.

"Mrs. Cole? This is Elaine Boynton, Clifford's friend. I was so sad to hear about Clifford. Yes. Yes. And so I feel just terrible that I missed the memorial service. Really? He said that? She's, uh, gone. Yes. A small, private one. Yes, I do. I'm sure they would. I understand. I was wondering where I could send a donation in Clifford's name. Does the family have a preference? Okay. Thank you."

30

What Would You Like to Say?

I HAD SPENT all day and evening yesterday on the phone. All I wanted to do today was get over to Cliff's loft and find the final few pieces of the puzzle. But there was one place I wanted to go to first, B & H Photo, to pick up Clifford's slides.

"This is olt," the pale, bearded young man in the yarmulke told me, examining the slip I handed him. "Vot made you vait so lonk?"

"I was busy," I told him.

Then he noticed Magritte, who had put his paws up against the counter to see what was on the other side.

"Oh, it's mine friend," the young man said, stepping forward and leaning over. "I'll get for you a kendy, vait, vait," and all in a stir, he reached into one of the candy dishes that sat at even intervals along the counter and pulled out a small Tootsie Roll for Magritte.

"He doesn't eat candy. It's not good for him," I said in protest. But I was too late. The Tootsie Roll was already in Magritte's mouth.

"He alvays eats a kendy ven he comes. Vot vould he t'ink if ve didn't give to him today a piece?"

But as I watched Magritte chewing, opening his mouth twice as wide as usual for each bite, all I could think about was the poisoned bait and how quickly and unexpectedly the whole world could change.

I put the yellow box into my pocket and headed downtown with the dogs. After I tossed the loft again, I'd sit down and look at the slides and have myself a good cry.

Walking downtown, Dashiell plodded along at his usual workmanlike pace, stopping only when I told him to wait at street crossings where the light was red. Magritte kept pace, darting to the side occasionally to try to catch a bit of paper that was swirling about in the wind. But as soon as we crossed Houston Street, Magritte's demeanor changed. He began looking up at me and whining, as if he couldn't contain himself. When we got to Greene Street, he pulled straight for home, and once inside, where I unhooked both leads, he dashed on ahead, passing his new home and going straight for his old one.

I knocked. After all, there seemed to be more people with keys than without them, and I didn't want to cause anyone undue fright. Then I un-locked the door, Magritte impatiently jumping up and down at my side. He was the first one inside when I opened the door.

Dashiell headed straight for the kitchen, looking for water. Magritte walked to the center of the front room and sat. Head cocked, as if listening for a sign that his beloved master was home, a sound, a scent, anything to hang his hopes on, he stayed in place without moving, as I did, watching him. Suddenly, his muzzle tilted up, his mouth made a small circle, and he let out the most heart-wrenching sound, a keening howl, not long and smooth like a wolf howl, but a piercing *awoo, awoo, awoo,* a pause, then again, *awoo, awoo, awoo,* the second time joined from the back of the loft by Dashiell's guttural howl, honoring his friend's misery the way a second hunting dog honors a point.

For a while Magritte stayed close enough to trip me when I tried to walk, following me to the kitchen, where I filled the water bowl and put the kettle up for tea. He stayed close by while I poked around in the cabinets for snacks, even trying to join me on the step stool when I was checking out the shelves I couldn't reach. When he found he couldn't reach me, he whined and paced. I let him be. Dogs have as much right to the integrity of their feelings as people do.

After pulling down some unopened rice crackers and—God is merciful and all knowing—an unopened box of Mallomars, I felt an envelope on the top shelf, the one I could barely reach, even with the stool. I managed to pull it forward with one finger, sliding it along the oak shelf until I could pull it to the edge where I was able to grasp it.

The envelope was blank, but there was a letter inside it.

"Honey," I read, still standing on the top of the step stool, one hand on the cabinet, bracing me. "For so many years I pushed aside my desire to sleep with a man, not just the desire for sex, but to lie in a man's embrace, to feel his strong arms around me, his warmth and sweetness mine hour after hour. I never had that until I met you. And much as I want that, want to be with you, sometimes I can't.

"I'm driven by demons now. There's something I have to do, now, to get out, and I want you to understand that your love is my saving grace, my life, and to be patient with me while I work this out."

It was typed and not signed. Had Cliff written it to Louis? Or to someone else? "Honey" could be anyone. And why had it been hidden, not mailed, given, faxed?

After making tea, I decided I should do my best to really make myself feel at home, despite the empty spaces where art had once hung. If I got comfortable, I might get more into Cliff's head and be able to sort out some of the incredible things I had found out the day before. I decided that music would be the first priority. Having noticed a tape deck and drawers of tapes in Clifford's study, I put on the light and began to look at Clifford's taste in music. But before I had the chance to consider Diana Ross over Barbra Streisand, I saw just the tape I wanted to hear. It caught my eye because it was loose, sitting on top of the other tapes. Miles Davis.

Workin'. I turned on the tuner and the tape deck, put the tape in, pressed the play button, and went to sit in the chair to drink my tea and listen while I thought about what to do next. Cliff had apparently made the tape himself, probably from a CD. There were other tapes he had made, carefully listing each cut in order on the paper in the box so that he would know what was coming and when. This tape, though, had no box. But Clifford was as obsessive-compulsive as you can get; even his copper-bottomed pots were polished. Why was this tape loose?

I went back to the drawer where the tapes were arranged not only alphabetically but by style of music, and looked for the jazz tapes, my finger running over the boxes—Chet Baker, Clifford Brown, Ray Charles, John Coltrane, Miles Davis, *Bag's Groove*, *Birth of the Cool*, and there it was, *Workin'*. I pulled out the box to read the titles of the cuts, but it wasn't empty. There was a tape in it.

I guess that's why he hadn't put the tape away, I thought, sitting back in Clifford's chair, at his desk, holding the box in my hand, turning it over to read the cuts. And while I listened to "It Never Entered My Mind," I began to think that the Clifford Cole *I* knew and loved was much too compulsive to leave a tape out where it could get dusty or to put a tape back in the wrong box.

For a moment I pictured the precise little lower-case letters with which he painstakingly titled his paintings.

I looked at the box in my hand, at the neat printing of each cut; underneath the last one he had taken the time to put down the name of each artist along with the instrument he played.

Was this a man who would leave a tape lying around loose?

I interrupted *Workin'*, popped in the unmarked tape, and pressed play.

"I have Magritte."

It was a woman's voice.

But it wasn't really a woman's voice. You don't work for Bruce Petrie for very long without being able to recognize the sound of a voice-changing telephone. I even had one someplace, probably with my good crystal, in the basement. Bruce had given it to me, "For Hanukkah." And when I'd said, "Bruce, you shouldn't have," he'd looked puzzled. "Why not?" he said. "It's your Christmas, isn't it?"

"I have Magritte," "she" said, enunciating carefully so that not a syllable would be lost. "If you want him back alive, don't tell anyone about this message. Come to the Christopher Street pier at four o'clock tomorrow morning. Come alone—alone, you hear, or the mutt dies. And bring a thousand bucks, you got that? A thousand, in small bills. Yeah."

The money was an afterthought. The money was clearly not the point of this. Which is why it wasn't taken.

I rewound the tape and listened three more times to the message that signaled the beginning of the end of Clifford Cole's life. Afterward, I put "It Never Entered My Mind" back on, hoping that I was finally on the right track and it wouldn't turn out to be my theme song.

Cliff had hidden the tape in the Miles Davis box. Did he think he'd need it again, later? He had hidden the letter, too. And one of the bills I had found, a fifty, in one of his jackets, had been tucked into the bottom of that long, skinny inside pocket that I always figured was for carrying glasses.

He hadn't told Dennis the identity of the person he had found out about. Hadn't told Louis about the kidnapping. It's only a dog, Louis would have said. Why take chances?

He was secretive, even before the events that led up to his death. I reached for the phone and called Information, to see if his phone number was listed. That's when I got the next big surprise of the day.

It seemed everyone involved with this case was full of secrets, and many of them were telling lies.

I took off my boots and padded out to the front room to make sure the chain lock was on. Paranoia was in the air, and I didn't want any surprises today, not from the ever lovely Veronica Cahill, and certainly not from the person with the big feet who was my neighbor in the ladies' room at Madison Square Garden.

I wondered if he had the key, too.

If he was the murderer, apparently he did. After all, Dennis didn't say the loft had been broken into as an explanation for Magritte's disappearance, had he?

I went back to the little red room with its orderly collection of tapes, CDs, and videos and, opening each door and drawer, found the slide projector, a huge collection of slides, all marked as to content, three fat photo albums, and an ample collection of

X-rated commercial videotapes, including two of my all-time favorites, *Scared Stiff* and Honorable Discharge.

There was another large collection of tapes, the homemade kind if you were to judge by the labels, all, oddly, with the same label, "The Cliff and Bert Show." I wondered if these were pornographic as well. I wondered who the hell Bert was.

Fortunately, I didn't even have to close the curtains to make the room dark enough. Since the den was an internal room, it was always dark.

Having determined to dig in and be comfortable, and since what's a movie without good snacks, I refilled my cup, took the box of Mallomars, and got Magritte settled on my lap. As I pointed the remote at the set and pressed play, I even answered my own question—who the hell Bert was.

Clifford Cole was on the screen, his round face tense, his smallish, close-set, brown eyes alert, as if he were waiting, his brown hair too long, my mother would have said, ringlets falling on his brow and curling around his collar, giving him an almost cherubic appearance.

"I watched the tape," he said, his voice nearly inaudible.

"And so what would you like to say?"

Bertram Kleinman's face wasn't on the video, only the sound of his voice, as seductive as bait.

"Well, when I was here last time and I talked about these feelings that keep cropping up, that come back from time to time—"

Clifford stopped speaking, and one hand went to his mouth, the fingers tracing his full lips from one side to the other, as if there might be traces of a meal he wished to wipe away.

"Well, when I viewed the tape," he said, drawing himself up, beating back what was coming, "that's just not true. It's not that they crop up from time to time. They're always there. Like weather."

"What does that feel like?"

"Like it's always raining. What I mean to say is, oh, it's so difficult to express, it's like the sun could be out, but it would be raining *inside*, inside *me*. I don't know why, but I'm carrying something around that makes me feel terrible. I know I'm not a terrible person, but I *feel* I am, do you know what I mean?"

"Yes, of course, Clifford. Can you tell me, when did this feeling begin?"

"Oh, it's been around as long ago as I can remember."

There was silence then, Kleinman saying nothing, Clifford looking down into his lap, as I had done so often, having arrived at Ida's office feeling blocked or sullen, not knowing what I was supposed to be saying or feeling, removed, as it were, for the moment, from my own self.

As I watched and waited, just as Bert Kleinman must have, suddenly the painful issue of the inability to create a human being from the clues of his life was no longer a problem. Here was the man whose murder I had been hired to solve, alive through the miracle of modern technology.

The technique had been around for ten years or so, predicated on the idea that watching the tape would let the patient see and understand things he had missed during the session, that seeing yourself respond, and not respond, would continue the process of education at home, between sessions.

Why not? Everything was on tape nowadays. People being born now would, in years to come, be watching themselves sally forth into life. What would they think, hearing those first cries at leaving the paradise of the womb for the harsh lights of the delivery room? What would they think, seeing themselves pop naked and greasy into the hands of a stranger?

I had pulled a tape from the middle, not paying too much attention to the dates. Waiting as patiently as Dr. Kleinman for Clifford to troll within and come up with something else to say—God, how I hated those blank moments early on in my therapy—I picked up the box and looked at the dates, four of them, four sessions on each tape.

Waiting, I began to think about Clifford's work, about the painting of Magritte at the window, the rain coming down indoors, inside Cliff. Those others, the gray paintings.

Now suddenly my mind was moving fast. I looked at the box in my hands, at the dates, then rewound the tape and looked for another, and another, all around the time that Dennis had said Clifford had come to see him and he was wild, pacing, he had found out something about someone, wasn't that what Dennis had told me? And that it had to be exposed, at any cost.

Exposed.

I had to look at the film, too, the slides, it was dark enough in the den, but first I had to find the tape, I was sure there'd be one, where Clifford found out whatever it was he'd found out, trolling within, I was sure now that that's where the discovery had been made.

Three hours and twelve minutes later, the Mallomars long gone, the dogs asleep on Clifford's big white bed, I finally found what I had been looking for.

31

Man, I Couldn't Stop

HE WAS WEARING a navy blue turtleneck, the golden-brown curls like a halo around his face, his eyes no longer pinched and small but as round, open, and vulnerable as a child's.

It had been coming for months, for ages, hour after hour, talking about low self-esteem, about his lack of confidence, about feeling ugly, this beautiful child of man, sweet-faced, sad, trying to make the bad feelings go away, trying to find out why, why some people could feel comfortable, even happy, but he couldn't.

"What would you like to say?" Bert asked as Clifford attached the microphone, pinching up a piece of his sweater and clipping it in place. "You look *so* sad today."

"I kept thinking about what you said, when I brought in the album, about how happy I had looked as a baby and as a young boy, and then the change, you saw the change, that later I never looked at the camera, only down, and that I looked so sad, almost frightened, you said. I kept thinking about that."

He wiped his palm over his lips.

He sighed.

"So I looked at the pictures at home, not the tape this time, the photographs," and his round, brown eyes began to shine with tears, his cheeks flushed, his nose and chin became pink, "and I kept seeing what you saw, I can see it now, I can't understand that I didn't *always* see it, and I kept asking myself why, and the more I did that, the worse I felt."

Clifford sat still for a moment, nothing moving except the tears running over his wet lashes and down his cheeks, falling onto his hands and lap.

"One day I'd paint for twelve hours, the next I'd stay in bed, keep my dog with me under the covers, not answer the phone, not go to Louie's house. I felt I didn't deserve to see him."

Clifford turned away, his lips pursed, brow knit, eyes closed. And waited. We all waited.

"That's how I feel," he said, his voice hoarse with emotion, "that there's something wrong with me, that I *deserve* to feel like shit."

Tears fell.

"But I don't know why," he shouted. "I don't know why."

"What are you feeling now?"

"Nothing." Sullen.

"You look angry now."

"I'm *not*."

Silence.

"That's not true, I am. Do you know what I did?"

"No, what?"

"I was taking out the pictures, so I could look at them better, first when I was happy, like you said, then later, when I was . . . not, like you said, when I was not happy anymore, when I was looking down."

Looking down now. Looking like a child. Pauses thick with emotion.

"I didn't mean to do it," he said, looking so young, so scared.

"What did you do?"

"I tore them."

"Which ones did you tear?"

"Mine. Me. But then Peter got torn, too. By accident. I tried to separate him out, so I wouldn't tear him, too. But he got torn. In half."

Now Clifford Cole was sobbing.

"I didn't mean to hurt him," he said. "I didn't."

And a hand appeared on-screen, offering a box of tissues.

Clifford wiped his eyes and blew his nose, and I watched as the sad face of a little boy was transformed and, like the sudden recognition of knowledge I'd never tire of seeing in the eyes of the dogs I used to train, Clifford Cole got the knowledge he'd been looking for, the full brunt of it, all at once, recorded on tape for posterity.

"I *did*," he said. "I did mean to hurt him. It was *Peter*. Peter was why I hate myself."

"Why is that?"

"Because he hurt me," Clifford shouted. "He fucked me. He abused me. I pushed it all away, but now it's back, now I remember what he did, that's why I began to rip him up!"

Triumph in his eyes, his eyes so old, so sad now.

"Tell me about it."

"All week it was coming back to me, weird, horrible feelings, and I'd be thinking about Peter or mad he hadn't called me, something stupid like that, only that wasn't it, wasn't the real thing, and I'd just feel like I was too ugly to go outside, I even hired this kid, Michael Neary, who walks dogs in the neighborhood to walk Magritte, and I stayed in bed, and then it came to me, like in pieces and I couldn't grasp hold of it, only see parts of it, but I knew it had to do with Peter, I don't know how to explain it, but I just did, and now all of a sudden I remember it all, what he did to me, when it was, everything.

"It started when I was seven and he was twelve, when my parents would go out and they'd leave Peter in charge of me, and he said he had things to teach me, because I'd be a man one day, and there were things I'd have to do, things I had to know, things he knew because he was older than me, and I had no idea what he was talking about, but I knew he was going to help me because he was my brother and I loved him. I trusted him. My parents, they always made this big thing about brothers, how you're loyal to each other, how it's forever, being a brother, that when they'd be gone, we'd have each other."

"And what did Peter want to teach you?"

"About girls. He said I had to know what to do with girls. That he'd *show* me. So he took me into our parents' room and he dressed me in my mother's clothes and he showed me."

"What did he do, Clifford? Tell me what he did."

"He hurt me." Sobbing now. "And when I cried, he said, Be a man, Cliffie, you have to know this, and Mommy and Daddy will never teach you, it's up to me, he said, because you're my brother and I love you, and I was so mixed up, because he said that, but he was hurting me, and after that time, he did it again and again, in his bed or in my bed or in my parents' bed, he'd put me in a *dress* and put lipstick on my mouth, all over my mouth and around it, big, grotesque, red lips, and he'd kiss me and he'd fuck me and he'd say, This is what you'll do when you get the chance."

He covered his face and cried, but when he took his hands away, his face had changed. He wasn't sad now, he wasn't frightened, he was angry, his face whole, open, strong, his eyes round and clear, sane, his demeanor adult, powerful.

"Then it changed," he said, strong in his knowledge, "and now *he* put my mother's dress on, and makeup, powder and rouge and lipstick, he looked so weird to me, but he said he was doing it so I'd know what to do, so I wouldn't make a fool of myself when the time came, so I could be a man. That's what he told me, so I could be a man."

"How awful for you."

"Gotta practice, he'd say. Gotta get ready. Gotta do it. That's what he'd say when I cried—Gotta do it. I was a *child*. I couldn't protect myself. I didn't know how. And there was no one there to do it for me. No one there to rescue me."

"That's what we're doing here, rescuing that child."

Clifford nodded, his gaze far away. Bertram Kleinman and I waited silently, watching Cliff see something from a long time ago, something only he could see.

"When I was little, before this, four or five, I guess, Peter used to make me alphabet soup, you know, from a can, of course. I still remember it," he said, his brown eyes glowing. "He'd bring the bowl carefully to the table, one of those flat, wide soup bowls with rims, and some of the soup would slosh up onto the rim of the bowl, and when it went back into the bowl, the letters that had washed up onto the rim would stay there, and he'd say, We need these, we need every letter, because there's a message in there. Where? I'd say, looking into the bowl of soup. In there, he'd tell me, there's a message for you in the soup. You just have to find it. And he'd hand me the soup spoon. Do you remember what a soup spoon felt like in your mouth when you were four or five, how huge it was?"

Kleinman must have nodded. Clifford smiled at him.

"That was my brother. Huge. I loved him. And he hurt me."

"What would you like to say to Peter now?" Kleinman asked.

Clifford sat still. I could almost feel the dizziness of his trying to think of what to say and the question of who you were, of how old you were, as you said your piece.

"He wasn't all bad," he said softly, almost inaudibly, his eyes down.

Clifford took a huge breath and let it go. He

looked up now, toward the direction from which the
hand with the tissues had come.

"I wouldn't like to *say* anything to him. I'd like
to hurt him."

"That's a very disturbing thought. Tell me about
that. Tell me what you feel."

Sullen now, Clifford sat staring, saying nothing,
for what seemed like forever, until finally Dr. Kleinman said they'd talk more about it next time and
the screen went black with thousands of swirling
white dots on it.

In a moment the next session began. Clifford had
on a flannel shirt, a deep rust, cream, and teal, his
hair looked darker, it looked wet, curls on his brow,
the rest smoothed back tight and straight, pulled
into a ponytail in the back. He looked stony as he
clipped on the microphone.

"I saw him. My brother."

He exhaled through his nose in disgust.

"And what happened between you?"

"I told him that I remembered what he had done
to me."

"What did he say?" Kleinman's voice full of emotion now.

"He *said* I shouldn't make a big deal out it. You
always were like that, Cuffie, is what he *said* to me.
What a pain in the ass you always were. Imagine.
He called *me* a pain in the ass!"

"How awful this must have been for you. How
painful."

"You're so thin-skinned, he said. I can't even
talk to you. That's just stuff boys do. You don't
have to make a whole production about it now, do

you, it was a million years ago, we were just kids, playing. That's how boys play, Cuff."

"And what did you say to him?"

"What *kind* of boys play that way, Peter? Tell me that."

"What did he say?"

"He got furious. *He* got furious. *Nor*mal boys play that way, he said. So I said, Yeah? How about *your* boys? Do your sons play that way? And he jumped up—we were in a fucking restaurant—and I thought he was going to smack me right in the face."

"What did you do?"

"I kept right on going. Man, I couldn't stop. He was putting on his jacket, and I was sitting there shouting at him. If it's so fucking *nor*mal, then I guess you wouldn't mind if everyone *knew* about it, would you? Like your *sons*. Or your *wife*? Or, and then I was laughing at him, the way he used to laugh at me, those nice folks at your school."

"What happened then?" Tension creeping into Kleinman's voice.

"He split. Ran out. Stuck me with the bill. You know, I remembered something else, Dr. Kleinman. I remembered that one time when we were kids, after he had started abusing me, I said I'd tell on him, and do you know what he did?"

Silence.

"He said he'd tell everyone *I* was a little shit-eating sissy. And they'd believe *him*, not *me*. And he laughed at me, laughed at his cleverness, at the trap I was in. After that, he used to call me that. In fact, in front of my parents, you know how kids always like to tease each other so that the parents

don't know what's going on? Well, he just short-
ened it to SES, shit-eating sissy, then just SSS, and
I'd know, SSS, like a snake. He'd whisper it at the
table or when we were riding in the car, he threatened me with it, he shut me up with it until I felt so
bad and so beaten that I shut away the whole thing,
everything he'd done, and later, now, I just *felt* like
a little shit-eating sissy, but I never knew why."

"Clifford, the word 'sissy'—"

"Faggot, fairy, queen, homo, you mean *that*
word?" he shouted. "Yes, and let's not forget sissy.
Sissy boy. He called me that, too. That, in fact, was
another of his favorites."

"Do you feel that what your brother did had anything to do with your sexual orientation?"

"No," he said. "Of course not."

He sat quietly, his eyes filling, tears spilling out
over the rims, not blinking, not catching those tears
with a tissue, not wiping them away with his fingers.
No, he just sat.

"Of course not," he whispered. "It had to do with
my feeling like a little shit-eating sissy. It had to do
with my always feeling inadequate, at fault, ugly,
stupid, guilty."

I thought I heard Kleinman crying, too.

"But my sexual orientation is God-given. Peter
didn't have anything to do with that. No matter what
I thought when I was a little boy, Peter is not God."

I heard Kleinman ask Cliff if he was all right, and
then static indicated that the session had ended.

A week later, Clifford needing a shave, Clifford
looking as if he hadn't slept in days:

"I told him blood will tell. I told him that Morton

was doing to Lester, his precious Lester, what he had done to me."

"You told him that over dinner?"

"No, I told him that by painting it."

Les and mor, for God's sake. Lester and Morton. Peter's boys.

That's why it wasn't at the show.

Peter had seen it the night that Dennis left the key for him. And after Louis had invited him to the opening, he'd done what any father would do. He'd gone back, to rescue his children.

"After that first confrontation, Clifford, what did you actually say to Peter?"

"I've been painting," he said. It was on his shirt, and in his hair.

Orange, like the basketball the young boy in the dress was holding.

Peter. In a dress.

So that's how he would hurt him!

"What do you mean, Cliff?"

"I've been painting the truth, painting him the way he really is, the way he should be seen. Oh, he thought he made *my life* a drag! Wait until he sees what I can do to *his* life."

Bitter laughter.

"But you haven't tried talking to Peter again?"

Silence.

"Maybe in time, Clifford, you'll be able to. Right now, you need time to deal with your own feelings, with this terrible pain, so that you will be able to let go of it sometime in the future."

Snort.

"He needs time, too, Clifford. All he can feel now

is defensive, but given time, if you tell him again
how he made you feel—"

"I *told* him. I also told him I wanted him to *feel*
how I felt. He's my brother, isn't he? So I want to
share with him how shame feels, how fear feels,
how it would feel to be threatened with exposure
and humiliation, all the things that I felt. Thanks
to him."

"You told him about the paintings? What did he
say?"

"He laughed at me. Who cares what you paint?
Who'll ever see what *you* paint? And then he
hung up."

"Listen, Dennis," I had said late last night when
he picked up, half asleep, "there's something bothering me."

"What?"

Well, to tell the truth, it was more like *wha*? It
seemed Dennis had finally gotten over his insomnia.
I forged ahead anyway.

"It's about those three missing canvases. Have
you thought about them at all?"

"Sure. I figured Louis took them to keep for
himself."

"Why take them off the frames?"

"A lot of people do that, roll the canvas so that
it takes less space, you know, store it in a tube.
Maybe he didn't have room for them. I understand
his place is really small."

"But he had one painting at the show that was
not for sale. Why hold three out?"

"He has that right. Maybe he didn't like them.

Or maybe he loved them. Maybe they were personal. Who knows?"

"I'd like to."

"*Now?* Couldn't it wait until morning?"

I looked at my watch. It was after two.

"Sorry. I'll catch you tomorrow. I mean tonight."

I had wanted to tell him everything I had learned, but it could wait. At least until I was sure.

The catalog listed fifty-three works. I thought that's what Louis had said, too—or was it Veronica? Yes, she had said there were forty-seven paintings and five pieces of sculpture, and that's what was listed. Everything accounted for.

Except what had been on those empty stretchers. Two works in addition to *les and mor*.

I jumped up without bothering to shut off the VCR and went right for the photo albums, taking all of three of them back to the desk. I opened the first.

The first album contained pictures of Cliff and Louie on a trip to Rome and Israel; from the looks of the other people occasionally in the photos, it was a gay tour.

The second album was a book of slides of Clifford's work. I took the loupe out of the middle drawer, took out one of the plastic pages, and, my eye to the lens, held it up to the light to see what was there. On this page, there were photos of *up* and *rising son*. Also the basenji sculpture, shot in various stages.

There were some shots of Cliff, in goggles and knee pads, painting, what looked like Saran Wrap around his watch, but it wasn't possible to be sure without projecting the slide.

The third album was the one I wanted to look at first, family pictures, the ones Bertram Kleinman had been shown, and yes, there was Clifford as a happy little boy, on a tricycle, with a litter of beagle puppies, holding hands with an older boy. A boy who was a little taller than he was and quite a bit stockier, even then. A boy holding a basketball against his hip. A boy whose head had been torn off.

I paged through the album slowly, studying Clifford's family, his mother and father, looking young and proud with their two sons, one, the younger, with blond curls, the other, the older boy, headless, and on and on, even until adulthood. Near the end of the book, I found Lester and Morton. In fact, I found the picture from which the painting in question had been made. In the photo, the boys stood close together, grinning falsely, clearly having been told to smile for the camera. Normal boys, like normal basenjis, not wanting to do as they were told. Not wanting to have their stupid picture taken when they could be playing war or climbing a tree instead. The painting, as I remember, was another story, a story of lewdness and fear, a story of incest and abuse, a story that said, Do your sons play that way? and Blood will tell.

Peter's wife, Linda, whom I had spoken to yesterday, was a short, square-looking woman with a round, flattish face, her hair neatly coiffed and sprayed, the hem of her unstylish dress landing primly beneath her knees, her children at her left, the ankles and feet of her husband to her right.

Bertram Kleinman's voice was coming from the television speakers.

Bert: "You said that to him?"

Cliff, crying: "Yes."

Bert: "You were able to get angry at him?"

Cliff: "Yes."

Bert: "This is marvelous, Clifford, a real break-through for you. This is what we've been working for."

Cliff: "But it didn't do any *good*. He just doesn't get it. The way he doesn't get that I'm an artist. Just because I'm his kid brother. I mean, even when I told him I had signed a gallery contract for my first show, well, my first *group* show, but still, he didn't get it. He didn't even congratulate me, Dr. Kleinman."

"What did he do?"

"He hung up on me. He said 'Shit,' and hung up. Do you see what I mean? What *good* did it do?"

Bert: "Clifford, we're not talking about changing Peter. Or erasing the past. We don't have the power to do either of those things. What we're talking about is *you*, we're talking about your ability to express what you feel. And toward that end, this has been a really positive step for you."

"I guess. I guess you're right."

So that was the Cliff and Bert Show.

I shut off the set and walked out of the little red room into the huge, hollow, empty studio in the front of the loft.

The light coming into the windows was from streetlamps, now, and when I walked over to the windows and looked out, I could see that it was raining.

It was raining inside, too. All around me, overhead, in every room, in the closets full of expensive clothes, in the kitchen hung with polished copper-bottomed pots, it was raining sadness. I had seen him now, heard him, felt him, listened as the secret of childhood abuse had bubbled up in therapy, but nothing I or anyone else could do would bring him back to paint in his studio, to wear his expensive clothes, to cook in those copper-bottomed pots, to walk his dog, to love his handsome boyfriend.

All I could do was make it as likely as possible that the person who killed him would be punished. I still had much to do.

32

Dashiell Was Ready

IT WAS AFTER seven and I was starving, so I went poking through the kitchen drawers for what every New Yorker has, menus. While I waited for my miso soup and tekka maki to arrive, I fed the dogs the last of Magritte's food and set up the slide projector in the studio, where I would be able to look at the slides on those huge, bare white walls.

When the delivery man buzzed, I salivated like Pavlov's dogs, buzzed him in, and waited hungrily for him to climb the stairs. I had the money ready. My dogs were ready, too. Dashiell was ready to lay down his life for me, or at least place his bulk in front of mine. Magritte, being a basenji, never wanting to be where he was supposed to be, was ready to escape.

I reached for the bag, handed the deliveryman

the money, and felt something warm and quick brush by my left leg.

The deliveryman headed down.

Magritte headed up.

I figured, what the hell, the dog has a C.D. So instead of chasing him up the stairs while my soup got cold, I called him. And he came.

The food was wonderful, and I ate most of it. Ex-dog trainer or not, there was no way I was going to disappoint my companions. Even if my newest law of private investigation is Never put anything into your mouth that was meant for a dog, there's no law that says you can't do it the other way around.

I turned on the slide projector, and the first slide appeared on the wall.

Uncle Miltie. The stocky guy in the housedress and cheap wig. His back turned. The cigar burning.

Click.

The second panel. Ash accumulating.

Click.

The third panel. Ash dropping to the carpet.

(Stomach tightens.)

Click.

The fourth and missing panel. Otherwise known as the truth, as rendered by Clifford Cole.

The subject of the work, in a dress, a wig, and the kind of orthopedic stockings my grandmother Sonya wore, had turned around.

He was grinning.

He was wearing lipstick.

Lots of lipstick.

A garish amount, in my opinion. Especially with *that* outfit.

Genderfuck is done with wit. This portrait was

done with malice. Be that as it may, once again we were face-to-face.

I had seen him first at the opening, even though he'd told Dennis he couldn't be there. He had been so impressed with the price of the basenji sculpture, he had whistled in amazement.

I had seen him next at Westminster, where he had wondered out loud how anyone could tell the basenjis apart. Where he had made dead sure he knew whose harmless bait to exchange for the tainted bait he'd meant for Magritte.

And when he'd heard on the news, no doubt, that a handler had died instead of a dog, that his clever ploy had failed to work, because after all he was not a dog person, didn't know the practices of the conformation ring, he had come back.

To try again.

Gotta do it.

He had followed me into the ladies' room. He had whistled then, too, whistled for Magritte, witness to murder.

My, I thought, studying his portrait, what *big* feet you've got.

Feed I'd know anywhere.

That is to say, feet whose *size* I'd know anywhere.

To the right of those big feet, there was even a title, neatly printed: *big shit-eating sissy*.

For once, without his head torn off.

33

Dead Ahead

I KNEW THAT Peter *could have been* at the opening before I learned that he *had been* there. I had learned that during one of yesterday's many phone calls.

"Mrs. Cole?" I had said when a woman answered.

"Yes. To whom am I speaking, please?" A voice like a dried magnolia petal, brittle yet still fragrant.

"This is Elaine Boynton, Clifford's friend. I was so sad to hear about Clifford."

"Well, of course you were, my dear. It was such shocking news, such tragic news."

"Yes."

"Were you close with my son?"

"Yes. And so I feel just terrible that I missed the memorial service."

"There was no service, Elaine."

"Really?"

"Why, yes. Clifford's brother, Peter, said he thought Clifford wouldn't want any sort of a fuss, wouldn't want to make his friends drag all the way down to Virginia. He said it wasn't necessary."

"He said that?"

"Well, it *was* basketball season, Elaine. His weekends belonged to the team. Don't even *call* me, Mother, he said to me. I'll call you when I get a chance. Both my sons are busy, busy men."

My bet was she didn't know Peter had moved out, had no number *to* call him at.

"Do you call your mother, Elaine?"

"She's, uh, gone," I said.

"I am so sorry, my dear. Was there a service for her?"

"Yes. A small, private one."

"I see. Well, I do feel that family and friends need the closure of a service. Don't you agree, my dear?"

"Yes, I do."

"Don't you think Clifford's friends would come to Virginia for a small service, once the weather gets a little kinder?"

"I'm sure they would."

"I'm so pleased to hear that, Elaine. I would like to meet my son's friends."

"I understand. I was wondering where I could send a donation in Clifford's name. Does the family have a preference?"

"Well, now, of course Clifford hadn't voiced such a preference. He was so very young." There was silence for a moment. "I'm sure any charity you pick would be just fine."

"Okay. Thank you."

"Thank *you*, my dear. Thank you for your affection for my son."

Ma son, she'd said. Delicate as a tank. I wondered if degaying the loft had more to do with Cliff's problems than his mother's.

More to the point, Peter had lied to Dennis about the service and had come to the opening to make bloody sure he hadn't missed anything when he removed the offensive canvases from the loft. He had taken *les and mor* and tossed the empty stretcher in the back of the closet. Perhaps he'd taken another painting out, an older one, and hung it on the empty nail. He'd taken the significant panel of *big shit-eating sissy*. And he'd taken a portrait of himself, a portrait where his mouth was twisted and cruel, his eyes cold, his cheeks even more red and doughy than they looked under the unflattering lights of Madison Square Garden. That last one I'd seen when I watched the rest of the slides I had retrieved from B & H. It was called *helen*, the name gay men use for an old queen. It turns out it wasn't only his sons that Peter had gone back to rescue. It was himself.

My guess was that the only record of these paintings would be the slides that Clifford meticulously took and filed of all his work. I was so grateful he had done that. The slides of the missing paintings were enough by themselves to make me *suspect* Peter.

And my day on the telephone had all but eliminated everyone else.

I'd found out from Louis that like so many other

SoHo galleries, the Cahill Gallery had come close to folding when the art-buying frenzy of the eighties had ended so abruptly, but because Veronica has the scruples of a scorpion—*his* words—she'd managed, mostly with manufactured hype, to keep afloat. Now they were just making as much as they could out of what Louis had inherited.

"Can you blame us, Rachel?" he'd asked me.

Marjorie Gilmore had clued me in on Doc. He was Herbert Hanover, Ph.D., founder and owner of Hanover Cryogenics. Frozen semen. He not only stood to lose a lot with Gil gone, he and Gil were both at the Illinois State Veterinary Conference when Clifford was killed. So Gil was already dead when I found out he had a perfect alibi.

I had ruled out Michael Neary, the dog walker. He was only seventeen. And Addie and Poppy; had they tried to off Gil or Magritte with tainted liver, they would have jeopardized Orion. Anyway, they're dog people. They might have gone after Gil, but never Magritte.

In my back-to-basics mode of yesterday, I had even called information to see if Clifford's number was listed.

"I don't have a listing for a Clifford," the operator had said, "but under new listings, there's a *Peter* Cole."

That was interesting.

I called and heard his raspy voice on his answering machine, one of those no-name, covert messages— you know: "You have reached 555-2486. Please leave a message after the tone and I'll get back to you as soon as I can."

As if there were a person alive on the planet who didn't know to wait for the tone by now.

Next I called poor, shapeless Linda Cole, in Woodcliff Lake. Of course she didn't tell me he'd moved out. Why should she have? Who was I that she should tell me her sad story?

Whether or not he actually was abusing his boys would be her problem. And theirs, of course.

My problem was that I needed proof.

He had been *so* clever.

He had asked Dennis for a key, when in fact he co-owned the loft with his brother. I had discovered this by dropping in at the real estate office around the corner and checking the *Real Estate Directory of Manhattan*, volume two, which listed the owners of the loft as Cole, C., and Cole, P.D. Banks prefer steady income to lump sums of money, which, as anyone knows, can disappear. In fact, they are sometimes "placed" in the buyer's bank account by a rich, understanding relative and, subsequent to approval, "re-placed" back in the owner's account. A secure job always has more weight with the bank.

He had removed, and probably destroyed, the paintings Clifford made to shame him. I remembered that when I had looked at Cliff's will, the codicils had been out of order. Peter must have checked the will to see where Cliff's paintings were going. He'd need to know that. But he couldn't have taken them that night. He had to return the key to Haber's, and even rolled up, the painting would have been noticed. No matter. That is, until he learned about the show. Then he had to act fast.

But he didn't know that Clifford kept a meticulous record of all his paintings by taking color transparencies of them.

Neither did he know that Clifford's therapy sessions had all been taped.

I was sitting on the floor in the big, bare, empty studio, hugging my dog now, Magritte curled and asleep at my side.

He knew when Clifford went to therapy, when he wouldn't be home, when he could use his key, whistle for Magritte, take him away to use as bait to get his brother out onto the pier, to make it look like the sort of crime no one would bust his ass to solve.

Peter had evidently used a voice-changing telephone, ninety bucks from Sharper Image. Probably bought it, used it and tossed it. Made his voice sound higher, like a woman's voice, to disguise his identity and maybe even to make it all sound less threatening to his brother.

But only a person who had never lost his heart to a dog could think that any scenario that put that relationship in jeopardy could sound less threatening. Less threatening than what—nuclear holocaust?

"I have Magritte." Three little words.

Sticks and stones will break your bones, they chanted in the schoolyard when I was a kid, but words will never harm you. Another of the lies I grew up on.

What did Clifford do while he waited? What did he think?

When did he write and hide the letter?

Why had he hidden the tape? Had he planned that *after* he got Magritte back he would take it to the police?

Did he get the message in time to get to the bank before it closed? Of course, with Select Checking, he could have gotten the thousand from the ATM by making two withdrawals of five hundred each. He had noted the amount he had taken out, not how it had been retrieved.

I laid my face on Dashiell's neck, breathing in the comforting smell of dog, and closed my eyes.

Frantic. He must been frantic, wandering from room to room—everywhere he looked, Magritte wasn't there.

Finally, it was time to go. He felt the money, a small lump, in his pocket. Not as much as it would be for a person. After all, Magritte was only a dog. That's what the police would have said. Louis would have said that, too.

He crossed West Street, the wind going through his clothes, and finally he heard him, heard Magritte, and his heart lifted like a piece of paper caught in a gust, swirling and joyous. He never saw the car, sitting there, motor off, he only heard Magritte. He began to run.

Peter sat across the seat waiting, watching out the back window of the rented car.

I had even found out where yesterday, by calling all the rental places as Mrs. Peter Cole, complaining I was overcharged. Thrifty Auto Rental, West Ninety-fifth Street, walking distance from his new apartment, assured me the bill was correct.

"We have the AMEX receipt, Mrs. Cole," they told me. "Shall I send you a copy?"

Difficult to rent a car without a credit card. Difficult to use a fake name when you need a credit card and driver's license.

Still, he'd planned so carefully. He knew he couldn't use his own car. Clifford would have recognized it. Had to think it out, think it through, find a way to stop the little shit-eating sissy from destroying his life. He had his name to think about, his reputation, his job. He had sons to protect.

His sons. How he missed them. There was another one who took things the wrong way, Linda, that cow, making a big deal over everything, couldn't even let him love his own kids in his own way, seeing faults in every little thing. Forcing him out.

The way his brother had forced him into *this*. Threatened him.

Both of them. Family! Well, fuck that noise.

It wasn't that he *liked* the idea of killing his brother, shit, he was no pervert, he wouldn't *enjoy* doing this, it just had to be done, Clifford running amok like he was, painting him as some old faggot, some helen, in a fucking dress, for God's sake, what would people think, and how would he earn a living, right, great, working with adolescent boys after *those* pictures were in everyone's face, his luck, the shit would end up in some museum, and then he looked up, and saw that his brother had passed the car, he was on the pier now, running, running toward that stupid dog of his, damn thing would be the death of him, and you know, he couldn't help it, he had to laugh at his own joke.

It's his own damn fault, the little shit, he just wouldn't let it go. I told him, Drop it already, I told him, that's how boys play, crying in the restaurant, his eyes all red, as if he were some girl, what would people think.

After the impact, he hit the brake.

Safe, he thought. I'm safe. Then, looking over his shoulder, he backed off the pier and was gone.

The car was coming out backward, quick as it went in, and Billy Pittsburgh ducked down, down, down, under his blanket and lay still as snow, stayed that way so long, maybe he fell back to sleep again.

When dawn broke, the gulls woke Billy, and, wrapped in his blanket, dragging his bag of bottles and cans, he walked partway out onto the pier, saw the dog was gone, saw the young white man lying on his back; and he turned around fast as could, knew just where he could take what he knew, trade it for some coffee, a place to sit and drink it out of the weather.

Turning his back to the wind, he headed for Tenth Street, for the Sixth Precinct, passing on his way the wrought-iron gate that led down the passageway that opened into the garden in which my cottage sat and in which I lay warm as the coffee cup he'd soon be holding in his hands, sleeping like spoons with my dog.

I don't know how long I sat there brooding, but it was dark out, time to go. I had seen a leather backpack in Clifford's bedroom closet. I took the significant audio- and videotapes and the box of slides I had picked up at B & H, put them in the backpack, and locked up the dark loft.

Walking home from Clifford Cole's sad, empty loft to my own cozy cottage, I kept trying to figure out exactly how I could make sure that Peter Cole would get his just reward. I had to get him. Had to.

Though I did not want to be the one to have to tell Adrienne Wynton Cole that she had lost *both* her sons.

Still, it had to be done.

That he deserved to be got, I had little doubt. But so far all the evidence was circumstantial, none of it conclusive. I had to be sure that if he was charged, the charges would stick, because nowadays people got away with all kinds of murder.

34

I Know Your Secret

MAGRITTE BEGAN TO whine, anxious to run free in the garden. The lock on the gate seemed stuck— all these gates were so old—but I wiggled the key, and finally it clicked open. I unhooked the leads, and both dogs dashed on ahead down the narrow, unlit passageway. I locked the gate behind me and noticed how relieved and safe I always felt to be home.

Except for the path, where it had been worn down by our feet, the garden was still covered with thick layers of snow, crusted hard on top so that there was a sound like crinkling cellophane when the dogs ran. It was a clear night. I stood still for a moment, looking up at the stars.

It was quiet in the garden, the way it rarely is in New York. Even that hum that newcomers to the city are so conscious of, that unexplainable constant din of background noise, seemed to have abated. When Dashiell sneezed, it seemed as loud as a thunderclap.

Inside, I toweled off the dogs, filled their water bowl, and made a fire. I thought about calling Dennis, but it was after eleven and I decided against it. It would be better to call him when I knew for sure what I was gong to do.

I thought about calling Peter Cole, too, but not then. I could call late the next morning, after he'd left for work, and leave a message on his answering machine. I could even use my own voice-changing telephone, if I could figure out which box in the basement it was in.

I know your secret, I could say.

Yeah.

Meet me at the pier. You know which one, and you know when. Don't tell anyone about this call, asshole, and bring five thousand dollars with you.

The price has gone up, I could say.

Right. I should wait alone on the Christopher Street pier at four in the morning for a guy who had already killed his own brother, like he'd have some compunction about eighty-sixing me.

He'd probably just rent a car and drive over me a few dozen times, just to make sure I didn't bother him again.

Growing up is murder. I'm glad I never tried it.

I decided to go to bed and figure it out in the morning, when I'd be seven or eight hours more mature.

But when I got upstairs and was taking off my snow boots, Dashiell began to pace and whine, going over to the window, pushing his nose against the shutters so that they rattled, then coming back to me and catching my eye.

I shut off the light, went over to the window, and, leaving the shutters closed, opened the slats so that I could see out. My bedroom window faced the main house, and as I looked across the deserted white garden, for just a moment I saw a flash of light.

It could have been from a car passing on Tenth Street, the headlights momentarily lighting up the dark house. Except that this light didn't flash across the house, appearing first in one room and then almost instantly the next, moving left to right from where I was, the way the one-way traffic did on Tenth Street. This light was only in the kitchen, nowhere else. It was an intense beam. The kind of light a flashlight makes.

I looked down at Dashiell and saw that his hackles were up, so I relaced my Timberlands and, keeping the lights off and not bothering with a coat, left the cottage and headed for the Siegal house to see what was going on.

I had only planned on taking Dashiell. Magritte was sleeping on my bed, and I had no reason to disturb him, but as usual he had ideas of his own. I felt him brush by me on the stairs, and he was first out the door, turning back toward us with his eyes afire, then play-bowing to Dashiell to start a game.

But Dashiell wasn't having any. His mind was elsewhere.

I followed him across the winter yard, the elongated shadow of the big oak flat on the snow in front of us, then crawling up the bricks of Norma and Sheldon's house.

There was light on the third floor now. I saw it

swing across the back bedroom Norma used as a study.

I unlocked the back door as quietly as I could, pulled it open, and left it slightly ajar, going first, while I had the chance, toward the front of the house to find out where someone had gotten in. I signaled Dash to stay by me, but he kept looking toward the stairs. Still, he obeyed, and Magritte trotted alongside, stopping here and there to sniff the strange territory.

It didn't take a detective to see what had happened. One of the front ground-floor windows had been broken. But this time someone had used a glass cutter and a suction cup, silently cutting a circle near the lock rather than noisily smashing the whole window. Someone had planned this, had cased the house and returned with the necessary tools to do the job.

My heart picked up its pace, knees high, arms pumping. If a heart could sweat, mine was sweating. I had thought I'd find another homeless person, some hapless creature just trying to find shelter from the cold. A homeless person with a glass cutter?

Had Big Foot's cab followed close enough to my own to see approximately where I had disappeared after getting out of my cab? Not knowing the Village, Peter Cole wouldn't be likely to guess the secret of what lay beyond the wrought-iron gate. He would naturally assume I lived in the main house. Or had he tried the gate? Was that why I'd had trouble with the lock?

I decided to go back to the cottage and call the precinct. I didn't think it was a great idea to take chances when my gun was in its show box in the closet rather than tucked into my waist and there were a bunch of lovely policemen just across the street waiting for a little excitement to enter their lives.

I gestured to the dogs and headed for the open back door. But when I stepped out the door, Dashiell was nowhere in sight. He must have misunderstood; whenever we had come in the past, he had gotten to search the whole house. And this time, his efforts would actually pay off. Apparently he was on his way upstairs; when I stepped out onto the small porch, there I was alone with Magritte.

I turned to go back and call him. After all, Peter's choice of weapons was pretty eclectic. This time around *he* might have a gun. But before I got the chance to take a step, the breath was squeezed out of me, a powerful arm around my throat, choking me, taking me off balance, and dragging me backward. I could smell the foulness of stale cigar smoke on his breath and clothing and smell the sourness of his sweat, even though it was below twenty and we were out-of-doors. I clawed at his arm and kicked back, but his grip only tightened, and when I opened my mouth, he clamped his other hand, in a leather glove, over it.

Suddenly he was dragging me closer to the house. I thought he was going to take me back inside where no one would have heard anything and he could have done whatever his beady black heart desired to me, but he didn't.

He did something far worse. He kicked the door shut, separating me from Dashiell. Once again, I was in danger and the only one there to help me was a twenty-pound basenji.

With the door closed and me under control, Peter began to whistle, that eerie little tune, four notes, a pause, the same four notes again.

That's when I remembered who it was that Peter Cole was out to get.

If I got it too, well, that would only mean he was being careful.

I could see Magritte in the center of the garden, keeping his distance.

Peter whistled again.

Magritte wasn't having any.

The choke hold tightened. Here was clearly a man who could do more than one thing at a time.

Maybe someone else had heard the whistle, I thought, but wasn't that just me whistling in the dark, so to speak? True, another garden backed up to mine, and beyond it was another house, one you entered from Christopher Street, one block south of Tenth. But those windows were so far away. And there was a wall at the back of the property, separating the gardens. What I loved about this place was privacy, but just then I was thinking maybe I had too much of a good thing.

I was shivering.

I tried to tell myself it was because I hadn't taken my coat when I ran out.

Suddenly the hand on my mouth loosened and I heard his raspy voice, a guttural whisper right at my ear.

"If you scream, I'll hurt you. Will you be quiet?"

I nodded enthusiastically, and the hand slipped off my mouth but the arm around my throat held tight. It was then I had a hopeful thought. He didn't know I knew who he was. He was behind me, whispering. Maybe he didn't intend to kill me. Maybe I could get out of this.

"Who are you?" I whispered, not wanting him to think I was crying for help and cover my mouth again. "What do you want here?"

"Shut up" he growled. I could feel him moving behind me, but I didn't know what he was doing. Then he spoke again, but this time that rough voice was up in pitch. Because it wasn't me he was addressing.

"Here, boy," he said. He whistled again. Four notes. A pause. The same four notes, only an octave higher.

Magritte cocked his head and lifted one front paw. But he didn't come closer. Instead, he began to whine.

Even a basenji, not exactly my number-one choice as a protection dog, knew something was wrong. Magritte had grown attached to me, and he could smell my fear as well as he could sense Peter's malice.

Again, "Here, boy." Then I could see his hand moving, waving about. He had something for Magritte, and he was trying to tease him closer. The hand moved where I could see it, thumb and pointer holding something small, something hard, something grayish brown.

Liver!

Magritte took a tentative step closer.

I didn't know how far Clifford had gone with Magritte beyond the C.D., but if he had, it was my only hope.

I screamed at the top of my lungs, "Go out! Magritte, go out!"

And as I did that, I realized I might have just traded Magritte's life for my own. I could literally feel the rage surge in Peter Cole. A hideous sound came from me as the arm around my neck jerked back. My knees buckled, and I thought I was going to pass out. But two things changed all that.

One was Peter trying to force the piece of liver into my mouth. I never ate it as a kid, and I sure as hell didn't want to start now, not with the smell of bitter almond filling my nostrils.

The second thing that happened was that I saw something move off to the side. And realizing what it was gave me courage.

I jerked my head violently from side to side. You don't grow up with a Jewish mother without knowing how to refuse food. At the same time, I lifted one two-ton Timberland boot and kicked back as hard as I could. It felt as if I only glanced off his shin, but I heard an *oof*, so I knew I'd hurt him, and before he got the chance to get even, and then some—this was surely a vindictive man—we were both pitched sideways into the snow. Now instead of bitter almond, I smelled the comforting odor of dog.

I was able to roll away, and as I picked myself up, I saw Peter Cole, his face gray with terror, a gray not unlike the one his brother used to paint him as the revolting pervert he was, holding his arm now not around my aching throat but up in front of his own face.

Dashiell was standing over him, the sound of an outboard motor coming from somewhere deep in his massive chest. Then, his face inches from Peter

Cole's, he barked twice. His tail was wagging. He was triumphant.

"Get him off me," he cried. But I ignored him. I turned to look at Magritte, and he was licking his lips. I panicked.

"Where's the liver?" I shouted.

Peter tried to move his arm, and Dashiell grabbed it in his jaws, stopping the movement.

"Don't move. Is it still in your hand?"

I could barely hear him. "No."

I turned back to Magritte, who was just sitting in the snow, watching us. Then I saw it, grayish brown, lying in the snow. I picked it up and walked over to where Peter Cole was lying on his back, terrified, under Dashiell, who never once took his eyes off his prey.

I wondered if he was as scared as he could possibly be. Or if there was room for improvement.

"Open wide, asshole," I said, holding the liver over his mouth.

For a moment, I saw what I had wanted to see. I could leave the rest up to the police. I pulled a plastic bag from my pocket and dropped the liver in, knotting it securely on top.

"Excuse me," I said to Peter. "I hope you won't consider me rude, but I have to use the john."

I turned and headed for the cottage and, after making the phone call I had to make, grabbed my sheepskin coat and went back out to the yard to wait for the police.

35

Up to Scratch

IT WAS SNOWING lightly on Saturday. In the morning Dashiell and I walked over to Bailey House to see Billy Pittsburgh and tell him the white man he'd seen commit murder was in jail. We saw Ronald, too, and we got to meet Jimmy McEllroy, who was only twenty-two and loved Dashiell, but we never did get to see Sivonia LeBlanc. She had died early on Thursday morning.

In the afternoon Dashiell and I went over to Dennis's loft to take Magritte home and collect our check.

"I still can't believe it was his own brother who killed him," he said after I'd caught him up on all he'd missed.

"Why not? It's the second-oldest crime. Right after stealing fruit."

If ever I'd heard an exit line, that was it. I stood and picked up my coat.

"Wait up," he said. "You never told me how Dashiell got out of the house."

"Dashiell," I said, and when he looked up from wrestling with Magritte, I pointed to the door.

He was up in a flash. He grasped the knob, turned his head, and, carefully keeping his grip, backed up.

"Only their door opens out, so he had to push instead of pull."

"Brilliant!" he *k'velled*.

"Yeah, yeah," I said modestly.

I had known Dennis less than two weeks, but it seemed I'd known him ages. I sometimes think detective work is like summer camp. You make friends and enemies in record time.

"I was at the Sixth yesterday," I told him as I put on my coat. "They have the tapes, the slides, and the piece of tainted liver Peter tried to shove into my mouth."

"We did so *well*, didn't we?" he said, sharing the credit as he leaned to kiss me good-bye. "We could be partners, Rachel, you know, a politically correct Nick and Nora Charles. And Dashiell—"

"Yeah, yeah. Dashiell could be fucking Asta."

"Exactly," he said with a grin, those lovely crooked teeth looking like piano keys after an earthquake.

But I already had a partner, I thought as I followed him down the stairs, his ears bobbing as he descended toward the street. One who had proven himself up to scratch.

Once upon a time I had saved his life. He had recently returned the favor.